THE IMMORTAL WARRIOR

The Immortal Bound Series

THE IMMORTAL WARRIOR

CHRISTINA FARLEY

Published by Everbound Press

Copyright © 2025 by Christina Farley

Library of Congress Control Number: 2025905707

www.ChristinaFarley.com

Cover and Interior Artwork: Trif Book Designs

Map Artwork: Veronika Wunder

ASIN: B0DHT2YXNZ

ISBN (hardcover): 979-8-9864624-8-6

ISBN (paperback): 979-8-9864624-7-9

ALSO BY CHRISTINA FARLEY

The Immortal Bound Series

The Immortal Legend (Novella)

The Immortal Secret

The Immortal Heart

The Immortal Warrior

The Immortal Crown

The Gilded Series

Gilded

Silvern

Brazen

The Dreamscape Series

The Dream Heist

The Dream Hunt

Adult Books

Fairy Tale Road

Middle Grade Books

The Princess and the Page

The Thief of Time

To Caleb, whose power is flight.

The Eien Kingdom
Garden of Tranquility
Training Pagoda
Bamboo Grove
Tōkai-mura
The Channel Sanctuary
Lake of Eternity

The Emperor's Castle
The Land of Kakurezato
Ami's Palace
Walkway of Eternity
Tethering Nexus
Hall of the Ring
N
W
E
S

1
INFILTRATION 101
ESTRELLA

Kyoto, Japan

The night cloaks us in its folds as we stealthily weave between the bamboo trees toward the imposing fortress. The moon, shrouded in the clouds' ghostly tendrils, offers just enough light to guide us. Our black clothing camouflages us against the darkness, but one misstep, one wrong move, and the guards patrolling the grounds will surely spot our movements. My boots step softly on the forest floor as I trail after Dion's dark form. He holds up one hand, indicating for us to stop.

Tristan and I freeze.

The sparks of Dion's electric powers shimmer across his skin as if eager to leap out in attack. Someone is close.

My heart thuds against my chest, a drum beating to the rhythm of my impending death. Every cell within me screams to turn and run, but my heart knows my future depends on infiltrating the fortress. I crouch in the shadows. My gloved hand clenches the hilt of my dagger tucked in its sheath, ready to unleash its full power on any attacker.

Behind me, Tristan's heated power drifts around my body as if calming my nerves. Ever since I started training with him at the Castle of Stará, I've slowly become more attuned to other immortals' powers. If only I could focus enough to use that ability to my advantage.

A form leaps out of the darkness from the tree bough above, and a curved blade glowing green swipes through the air.

"Watch out!" I whisper-yell.

Dion ducks then attacks. A sharp, quick bolt to the chest. The guy shudders, veins of white electricity shimmer across his whole body, making it glow.

The attacker cries out and then goes silent.

"Don't want to be him when he wakes up," Tristan whispers.

Dion's arm slowly lowers. *All clear.* He creeps on, his lithe form moving through the shadows, a lethal weapon ready to strike. Soon we're at the base of the fortress, a section in the wall covered in vines and bramble.

"What is this place?" I ask warily.

"It's the Eien Emperor's stronghold," Dion explains.

"Are you freaking kidding me?" Tristan asks. "This is a terrible idea."

"That's why I didn't tell you about it earlier," Dion says as he combs the stones carefully, searching for the opening that was promised, but the longer he searches, the louder my heart starts thudding.

"I don't like how exposed we are," I say, eyeing the top of the walls.

"It's only a matter of time before a patrol pops by," Tristan says. "You sure you trust this contact of yours?"

"Positive," Dion spits out.

"Who exactly is this contact?" Tristan presses. "How do we know this isn't some sort of trap?"

"Guess you'll just have to trust me," Dion says.

"I don't trust a Nazco further than I can spit."

"Thanks, I appreciate that," I say sarcastically, fisting my hips.

"Other than you, of course," Tristan says with a grimace, rubbing the back of his neck.

I roll my eyes and step up to the wall. "It will take all night to search this section," I mutter. "Let me see if I can find it."

Taking a deep breath, I focus my senses, trailing my palm across the stone and vines. I shove aside the sensation of the cool breeze flowing across my cheeks, the warm scent of the earth beneath my feet, and the chirp of the crickets. Instead, I scour for the bands of power flowing around me. Dion's and Tristan's are the most obvious, and then there are the walls, infused with the strength of rock power along with something else.

A deeper power tingles to my right. It has a different humming thread to it than the stone. I scrub away the vines to uncover a small doorway. An imprint of a circle with a bird in flight at its center.

"You found it." Dion stares at me with pride in his eyes. "Nicely done."

He pulls out a disc that looks like a half-dollar coin and

presses it against the symbol. The doorway softly clicks and creaks open.

"Whose symbol is that on the door?" Tristan asks warily as we dart inside.

"Our contact's," Dion says and turns to face Tristan. "If you're going to question me at every turn, you should leave now. We don't have time for second-guessing. If any of us get caught, we'll be executed without a trial."

"Leave?" Tristan's eyes flash. "Just when things are getting interesting? Think I'll stick around. You know, the whole 'keep your enemies close' thing."

"Seriously?" Dion snaps. "That's your response?"

This is my fault. I'm the one who wanted them both to come with me when we escaped the castle. "We need him, Dion, and you know it," I say before slipping inside the fortress. "There's strength in numbers. Now which way do we go?"

The two follow me inside. It's a long tunnel where we could go left or right. Dion holds up the disc, which illuminates when he faces right.

"Right it is," he says, and the three of us take off down the corridor at a light jog. Voices echo against the cold stone up ahead, warning us that guards are coming. Dion grabs my arm and yanks me into a small room on the left. Ghostly orange flames flicker from torches, glinting off weapons stacked along the walls. Large bins are set in the center of the room, full of glistening balls of green liquid. The power from within them sours in my mouth.

Poison.

The guards are speaking in Japanese. I understand a smattering of it, so I must have studied it in my former life.

Professor Henrich told me he thought I attended some Nazcoian school, the Midnight something, he called it, which was for those with high powers.

"I think they're coming in here," I whisper.

Dion grimaces. "Hide."

"Where's Tristan?"

"He's a big boy. He'll be fine."

We duck behind one of the large bins.

"Did I attend a school called Midnight?" I ask.

He lifts his eyebrows. "This is hardly the time, but yes. The Midnight Academy. Why?"

Interesting. The professor was telling me the truth. I'm about to explain just as two guards walk inside. I hold my breath as they discuss how much they hate the night shift. Dion checks his watch.

Five minutes.

It's a timer that counts down our entry window to wherever Dion's contact arranged for us. His jaw tightens.

"Are we tight on time?" I whisper.

Dion shakes his head, dark eyes warning me to be quiet.

"I don't know why these need to be reorganized," one guard says.

"Busy work." The other shrugs. "Trying to keep us out of trouble."

Dion's eyes flash to mine. "We can't sit here while they rearrange the whole blistering room."

"I've got an idea," I say.

But before I can offer it, Tristan pops into the room, a mischievous grin on his face. "Well, hello, there."

The two guards jerk with surprise. One drops the dagger he was shelving.

"Who are you?" the other asks, fumbling to pull out his sword.

"You wouldn't happen to know where I can find some good coffee?" Tristan asks, advancing on them lazily, but I don't miss how taunt his muscular arms are. "I'm in desperate need of some strong brew."

Then with sudden speed, he grabs the guy and smashes him against the wall.

Meanwhile, Dion leaps up, grabs a shield off the wall and knocks the other on the back of the head. Both guards crumble to the floor.

"Come on," Dion says. "We're running out of time."

The two take off out of the room, and I follow, snatching up one of the green balls because it's always a good idea to be prepared. Adrenaline surges through my veins as I pump my legs. I'm glad we took the time to change clothing once we left Slovakia and entered Japan so I'm not encumbered by my ballgown, but we've been on the run for over twenty-four hours since we left the masquerade ball, and I can feel my body breaking down.

My muscles twinge from running. My bones still ache from being slammed to the ground by Valeska. Tonight has taught me I'm hardly in good shape. If I'm going to be able to help my friends, I need to become stronger. If I survive tonight, I promise myself I'll train harder.

We careen around a corner only to stop short when we find two guards standing up ahead at a post.

"We've got more target practice up ahead," Tristan says.

They spot us and jerk to life, lifting their spears and pointing them at us.

Dion shoots out a bolt of electricity at them that

shivers over their bodies, causing them to drop their weapons as they cry out in shock. But they manage to press an alarm.

"Way to be subtle," Tristan grumbles as we take off once again.

"We don't have time to be subtle," Dion says as a wailing sound fills the air. "We've got minutes to cross the gate before it closes."

"I'm starting to second-guess this arrangement with your contact," Tristan says as I stab an oncoming guard and continue running. "Every second here, we're putting Estrella's life in danger."

When we arrived in Kyoto, Dion explained the plan to us. He would bring me to meet a powerful immortal who could help me get my powers back. Except this contact only gave us a small window of time before the entrance to their complex is closed off until the next quarter moon.

"Both of you stop arguing," I say, gasping for air as we hunker at the base of the stairs. "We have to work together if we're going to survive this place."

The two grumble in agreement, and we take off again, racing up the stone stairwell. It spills us into a courtyard outside, full of training equipment and military gear. The cool night yanks at my long braid trailing behind my back and snaps against my black jacket. Those same strange pumpkin-colored torches ring the perimeter, illuminating the grounds in an eerie glow like jack-o-lanterns lined up on All Hallows' Eve. A second-story walkway curls around the courtyard, packed full of guards patrolling it.

A long wooden bridge spans across a pond where glowing lily pads and iridescent flowers bob on its surface.

They're so beautiful that I want to stop and take it all in, but Dion is pointing up ahead.

"There it is," he whispers.

My attention pivots to the glowing red gate at the end of the bridge. It's made of two upright pillars that support two horizontal crossbars, one slightly curved, the other straight. The center is dark and shimmery like an inky pool of water.

"How are we supposed to cross that without being seen?" Tristan asks.

"Like a ninja," Dion says, which earns him an incredulous look from both of us. "Let's go."

He takes off.

"I sure hope this contact of his can help me," I grumble.

"I'll take the rear," Tristan tells me.

I race off after Dion, my heart tumbling around in my ribcage like a bird in flight. As we get closer, doubts storm my thoughts. There's no way we can make it. The odds are impossible. The gate is too far, and there are too many soldiers here.

"Intruders!" a guard yells out from above.

The boom of a gong rings across the area like a death knell. My lungs burn, but I force my legs to move faster. Shouts from the other guards rise up. Arrows zing down from above, landing inches from my feet, pinging like rain pellets. Dion waits for me at the bridge's entrance as I sprint up to him.

"Keep running," he orders. "Don't stop until you pass through the gate."

"I'm not leaving you," I say, turning to find Tristan just behind me, his flaming sword already clashing against three guards.

"Run!" Tristan calls over his shoulder.

I grit my teeth as I spot five more guards barreling up to fight Tristan and Dion. There's no way I'm letting these two sacrifice themselves for me.

"Hold your breath!" I call out.

I hurl the green ball I picked up in the weapons room, aiming just behind the first group of guards. I pray it's really poison. The glass ball shatters at the feet of the guards. Emerald-green vapor rises into the air. Instantly, the guards start choking, clenching their throats and dropping to their knees.

The three of us back away and then dash across the bridge in a full sprint, my boots pounding against the wooden planks beneath me. Arrows whiz around me. I duck and twist, barely missing their sharp tips.

I'm nearly at the gate when a form rises out of the water's depths like a monster who's been rudely awoken. A Samurai warrior hauls himself with surprising agility onto the bridge, landing directly in front of me, water dripping from his body. I stop short and hold out my dagger before this giant. Tidebreaker flashes stormy blue, ready to strike. I don't have to turn around to hear Tristan and Dion battling behind me.

He grins at my weapon as if it's a child's toy. His plated armor is a mix of stone and leather. A long pointed beard hangs from his chin, accentuating his lethal persona. In either hand, he clutches two stone swords. Fear claws at my chest. He's a Stone Wielder.

With a growl, he whips them through the air like they're feather-light. I leap backward milliseconds before his blade can cut me in half. He comes at me again and again, swooping arcs in a deadly dance.

Tidebreaker clangs against his blade. The power of the Samurai shudders through my body, sending a sharp pang up my arm. Somehow I manage to hold onto my dagger. But this warrior is relentless. With a growl, he lunges in attack once again.

Too fast. Too strong.

I scream, waiting for one of his blades to finally find its mark.

From behind, Dion dives between me and the tip of the sword. It slices across Dion's side, carving him open.

Dion's cry of pain erupts through the chaos. I scream, reaching for him, but Tristan's strong arms lift me off the ground before I can come to Dion's aid. He hurls me through the gate.

"No!" I cry out, twisting around as my body hurtles through a swirl of darkness.

The last thing I see is Dion and Tristan facing the warrior on one side and a horde of guards on the other.

2
THE HIDDEN REALM
ESTRELLA

Kakurezato, Japan

My body crashes onto hard stone, pain shooting up the side of my arm from the impact. Stars swirl through my vision. I groan.

"Well, well, well," a smooth, melodic voice says not far from me. "Look what the cat dragged in."

I blink away the dizziness and push myself up, taking in my surroundings. Rectangular lanterns sway from shifting trees, casting patterns from their geometric designs. The air smells intoxicatingly sweet like blossoms in full bloom. A shockingly beautiful woman stands on the path before me with two men on either side, pointing sharp-tipped, silvery swords at me.

Great. And here I thought it would be safer on this side of the gate.

I study the woman, a knowing smirk curled on her ruby-red lips. She's wearing a silk dress dotted with pink cherry blossoms. Its side cuts are high, revealing toned, muscular thighs, warning me to not be deceived by her dress. A thick sash hugs her waist, and her low-cut bodice shows off a gemmed necklace, nestled between two plump breasts. Unlike the two men beside her, I don't feel a lick of power emanating from her visik.

Which is strange, considering this place is dripping with powers.

Could she be a mortal?

I shake my head. I don't have time for these thoughts. I need to go back through that gate to help Tristan and Dion. I grimace as I stand and stumble back toward the black-pooled gate.

"I wouldn't go back through that if I were you," the woman calls to my back. "They'll kill you."

"My friends need me," I say.

As if saying the word, both Tristan and Dion come crashing through the pitch-black void and tumble onto the stone, joining me in whatever place this is. Even in the semi-darkness, I don't miss the blood soaking through Dion's jacket while more blood drips down Tristan's arm.

"Dion! Tristan!" I rush to them, wanting to throw my arms around both, but stop, unsure of whom to go to first. My heart squeezes in confusion. "You made it, but are you okay?"

"Barely," Tristan half-growls, crouched as if preparing to decapitate these guards too. Blood is smeared across his face. He's fierce as a lion, ready to rip apart any who come too close.

"You are safe," Dion tells me, but his words are slurred. "That's all that matters."

I spin to face the woman, anger welling up inside me, a furnace ready to explode. "Who are you and where are we? Will you help us? My friends are hurt."

"Welcome to my realm, Kakurezato. My name is Ami and this is my trusted advisor, Sensei Haruki." She steps closer to Dion, clucking her tongue and swiping a finger along his jaw. Protectiveness—or is it jealousy?—rears up inside me. "Utter dedication. Quite inspiring."

"You can keep your hands to yourself," I growl at her.

"You should've warned me there would be a whole battalion of warriors," Dion tells Ami. He clenches his jaw, his body shuddering.

"I needed to see if she was worthy," she says. "I don't just let anyone pay me a visit. I'm particular."

I touch Dion's arm, feeling the intense heat. I glare at Ami. "That Samurai blade was poisoned. He needs medical attention now."

"You can be assured, Estrella," she says smoothly, "Dion's every need will be met and he will be well taken care of."

"You know our names," I say as realization hits me. "You're our contact."

"Yes, I am. But you, I was not expecting." Ami's gaze swivels to Tristan. She taps her finger against her chin. "The Prince of the Sabians. Fascinating, but you were not a part of the arrangement."

"Surprises are my specialty," Tristan says, shooting her a wary look.

"You must leave," she says, waving lazily at the gate. "Now."

I can't take her treatment of Dion and Tristan any longer. I step in front of the two men, cross my arms, and level my gaze at her.

"I don't know what deal you made with Dion to let me come here," I say, "but we've come a long way and battled through Nazco, Sabian, and now those Eien warriors just to speak to you. Humor us for a moment and tend to these men's needs."

"You've got fire for a girl who has lost her powers," Ami says. "Either that or you're just foolish."

I swallow the fear climbing up my throat and lift my chin. "So is that a yes?"

Ami smirks, eyes glittering, and that's when I realize they're blue. I hold back a gasp. Ami is a Channeler, and heaven help me, I bet she's the one Dion arranged to train me. She flicks her fingers, indicating for us to follow her. My heart sinks. I may have just made an enemy of the one person who could actually help me.

Her two guards trail alongside the three of us. Dion stumbles and I grab a hold of his arm to support him.

"Thank you for bringing him through the gate," I tell Tristan. "You saved his life."

"I didn't have a choice because he was leading us," he hisses, looking anything but pleased. Wild blond curls hang over his eyes, and his large frame looks like he's tempted to spring and behead Ami's two guards. "This is why I don't trust Nazco."

The stone path cuts through a canopy of cherry blossom trees, lit by lanterns glowing buttery yellow in the evening.

Fireflies buzz around us as if welcoming us to this new world. Up ahead, a multi-tiered wooden palace is silhouetted against the night sky. Steeply pitched roofs covered with tiles curve upward like a traditional pagoda. The eaves extend far beyond the walls as if protecting the layers from rain and snow.

I wonder how many immortals tend to these grounds because the whole place is drenched with power.

Ami leads us up a long stone stairway to the main entrance. More guards stand at attention, stiff as statues by a giant golden circle with the same symbol that was on the wall outside—a bird in flight. By the time we step inside the large room complete with wooden beams crisscrossing above our heads, Dion can barely keep his head up. His whole body leans heavily against me. Ami claps her hands, calling for servants.

"You must let her train you," Dion whispers into my ear. "But never trust her."

I want to argue with him that I don't want to train with someone I can't trust, but I'm too worried about Dion so I nod. Tristan and I help him onto a low cushion on one of the mats. His eyes land on Tristan as his whole body begins shuddering.

"It is not safe for you to stay here," he murmurs loud enough for only Tristan and me to hear. "You should leave. I don't trust her."

Tristan's eyes darken. He glances over at Ami and her guards. "I think it's best if I stay. At least until you're back on your feet."

Dion's eyes flutter shut. Fear shoots through my veins. I cling to his hand, wishing I had power to give him.

"We need a Healer," I call out. "Now!"

Ami's head snaps in our direction, and concern finally registers across her face. "Tamaka!" she yells, and a small woman hurries into the room, bowing. "Take care of this man. If he dies, you will join him."

"Yes, master," Tamaka says, dips his torso.

I should be happy with Ami's commitment to Dion's survival, but there's something about her urgency that nags me. Why is she so concerned about Dion? The guards rush over to pick him up and place him on a stretcher. I wring my hands in worry. Should I let him out of my sight? Or perhaps I should focus on helping Tristan. My emotions swirl all through me in confusion.

"What about Tristan?" I say. "He's also hurt."

"That will come with a price," Ami says, sashaying over to join us.

"I feel great," Tristan says, his glare still firmly in place. "Ready to send a few more warriors to join their comrades in the afterlife."

"So brave, this one," Ami says, eyes sweeping over him with calculated precision. "But he isn't staying long enough to be attended to."

The thought of losing Tristan from my side and being here alone, unprotected by the Eien, terrifies me. A wave of dizziness and fear threatens to break me down.

"Would you enter enemy territory without one of your guards?" I ask her. She doesn't answer right away, which tells me she's not used to being challenged. Oddly, her eyes glitter and her eyebrow ticks up. I think she likes it. "That's what I thought. Tristan stays until Dion is fully recovered."

Ami's eyes slide to stare at Tristan and she shrugs

nonchalantly. "I suppose it wouldn't hurt to have a little added eye candy here. At least for now. Estrella, you will want to rest. Tomorrow you and I will start your training."

There are so many questions crowding my brain but there's one that is screaming the loudest.

"Why have you agreed to help me?" I ask, narrowing my eyes. "Obviously, you're not doing this out of the kindness of your heart. What's in it for you?"

She lifts her eyebrows. "Dion didn't tell you? Interesting."

The heat of Tristan's power flares up beside me like it does when he gets angry or upset.

"What did Dion promise?" I ask in a low voice.

"You'll have to ask him that," she says vaguely. "My servants will escort you and your...guard...to your room. The moment you hurt any of my staff or break any of my rules, I promise you will regret it. I will see you, Estrella, at dawn for your first training session. It will be painful."

Panic spears my chest but I quickly thwart it. "I will be ready," I say.

She breezes out of the main room and down a corridor, the ends of her dress flaring up in her wake. The moment she leaves, I search Tristan's face to find his eyes as stormy and dark as the ocean before a hurricane.

"Did I make a mistake coming here?" I whisper to him.

"I don't trust her or Dion," Tristan says, his eyes shifting to focus on me as if I'm his entire world. "But I'll do everything in my power to protect you."

3
WHO CAN I TRUST?
ESTRELLA

Kakurezato, Japan

A servant wearing a white kimono shuffles over to stand before us. She bows. "If you would come this way, please."

Tristan and I trail after her along the wooden floors. His large frame takes up most of the space in the corridors. The palace is lit by paper lanterns with geometric wooden frames. Screens decorated with flowers and mountain scenes are set up along the way, emitting a calm and peaceful atmosphere. This place is the epitome of serenity, and yet, every fiber of my being warns me that each breath I take is a gift.

We're taken to a square room with cedar plank floors and smooth wooden walls. It's so foreign compared to Nadia's and Tristan's castle in Slovakia. Straw mats are placed strategically by the entrance, the wall, and the bathing area. A single bed, set on a low bed frame with a cream-colored spread, is situated before a glass wall, over-looking subtly lit gardens.

"Can everyone look into this room?" I ask, feeling like I'm a caged animal on display.

"This shoji screen will offer privacy," the woman says.

She takes the end of the sliding door made of wood and translucent paper and rolls it across the wall. My tension releases. After everything I've been through, it doesn't take much to get me thrown off. I spin around and assess the rest of the room. But there isn't much else in the room other than a jar of bamboo sticks, a chest, and a low table. The opposite wall is a mural of rounded mountains and a maple tree, its leaves sunset red.

"In the chest," the woman continues, "you'll find clothing for sleeping and training. Food will be served soon."

"Please send in bandages and ointment as well," I say.

Her gaze whips to Tristan, and there's no mistaking the fear in her eyes. Not that I'd blame her. Between the blood smeared across his face, wild hair, and muscular body, he looks like he could rip her in half any moment.

Actually, he probably could.

She swallows, saying, "I will see what I can do."

With a bow, she slips out through the sliding door, closing it gently behind her. I turn to face Tristan.

"I have to admit," I say, "the whole atmosphere of Ami's realm is soothing."

"I don't trust her or this place," he says and marches

around the room, inspecting each corner as if searching for a trap.

"You don't trust the Eien?" I ask. "I thought the Sabians and Eien were allies."

"Allies? We are allies with the Caladrians. You could say the Sabians and Eien tolerate each other. Mostly."

I nod, but it's clear I need to get a better understanding of the politics of this immortal world that I'm being dragged into. "We need to attend to your wounds," I say.

He glowers at the room as if it's full of booby traps. "I'll be fine."

"If you want to protect me," I flash him a knowing smile, "you need to stay healthy. Now take off that jacket and let me have a look."

"Ah, ordering me to undress now?" He winks and starts unzipping his jacket. Halfway down, he winces.

I roll my eyes. "Here," I say, stepping up to him, "let me help."

His presence drapes around me like a warm blanket.

"I feel a little guilty about bringing you into all of this," I say. "I asked you to come, but I didn't know it would be this dangerous."

"I wanted to come." His voice is low, and I feel his eyes on me as I pull down on the zipper of his jacket.

I'm thankful that Dion's contact provided us with armored clothing. I'm realizing he saved all three of our lives. The zipper of Tristan's tight leather jacket crackles through the tight silence. Beneath, his rippled chest is hard against my fingers. My gaze follows the zipper's path down to his stomach and well-defined hips. I gulp and swallow.

Pull yourself together, I order myself. I need to focus on getting him healed, not ogling his stacked form.

Gently, I push the jacket off his shoulder. It drops with a thud to the ground. My eyes assess him for injuries. A jagged cut has sliced open the side of his arm. The blood covers his arm and has caked up on the wound, but it's black and angry.

I run a finger along it, testing to see if there are any residual powers from the blade. Sure enough, a biting sensation snaps at my skin. I jerk my hand away.

"You've been poisoned as well," I say. "Not as bad as Dion, but we need to wash it out."

I direct him to the tub. Beside it is a stand with a scrub brush, towel, and bar of soap.

"Is this your way of trying to get me naked, Estrella?" he teases, grinning wickedly.

"Hardly." But my face burns. "I'm trying to save your life. You can keep the rest of your clothing on."

I push him onto the edge of the tub and begin running the water. With the towel, I gently scrub away the poison and blood caking his arm and face. As my hands run over his body, my pulse kicks up. My eyes skim over his bare chest and my heart hums being so close to him. He stares up at me, eyes soft and vulnerable. We've been through too much together, and yet, somehow not enough. Ami wants him gone, but how can I let him go? We're so close that I could lean down and press my lips against his.

"Thank you for coming with us," I finally say in a whisper. "You risked your life for me and Dion. I owe you."

"You owe me nothing." His voice is gravely deep. "I made the choice to come with you, my love."

My heart stutters at those words. My love. Am I his love? Do I even deserve him after everything that happened back at his castle?

"I know your people want nothing to do with someone like me. I don't belong—"

He rises and his uninjured arm drags me against him. His mouth finds mine, smoldering heat that melts me into a puddle. I sink into the kiss. The cloth drops from my fingers, and I run my palms up his chest and then cup my hands behind his neck to pull him even closer to me.

A thrill whirls through me. There's something about kissing Tristan that whisks me away from all the madness that we've had to survive, leaving behind just the two of us. Our love is a cocoon against the rest of the world that clamors to rip us apart. His people hate me. He's supposed to be my greatest enemy and yet here we are, creating a world of our own.

His hot lips trail along my forehead, sending shivers up and down my spine. Strong hands stroke my back and our kiss intensifies. His mouth nips at my bottom lip and then his lips drag to my ear, hot as the sun. I gasp and skim my kiss, wild and untamed as him, down his neck.

The sound of the sliding door cuts through the haze of our passion. I quickly pull away and turn to find Ami, a wicked grin on her face. I push back the loose strands of hair that have fallen out of my braid and stand taller, calming the racing of my heart. Tristan instinctively shifts his body so he's in front of me.

"Isn't this fascinating?" she says. "I brought you a Healer. He has the cream that the Prince will need to cleanse the poison from his system. But it will come at a price."

"And that is?" I narrow my eyes.

"The Sabian Prince must leave now."

Leave? Yeah, that's not happening. "Why? You agreed he could stay until Dion gets well."

"He's a distraction as you've just demonstrated."

She knows I'm a Channeler, which means she also knows that with him, I've got powers. Without him, I'm only as powerful as those I can channel through.

"I won't agree to that," I say.

"Then the poison will slowly seep into his system and drive him mad."

This woman is conniving and dangerous. She's put me against the wall and knows I won't sacrifice Tristan to get what I want. As much as I wish I was strong enough on my own, I know I'm not. I'd be an idiot to stay here without someone at my side.

"I'm not leaving her unprotected," Tristan interrupts.

"One day," I finally concede.

"I now see why the Empress was so eager to get rid of you," Ami says. She nods to her Healer. He goes to Tristan and begins slathering on the cream. "You have a deal, Estrella. Always remember that nothing comes without a price. I will see you at dawn."

The moment Ami and her Healer leave, Tristan turns on me.

"I can't leave you here alone," he says.

"Dion will be here." As soon as I say that, his face jerks back like he's been slapped and I wish I could pull back my words.

"I don't trust Ami nor do I trust Dion. They both have an

agenda and you know it's true. They made some sort of deal, which he conveniently did not tell us about."

"He hasn't exactly had time to explain things."

"Like he never had time to explain to you in Florida that you were an immortal with powers?"

I press my lips together and turn my back to him. Tristan's one hundred percent right, except why do I still trust and believe in Dion? It's like something deep inside me understands him in a way that I can't explain.

"When Dion gets better," I finally say, "I'll talk to him about this agreement he made with Ami. How is your arm? Did the Healer's cream help?"

He nods stiffly. "It will be fine. I'm going to call Katka and check in. My parents will be worried."

"More like furious," I mutter. "I hope they don't hate me."

"They would never hate you," he says as he makes the call.

I cringe, thinking about how I left. How many people got hurt by me trying to escape? What must they think of me, knowing that I ran off with a Nazco and their Prince? My heart still hangs heavy remembering how that one Nazco who'd exposed his undercover status died trying to help me escape.

"Katka," Tristan says and puts her on speaker, "it's me. I'm checking in."

"You have a lot of nerve calling me," she answers. "What is happening? Everyone is saying that the Nazco Channeler has bewitched and kidnapped you?"

Tristan rolls his eyes but I sag onto the bed, hating how true her words sound. I can see myself from her point of view. It's not a pretty picture. Guilt flames up inside me. I should never have asked him to come with me. He's sacrificing his reputation just to help me.

"I'm with her in Eien territory," Tristan explains. "We're working with a Channeler here who has agreed to help Estrella get her memories and powers back."

"Really?" Katka's voice sounds surprised, if not still skeptical. Then there's a shocking pause. Is Katka really at a loss for words?

"Are you still there?" Tristan asks. "I need you to tell my parents that I've got everything under control."

"So what happened the other night at the masquerade ball was your version of things being under control?" Katka asks.

"That was Valeska and her friends," Tristan says. "My intentions have never wavered."

"Your job was to get Estrella to trust you so you'd convince her to join us. Putting your own people in danger was not part of the plan. And manipulating Estrella to join us by kissing her wasn't either."

Tristan's eyes flick to mine. My heart sinks. Had our relationship only been a way to sway me to join the Sabians? I look away, unsure what to think. I knew they wanted to help me regain my memory and powers so I'd consider becoming their next Conduit, but the last thing I wanted was to put a rift between him and his people.

"Just pass on my news to my father," Tristan says, rubbing his forehead. "I'll be in contact again when I have another update."

He hangs up and crosses the room to stand in front of

me. "I didn't kiss you to manipulate you. I kissed you because I have feelings for you."

After how things ended with Dion, I admit that what Katka said hit a little too close to home. Threads of distrust wind their way around my chest.

"Right now I don't know what to believe or think other than it seems like no one wants us to have a relationship."

"That might be true, but it doesn't change my feelings for you."

He eyes me, tormented, and then steps closer, trailing his fingers along the edge of my jaw. The heat of him ebbs and flows around us, a shell against the storm set against us.

"We haven't really talked about...us," I finally manage. "Or what we shouldn't be or do." My body warms just thinking about that passionate kiss we just shared. "But I'm a Nazco, no matter if I forgot who I was or not. And you're a Sabian Prince. Even if I wanted us to work, I don't know how it's possible."

"You're right." His voice is soft as feathers and laced with pain. "Yet, I wish you weren't. But there must be a way. We can figure it out, I know it."

"Maybe." Or maybe not. I sigh. "Let's not worry about it right now. You need to rest and get healed up. It's been a long time since either of us got sleep." Today has been too much and far too long. My nerves are jumbled and I feel ready to break into a million pieces. I pad over to the chest and pull out a soft gray kimono-style jacket and matching pants. "I'm going to take a bath and get some sleep. Apparently, tomorrow is a big day."

Tristan nods and I know he's trying to hide his disappointment, but he has never been a good liar. "You take the bed. I'll sleep on the floor."

"That's probably for the best," I say, watching as he settles himself on a mat, placing his sword by his side. A deep ache fills me. It's the right choice, but deep down I just want to curl up in his arms where the world is safe and warm.

4
AWAKENING THE INNER POWER
ESTRELLA

Kakurezato, Japan

A sweet breeze whispers across my cheeks, smelling of blossoms and pine as Tristan and I head down the wooded path, following our guide toward the dōjō where I'm supposed to meet Ami for my first lesson. I'm wearing the soft gray training tunic and matching pants I found in the chest.

We pass through a thicket of bamboo trees, which opens into a garden area, complete with a small pond with a bamboo fountain in its center. A narrow, railing-free bridge arches over the pond into a single-story wooden building with a curved, gray-tiled roof. Our guide stops and turns to face Tristan.

"You will stay here," he says.

"I'm not letting her out of my sight," Tristan replies. Dark circles ring his eyes. His face is paler than usual. Even though I slept fitfully, when I did wake, he was sitting, facing the door, his sword slightly illuminated across his knees as if eager to be used.

"I'll be fine," I say, lightly touching his arm. "I'll be just through that doorway. You should rest."

Indecision flickers across his features, but finally he nods.

"I'll be waiting then," he tells me as I cross the bridge.

I toss him a smile before entering the dōjō, trying to hide the fact that my heart is pounding and my muscles are in rebellion against each of my steps. Just being in Ami's presence unnerves me, but to rely on her for my training is even more unsettling.

After I take off my slippers as my guide instructs me, I step inside. I find Ami sitting cross-legged in the center of a spacious room made of natural wood and exposed beams overhead. Her eyes are closed, and her face is illuminated by the pale yellow light filtering through the paper screens. Quickly, I assess the area to see who else is here. Japanese calligraphy scrolls hang on one wall while another wall is filled with katanas, short daggers, and long poles.

We are alone.

I pad over to her and settle onto the floor, crossing my legs.

"Close your eyes," she says, so softly I almost miss it.

I swallow my fear and obey.

"Now breathe in deeply," she instructs. "Stretch out your senses. Feel the powers around you. The visik of the immortals and the powers infused in objects and the land. Do you sense them?"

I take a deep breath and follow her instructions. Tristan's powers flicker strong and heated not far away. At first, that's all I feel, but then I notice the flutter of powers within the weapons on the walls. My eyes pop open, and I glance over at them, hanging proudly on the walls.

"Yes," she says, her eyes now open, "those weapons are power-infused."

"And the ink on the scrolls," I add. "Although I don't recognize the power source."

"Impressive."

"The bamboo trees, too? How is that possible?"

"You are more attuned to your powers than I expected from someone whose memory was wiped." She rises to her feet and strides over to her weapons wall. "Now let's see if you were trained in the way of the sword."

She snatches a curved blade off the wall and holds it out to me. Once I take it, she grabs one for herself and returns to the center of the room. She bows.

"We're supposed to bow before a fight?" I ask,

Her lips twitch. "Nazco would never bow. They have no respect."

Before I have a chance to respond, she attacks. Her blade flicks out as quick as a whip. Clumsily, I hold up my katana in defense, blocking her strike. The impact jars against my arm. In a fluid lunge, she attacks again. I parry, our swords clashing. Steel sparks into the air.

There's something familiar about the movements and my muscles respond but they are sluggish and weak. I must have learned something about the craft of fencing, but all I have to show for it is a hint of muscle memory.

The power of the blades hums in the air, visik begging to be used. The hilt of my sword shivers electric across my palms. I allow it to soak into my body.

"You're reacting and poorly at that," she responds. "Dig deep and allow your muscle memory to take over."

"What if I wasn't trained to fight?" I ask.

"Then luck hasn't found you today."

She pivots and sweeps her sword in a controlled arc, aiming directly for my side. I leap backward, feeling the hum of her sword swishing through the air, a millimeter from gutting me open.

Fear chases up my spine. She isn't playing around. I grit my teeth and focus on our blades. She presses forward and I faint left, only to jerk right. I swing at her shoulder, but she blocks me effortlessly. Our blades flash and whirl through the air, faster and faster.

She's a master while I can barely hang on. Sweat drips down my face. My arms burn. My breathing is ragged, even with the power of the sword surging through my veins. Soon, my movements become too slow. Brute strength isn't enough to overcome my lack of skill. In a sweeping motion, her blade aims for my legs. I twist at the last moment to avoid being cut and fall to the floor.

She looms over me, her long, dark hair trailing across my chest. Her blade points at my throat.

Tristan storms into the room, sword flaming. "Step aside or I will kill you," he orders.

Ami rolls her eyes and withdraws her sword. I scramble to my feet, my heart hammering.

"Do you really think I would kill her?" Ami asks him.

He doesn't answer. His stormy face says it all.

"That's the easiest thing I could do to her, but no," she says, walking back to the wall and placing her sword on the hook. "I wanted to see how far she could go when pressed. She needs training if she wants to survive in the immortal world. She is not ready, and you storming in here hardly helps. This is why I want you gone from my realm. You are hindering her training."

"I've got this," I tell Tristan. "But thank you. Your presence means a lot to me."

He steps back without a word and storms out of the dōjō. I return my sword to its place.

"I know you say he's hindering my training," I tell her, "but he's saved me numerous times. I trust him with my life. You, I definitely do not."

She presses her lips together and leads me out to the veranda where tea is set up on a low table. I settle on the cushion opposite her as she pours us tea.

"I'm assuming you know the basics of how a Channeler operates," she begins.

"I've been learning and Queen Kelli taught me a lot. Like how I can pull powers from other immortals and use them. How to use powers infused into objects."

"Good." She sips her tea. "The queen's daughter—Tristan's sister—was a Channeler. Ivana was powerful for her age but too trusting. That is why she's dead."

I jerk at the harshness of Ami's words. "You knew her?"

"But of course." She eyes me. "She was a Conduit."

"And you." I swallow. "You're the Eien Conduit, aren't you?"

She nods, studying me carefully.

Instantly, a million questions hammer at my brain. What is it like? How do you become a Conduit? But the most burning question leaps from my lips as I say, "Tristan tells me that I, too, was a Conduit. Did you know me before I lost my memories?"

"No, but that's only because the night you entered the World of Between and passed your test, you were also excommunicated and cast out from the Nazco without your memories."

"So you know what happened to me."

She laughs. "Oh, yes. When it comes to news about Conduits, I make it my business to know."

"The deal Dion made with you was to help me get my powers back, wasn't it?"

Her dark blue eyes study mine. "Yes. And that is what I will do."

"But why? You obviously don't like me. I don't see what you have to gain from this."

"I am doing it because I hate the Empress with every fiber of my being. Considering that she took away your powers, it stands a chance you'd like revenge. If you had your powers back, would you help us overthrow her?"

"Yes, absolutely."

She grins and her eyes sparkle. "That was what I had been counting on."

"So you think it's possible for me to get my powers back then?"

"Not likely, but I have yet to see this happen with a Conduit so I am willing to give it a try. And I do love a challenge."

"There's something I need to be honest with you about as well," I admit. Her thin eyebrows rise. "The Sabian's Dragon Seer sent me to you."

"What?" And for the first time, I think I've caught Ami off guard.

"She said I needed to find you and have you take me to the World of Between. There I'll find what I seek."

"The World of Between?" she sputters and then laughs hysterically. "You would never make it there. The Ring would consume you in its starlight before you could even set a toe inside."

"A ring? What do you mean?"

"The Ring is the entrance into the World of Between and only a powerful Channeler can soak in the force of its power to travel through the portal. Most Channelers don't even try because very few are powerful enough to survive the entry. I doubt your powers are enough to enter the World of Between."

"But I did once before, so there must be something I can do."

She looks away, staring at the pond. "There is something. But it's a great risk and highly dangerous."

"I'm not afraid of risk or danger," I say firmly. "I want to do it."

5
POISON CAN BURN THE BONES

DION

Kakurezato, Japan

Fire wakes me. *Fates alive, I'm burning.* Gasping, I jerk to sit up. Cool hands press a wet cloth to my forehead. It does nothing to calm the flames raging through my veins.

I blink past the crimson coating my vision. A young woman frantically dips the cloth back into a basin of water, her dark brown eyes clouded in worry. She's wearing a white wrapped tunic and pants. Her jet-black hair is pulled back into a bun strapped in place with a decorated long pin.

"You must rest," she says in her lilting Eien accent, pressing the cool cloth to my bare chest.

I frown, the pain making it almost impossible to think properly. Sweat pools down my face. My chest is slicked wet.

Something on my arm catches my attention. It looks like a tattoo of a bird in flight. I know for a fact I've never gotten a tattoo. This is troubling.

"Where am I?" I ask the Eien Healer. My voice cracks, tired. Burned out.

"You're in the home of Ami, the Great Conduit of the Eien."

"Ami?" The name is vaguely familiar. I press against the fiery burn until the fragments of memories snap into place, one by one.

I made a deal with Ami, the Eien's Conduit. She would help Estrella get her memories back. I'd make sure Estrella gave her the location of the lost Temple of Fates. Except the moment we signed the binding agreement of powers, I feared I made the wrong choice.

No. This was the right choice.

The only choice.

"Estrella," I whisper. She's here. Alive and well. I need to find her, warn her to be careful around Ami, who I hardly trust. The Eien may not be fierce enemies with us like the Sabians are, but our peace is fragile as glass. Grunting, I swing my legs over the edge of the mat. "Blistering stars, what is wrong with me?"

"You can't leave," the Healer says, holding me in place as my body sways from the movement. "You were stabbed by a poisonous blade. If left unattended, it will eat away at your powers and mind."

"There must be something you can give me to speed things along. I can't just sit here like an absolute fool."

"You are hardly a fool! You fought against our greatest Samurai warrior and lived."

"The Stone Wielder?" I nod, the memory poking through the fiery fog of the poison. He had been the perfect foil against Tristan and me. They sent him because both my lightning and Tristan's fire powers fell meaninglessly on his rock skin. "Yeah, he was really fun. You must have some sort of herbal tea to help me out."

She sighs and pours brown liquid into a round teacup with no handle. "This should help. I couldn't give it to you in large doses before because you were sleeping. Drink it slowly. It will burn going down."

"Worse than it already does?" I dare ask, taking the drink.

"Yes." She flashes me a sympathetic look.

"Saúde." I hold up the teacup in a toast and then gulp down its contents. I expected the liquid to be hot, but it's as ice cold as the Antarctic Midnight Lands.

The cup falls from my fingers.

The Healer cries out, but her voice falls away as the liquid charges through my body. It slides through my veins, a burning ice. It coats my muscles in a glacial chill. My vision swims with blue. I clench my fists and focus on not passing out and wait for the pain to subside.

Heaving deep breaths, the heat of the poison fades somewhat, and my vision clears.

Soon, I'm able to rise to my feet. I'm wobbly and my hands shake as I reach for my freshly washed pants and shirt on a low table. I'm still so hot that the thought of putting anything on my skin is not ideal, but I can't go around naked.

Especially with Ami's mark tattooed so prominently on

my chest. The bird wasn't a tattoo that I got for fun; it is a representation of Ami's and my agreement.

Estrella must not see it.

Ever.

I can't let Estrella know how tightly Ami and I are bound. Both of us placed a portion of our powers into our signature as we signed that binding document. If either of us breaks the agreement, our portion of power is given to the other.

The Healer helps me dress. It takes nearly all my effort, and I'm forced to sit to recover before heading off to find Estrella. Thankfully, my phone is still with my limited possessions. I texted BJ the moment we exited the Water Channels into Kyoto to tell him that we were safe, but I want to give him an update.

BJ answers on the first ring. "Brother!" he says in a tone thick with worry. "Tell me you're okay and made it safely."

"I'm alive. Is there any news on the Nazco front about our escape?"

"None that I'm hearing about so far," he says. "Or at least the Sabians haven't mentioned it outside of their sphere. They must be keeping things very tight lipped. But the Empress has been asking for you."

"What did you tell her?"

"That you were very close to securing Estrella. That seemed to keep her happy."

"Good. We'll use that to our favor." I rub my eyes, trying to focus. I glance over at the Healer and move away, hoping she didn't overhear what BJ just said. "I need you to do some research for me. See if you can find any other cases where

the Empress used her scepter to implement the memory implant. Especially if any of them got their powers back."

"Didn't you already spend months looking into that after Estrella was taken away?"

"Yes." I lean against a doorframe. "But you're so much better at that sort of thing."

"Are you sure this is all worth it? Are you sure she's worth it?"

"Call me when you've got something."

I hang up, not wanting to get into a discussion with him. His words hurt more than I care to admit. It's obvious that Estrella and Tristan have formed a bond. And I get it. He rescued her. He has been trying to help her. But now I'm here, and I need to step it up and be there for her.

The Empress's deal still haunts me. She said if I brought Estrella to her, she could wipe Estrella's memories of Tristan. Tempting as it is, the thought of manipulating Estrella's mind makes my stomach roil.

I finish buttoning my shirt and head for the door.

"You can't leave, Master Cabral," the Healer tells me. "You are not completely healed."

Ignoring her, I head out into a long hallway of paper screens, emitting a pale glow from the sunlight outside. After asking the plant nurturers tending the gardens for Estrella's whereabouts, I hurry down the path toward a tiered pagoda with three curved tile roofs.

Estrella is standing with Ami at the bank of a pool beside the pagoda. Her long golden hair is braided down her back, and she's wearing a training tunic and pants similar to what Ami is wearing. Even though my whole body aches and each step takes effort, my worries ease to find that she's looking healthy and well.

When I step into the grove, I find Estrella and Ami aren't alone. Tristan is standing off to the side, a scowl printed on his face, and there's another immortal woman who is wading into the pool, wearing a shift that's almost translucent. What is happening?

"Estrella," I call out.

Everyone turns at the sound of my voice. Estrella's face brightens and just seeing her again fills me with renewed energy. She hurries to me and every muscle in my body wants to scoop her into my arms. When she reaches me, she hesitates as if she's not sure how to act or even if she should touch me.

A pang rattles my bones as I realize what's become of the two of us. It's like we've both grown up and the world that we once existed in has been washed away, taken by the winds of a tornado. We're now standing in its rubble, trying to figure out what is left and how much survived.

I don't know how to be the man I was once with her. In fact, it hits me how little we know about one another. So instead, I try to smile.

"Estrella," I say. "I'm glad you're safe."

"You look…" Her eyes search my face, and a crinkle pinches between her brows. "I'm glad you're okay, but you should rest."

Tristan joins us. "Looks like you might survive," he says.

"Appears so," I tell him. "I have you to thank for it. I suppose I owe you a life debt."

"We may not be friends," Tristan says, "but my world is too full of enemies. You owe me nothing."

I nod at him warily, my gaze shifting between him and Estrella. How close had they become while she was in Sabian territory? Why is a Sabian Prince risking his life to protect her? Dread pools into my gut. What has she promised him?

"Dion," a melodic voice calls from the pond's edge. *Ami.* I stiffen. "You're holding up Estrella's training."

My gaze follows hers to the woman wearing the shift climbing into the water. Once she reaches the center, she waits, standing there patiently.

I frown. "What sort of training is this?"

"This is Mai," Ami says. "She is a Reflector."

"Why do you need her for Estrella's training?" I ask, suspiciously.

"Ami doesn't think I'll survive the Ring test," Estrella says. "She wants to see how much of my powers are still flowing through me."

"I remember when you took your Ring test," I say softly.

Estrella's eyes widen. "You do?"

"When you returned, holding that ball of blue fire, you were a star sent straight from the skies to save us all. I was so proud of you. We all were."

Estrella bites her lips and tears spring to her eyes. "But obviously not enough." She goes to reach for my hand but stops, which pains me. "Why did the Empress do this to me? How could she after I brought the Nazco their powers?"

"That is the question of the hour," Ami says.

"It's complicated and something we need to talk about alone." I nod at Tristan and Ami. "But I do know she was afraid of you. Still is. Which is why I believe you can regain your powers as a Conduit."

"She has been practicing back at my home," Tristan says. "I was training her, but I'm hardly an expert on the ways of a Channeler much less a Conduit."

"You were training her?" My eyes widen in realization. "Ah, you want her to become your next Conduit? That's why you are here and why you went to such extremes to extract her."

"At least he was willing to tell me the truth," Estrella says stiffly. My words hurt her, but she needs to face the truth.

"That's impossible," Ami interrupts. "As a Nazco, she will only be able to manipulate Nazcoian fire. She could never be a Sabian Conduit."

"Are you sure?" Tristan asks, brows furrowing, and his gaze catches Estrella. She too looks upset.

"She's lucky if she can even wield Nazco fire," Ami says. "At this point it is a far-fetched idea if she can't even enter the Ring."

"Why do you need to go to the World of Between?" I ask Estrella. "It's far too dangerous. I think you need to focus on regaining your memories by activating what powers you have instead."

"I spoke to the Dragon Seer," she explains. "She said the answer to what I sought was in the World of Between."

"And how will this Reflector help you discover your powers?" I ask.

"She will submerge into the pool and her body will become a reflection of Estrella's," Ami explains. "Think of Mai as a mirror. When we look down at her, we will see where the powers flow through Estrella and how much."

"Except there's a risk," Tristan adds, "which is why I don't think this is a good idea."

"What risk?" I ask, studying Ami carefully. We may have made a binding agreement, but if there's anyone who can find a way out, it'd be her.

"If an immortal is weak or their defenses are down," Ami admits, "the Reflector could take their powers from them. Which is why we must all hope Estrella is stronger than that."

"I don't like this," I say warily. "It feels like a trap."

"Exactly," Tristan agrees.

I cross my arms, hating that Tristan and I agree, but also glad because between the two of us, we may be able to sway Estrella.

"Do I have any other options?" Estrella asks.

"The only other option is to train some more," Ami says, "and then hope you survive the Ring."

My heart stills at the thought of her not surviving the Ring test. I think back to the hours right before her test in the Midnight Kingdom before she lost everything. Estrella and I met secretly in the ice cave. Since she hadn't graduated and relationships were strictly forbidden for all Midnight Academy students, we always had to take precautions to make sure no one saw us. I kissed her that night knowing it might be our last kiss.

Here we are all over again, dealing with the very same fears.

"I think you need to focus on regaining your memories," I say. "We can worry about the Ring later."

"Lexi was kidnapped and taken to the Midnight Land's prison." Estrella bites her bottom lip and looks off into the bamboo thicket. "Time is not on my side. This test might show me what I'm dealing with."

"Or it could give this Conduit access to all of your powers," I say, glaring at Ami.

She huffs and rolls her eyes. "You have so little faith in me, Dion. I'm surprised, all things considered."

"What things?" Estrella asks warily, her crystal-blue eyes focusing back on me.

Ami is trying to distract Estrella once again and I'm getting tired of it. Actually, I'm finding it hard to continue to stand at this point thanks to the remnants of the poison.

"I believe in you, Estrella," I say. "I think given time, you could recover some of your memories, which might allow your powers to come back."

"Thank you for believing in me," she says. "But Lexi and all the girls at Nadia's are like family to me. They are suffering right now. I can't live with myself, knowing I haven't done everything in my power to help them." She steps up onto the arched wooden bridge and nods to the girl in the pool. "Which is why I need to do this."

6

TESTING THE WATERS

ESTRELLA

Kakurezato, Japan

Am I foolish for doing this? Maybe, but I didn't suffer everything I've gone through to only back down. I have committed myself to becoming a warrior, to fighting for those I love. I nod to the girl in the pool. She sinks below the water's surface.

"Hold out your arms," Ami instructs, and I obey.

Mirroring me, the Reflector stretches her body out like a floating star. Since this bridge doesn't have a railing, one step forward could send me plunging into the pool.

"You will feel a pull," Ami says, coming to my side. "When you feel that, don't release your powers. Hold them tight."

Tristan and Dion silently inch to the water's edge. Around me, the forest is quiet as if it's holding its breath, waiting. My muscles tense up in anticipation. I'm ready to fight against her pull, but also fearful that when we see my reflection, I'll discover what I already know deep down inside.

That I'm not enough.

The Reflector's powers reach out with cold, icy fingers and curl around my essence. I shudder. She tugs. Instinctively, I clamp up my defenses. I'm a vault, iron bars encasing me.

"Very good," Ami says appreciatively. "You've been trained well."

"I suppose," I say. "I did it more out of instinct than anything else."

I dare a glance at the two guys by the shoreline. There is fear in Dion's eyes while Tristan's hand has crept to the sword at his hip, his body leaning forward as if he's preparing himself to leap into the water.

"Now we shall see how much of your powers you have lost," Ami says. Her voice is laced with anticipation.

The woman in the pool begins to transform right before my eyes. Her dark hair washes out until it's pale yellow, weaving itself into a single braid—just like mine. Her skin becomes milky rather than olive, and even her clothes mimic mine.

I gasp. "It's like I'm looking at my reflection."

"How much longer?" Dion asks, gruffly.

"Just a moment more," Ami whispers, her eyes laser focused on the Reflector. "Since you are a Nazco, we should see a blue cloudy haze. When I did this test, it was green for Eien."

A shimmering iridescent glow begins to spread across

the Reflector's body. It sparkles. It reminds me of something. Ice and snow, glistening like diamonds under an endless blue sky.

"Fates alive," Dion says. "It's working."

"Pay attention to how comprehensive it is," Ami instructs, leaning forward. "It should completely cover her whole body, the thicker the mist, the stronger she is."

I hold my breath, scanning my reflection. The glow solidifies, a swirling mist drifting across my form.

"Look at her head," Tristan says. "The top right of her brain is void of the blue."

"That is where the Empress struck Estrella with her scepter," Dion whispers as if the memory still cuts through him.

His words spark something inside of me. A woman, pale as snow, with a crown of ice looms over me. She points her scepter at me. A flash of blue light sears my vision and pain lances across my mind. I cry out. The pain. The treachery of betrayal.

The hurt.

My grip on the iron bars within me snaps open. I try to break free of the Reflector, but I can't. We are locked in as one.

"Release her this instant!" Tristan leaps into the water, standing between the Reflector and myself. He holds the tip of his sword to the Reflector's neck.

The Reflector lets go of my powers and her hold on my essence snaps free. My knees buckle beneath me. Dion rushes to my side, catching me as I collapse.

"Estrella," Dion whispers. His arms encase me. "Tell me you're okay."

I blink away the nightmare of the memory and sink my head against his chest. My body starts shivering uncontrollably.

"The Empress," I say. "I saw her. I remember her."

Dion's eyes darken. "The marrow of her bone is foul."

"She pointed a scepter at me. The pain from it." I swallow the fear creeping up my throat.

"That was when she took your memories from you," Dion says.

"I thought it was a Wraith's blade," Tristan says as he and the Reflector splash out of the pool. He still has his sword pointed at her.

"You may go now," Ami tells the Reflector. "Find Sensei Haruki. He will pay you for your services."

"Yes, my master," she says, bowing deeply. With a furtive glance at Tristan's sword, she hurries away.

"The Wraith's blade is the usual way memories are taken." Dion helps me to a bench. He sways a little on his feet, which tells me he's not doing well himself. "But this time, the Empress had a hand in it. Which is why potentially, she could restore Estrella's powers."

"You think she has a plan for Estrella?" Ami asks. "Because based on what we saw, Estrella's powers are weaker than I'd like to see for a Conduit, but they are mostly intact. Everything except that one part of your mind."

"So what does this mean?" I ask. "Am I strong enough to enter the Ring?"

"You are close," she says. "Perhaps with some training, we could strengthen your visik and mind. Or you might be consumed by the Ring's power."

"Considering that I don't know what this Ring is or how

it really works," I say, "I think it's evident that I need time for training. Unfortunately."

"I will train you," Ami says, "but right now it's time for the Sabian to go."

Tristan sucks in a deep breath, clearly annoyed by Ami's treatment of him. "I'd rather stay."

"I will not have two high-powered immortals in my lands who are bonded and loyal to another Channeler," she says. "You must leave or I will not train her."

Ami's outburst surprises me. "Bonded? What are you talking about?" I ask.

"That's right, you've forgotten your training." Ami plucks a lush pink flower, studying it. "It is something we will discuss in private."

"That sounds cryptic," Tristan says.

"Because it is." Ami shoots him a wry smile. "The time for you to leave is here. Sensei Haruki will escort you out."

I leap to my feet. "How can I be assured he won't be attacked when he leaves? The Eien fortress guards were not so welcoming. And he's still injured."

"I'll speak to Sensei Haruki," she says. "He will escort him to the Water Channels."

I turn to Dion. "I'm going to walk Tristan out," I say. "Get some rest. Then we need to talk. I have so many questions."

He rakes a hand through his short, dark hair and slowly rises as if the movement brings him pain. "I want nothing more than to talk. We have much to discuss."

Ami leads Tristan and me through the winding path of the bamboo forest. My feet drag every step. I don't want him to leave. He's been there for me through so much that to be separated from him feels terrifying. And yet, deep down I know our relationship is impossible. The memory of the way his people looked at me still hovers in my mind. Even under his protection, Sabians relentlessly tried to kill me. If they were to find out that we were a couple, it would only give them more reason to kill me.

And distrust him.

The path spills us out into the main area of her land. The daylight gives me a clearer view of the traditional-style buildings and sweeping gardens. Cherry trees line the main walkway, their blossoms in full bloom. The fragrant air is full of power. Pink petals rain over our heads like they're bidding us farewell as we head toward the large gateway we just escaped from.

"Wait here," Ami tells Tristan at the entrance. "Haruki will be here shortly."

"I'd like a moment alone with Tristan," I tell Ami.

Once she leaves, I take Tristan's hands in mine, and I stare up into his face. I try to memorize that strong jaw, those stormy blue eyes, the way his hair falls across his forehead as if it dares to run wild. Will I ever see him again? Can I survive without him?

"Last night," I swallow, "we left things unsaid. The truth is whatever this is between us is impossible. Your people want me dead."

"Not everyone," he interjects.

"You're their next ruler. How would your people handle our relationship?" I ask. He looks away, jaw tight. "Half of your people would despise you if they saw us holding hands like this. The other half would always be suspicious of me since I'm a Nazco. Someday, you'll rule in your father's place. How will your people be able to trust you if you're with your enemy?"

"They don't get to choose who I'm with."

"Which gives them a great reason to rise up against you." He presses his lips together when I say that. It's clear that he has been thinking these very same things. "Plus, now that we know I can't be your Conduit since according to Ami, I can't wield Sabian fire, there's no reason for you to even be here. You have far more important things to do than babysit me."

"I choose to be here because I want to be with you. I want to help and protect you. It's as simple as that."

"I don't want you to leave," I say, my chest feeling hollow, ready to collapse.

"Nor I." His eyes burn, fastening into my soul.

"But you must return to your people," I say firmly. Like I believe it. "They need you. I'll never forget what you did for me. You saved me. More times than I can count."

"When I first saw you in that art classroom, I knew I'd never be the same. You've changed me, Estrella. And I'm glad for every moment of it."

His words cut deep. Can I imagine my world without him? I can't even think about that.

"Will we see each other again?" I wonder.

"I feel as if our souls are tied to each other. If that's so, then maybe."

He leans forward, and closing his eyes, presses a kiss to my forehead. Heat whispers across my skin. I'm desperate to cling to him. To kiss him deeply without holding back.

With a deep sigh, he pulls away as if the movement

takes great effort. He hands me his phone. "I want you to have this. In case you need to contact me."

I take it, curling it in my palm like it's a life source. "Or Katka?" I ask, teasing.

His smile is pained. Haruki strides up, nodding to Tristan, ready to go.

"Please," Tristan begs, "give me one final task. Tell me how I can help you."

My heart throbs. I should release him of any ties to me. Except my heart is selfish, and I can't completely let him go.

"There is one thing," I dare whisper.

He leans in closer. "Anything."

"My friends at Nadia's. Can you check on them? Make sure they're okay? After what happened to Lexi, I'm scared for Jamie, Zayla, and Mara. All the girls."

His face brightens, and he nods, standing a little taller. "You have my word."

"Thank you." Just hearing his promise, my fears for my friends ease.

Then he turns and strides confidently toward the gate with Sensei Haruki. I stand still, watching as they slip through the swirled blackness of the gate, disappearing.

I clutch the phone tighter, my heart ripping in half. I hate that I can't control my emotions. Deep down, I know he's not mine to have. He's a prince and a Sabian.

While I'm just a powerless outcast whose presence will only threaten his throne.

I must remember this if I care for him at all.

7
THE SECRETS OF THE CHANNELER
ESTRELLA

Kakurezato, Japan

When I return to the bamboo pond, Dion is gone. I spin around, searching for him, needing to talk to him and get answers to the million questions screaming to be answered.

"I sent him back to the Healers," Ami calls from across the bridge. "He looked at Death's door. I told him to join us for dinner should he wake in time."

"Will he be okay?" I ask, debating between finding him and letting him be. It's probably best that he's gone. I'm already an emotional wreck.

"If he rests, it's likely he will overcome the poison. The fact that he's running around is a testament to his strength, but he must rest. Now come. We have much to discuss."

She's right. I need to give Dion time to heal. Later I'll get the answers to my questions. Like what was life like for me in the Midnight Kingdom? What kind of person was I? Who were my friends? Where are my parents?

Most importantly, why didn't he tell me the truth of who I was while in Florida?

I let out a long breath and join Ami. The questions will have to wait.

"This place is beautiful," I say as we stroll along the path, tall bamboos spearing up on either side like sentinels. "Is this place really yours?"

The thought of having my own place feels unreachable. Right now, I don't even know where I belong or who I can trust.

"The Emperor and I have an agreement," she says. "He lets me do as I wish in my land and offers me protection. Meanwhile, I provide him power from the World of Between and leave him be."

"Sounds like a simple arrangement. Too simple based on everything I've learned about this world of the immortals."

"Betrayal does that to one."

Her words hit hard against my chest. These past few days have been a constant reminder that I don't belong and I'm not wanted.

"It still doesn't make sense that the Empress would get rid of the one person who could provide the Nazco with power," I muse. "There must have been something I did wrong. But if it was so horrible, why let me live?"

The path spits us out of the forest along a winding river. In the distance, rounded morning-blue mountains are dusted in snow.

"Excellent question," she says, "and why I believe all is not lost for you."

I stop mid-stride and face her. She pauses, stiffening as if sensing my walls rising up. "You've taken a great risk to bring me here, and based on that attack outside of your gate, I'm guessing your Emperor has no clue you're training me. There's more about this deal than you're letting on."

Those clear blue eyes, so similar to mine, study me carefully as if she's choosing her next words carefully. Her fingers play with the ruby-red necklace that hangs from her neck. Power swirls within its surface. It reminds me of the necklace that Dion gave me tucked away in my belongings.

"I already told you. I want to take down the Empress."

A chill clamps against my chest. "And what will he give you in return?"

"That is not for me to answer. Right now you must focus on your training."

She takes off again down a wooden bridge that crosses the river. Huffing, I clench my fists and march after her. It irks me that she and Dion made some sort of deal without my approval. She may be cryptic, but I'm determined to get answers and find out what exactly I'm dealing with. I try another angle.

"When we were training earlier," I say, the wood of the bridge creaking beneath my boots, "you mentioned I had bonded with Tristan and Dion. What was that about?"

This stops her and she leans against the railing, facing the mountains bathed in pink mist. I join her.

"It's a well-kept secret among Channelers, but based on how loyal these two are to you, you three must already know the truth."

"If I knew the truth, I wouldn't be asking."

"High-powered Channelers not only have the ability to take another immortal's power, but they can also give it back."

I nod. "That I know. Tristan showed me how to do it. He learned it from his sister."

"If an immortal does this with a Channeler willingly, over time, it can form a bond to that Channeler if both participants are in agreement."

"Both Dion and Tristan allowed me to channel their powers during a battle." My heart squeezes. "Are you saying they're only loyal to me because of that?"

"They choose to bond with you, but sometimes those emotions can be confused with love."

"None of us really knew what we were doing when they let me use their powers. It was purely a survival instinct. If we didn't, we would've been killed. Did the people here choose to bond with you?"

"Every immortal in my land has and they are loyal to me. They have agreed to willingly give me their powers when I need it."

"And you in turn amplify their powers. That's how you can create a beautiful land like this." I think about the glistening water where plump koi fish swim, the pink-laced clouds, and the blossom-drenched air. "Without your powers heightening theirs, they are limited. You make them stronger."

"Channelers who are the strongest and most feared are also the ones that have built a loyal following."

"How do I know if someone wants to be with me for me, not the power I can give them?"

"You can't and honestly, it doesn't really matter as long as both parties are satisfied," Ami says. "The power within other immortals responds eagerly to our amplification of it."

"Neither has told me that they love me." I swallow, looking down at my boots. Except Tristan had called me his love, didn't he? Could Dion and Tristan only be interested in me because of the bond? That thought makes my insides feel hollow and empty.

"Love and even passion stirred with our powers is intoxicating," she says with a knowing smile. "Trust me, it's one of the perks we have most have no idea about. The bonding must remain our secret. Over the past few centuries, few Channelers have been born and those with great power are even fewer. Which makes us rare and powerful."

Understanding hits me. "And dangerous."

"Exactly."

"But others must know about what we can do."

"Channelers work hard to keep as much of the knowledge of our powers closely guarded. Most immortals fear us already. They know that with one touch, we can sap their powers from them. Think of how people would respond if they knew how dangerous we really are."

"The Empress must know. That has to be why she excommunicated me."

"Perhaps." Ami tilts her head to the side, pursing her red lips. "Probably."

We continue down the walkway, heading toward a four-tiered pagoda perched on a tiny island in the middle of the river. An emerald glow spills from the windows.

We pass under another gate, and as we do, a shiver slithers over me like someone has inspected every inch of my body and decided to let me free. She shoots me a wry smile.

"Did you feel that?" she asks.

I nod, shuddering. "It was a strange sensation."

"It's a barrier that only a Channeler with high powers can pass. Everyone else dies."

I glare at her. "I guess it's lucky that I'm still alive."

She laughs, almost like she's drunk on the power of what she can do.

Maybe she is.

We step inside her Channeler pagoda. The scent of sandalwood soaks the room. The interior has a temple quality to it. Wooden floors stretch across the ground and intricate woodwork crisscrosses above our heads, spanning upward, layer after layer. Gilded artwork is inlaid into the wood.

"What is this place?" I ask.

"Every Eien Channeler who shows the aptitude for higher powers is brought here to be assessed and trained by me. You might say I'm a control freak."

"Or you don't want another Channeler taking your place?" I shoot her a lifted-eyebrowed look.

"You're catching on."

In the center of the place burns a green ball of fire. Its flames lick the air like serpents, eager to sink into the souls of immortals. It reminds me of the Sabian flame that Tristan showed me.

"The power source of the Eien," I say.

"Not the main power source." Ami circles the pedestal. "That's in the Emperor's castle. I like to keep a little extra here in my land. You won't tell him, will you?"

Our eyes lock. She has been sharing information with me that she would kill to protect. For some reason, she wants to be allies. If only I knew her endgame. She obviously has one. An immortal with a land like this has purpose, intention.

Of course, to say no to her would be suicide. Here, with the Eien's power source radiating from the pedestal, I'm weak, and we both know that. And yet, it's also a moment where I must decide whose side I'm on. Hers or everyone who isn't.

"Your secrets are safe with me," I say.

Her shoulders relax. "Yuto!" she calls out. "Come!"

There's a thumping sound and then footsteps clattering down a tiny set of stairs off to the side. A bald man wearing a coffee-colored robe scurries across the room. He throws himself at Ami's feet in a deep bow.

"Your greatness," he says. "How can I serve you?"

"Stand. I'd like you to meet Estrella." She switches to English, which I'm grateful for. "She's the ex-Nazco Conduit."

The man rises and turns to face me, eyes widening in horror. "Nazco? What is she...I mean...why is she..."

"She's here to train as a Channeler. We're trying to help her regain her memories and powers."

"Excellent. Of course." He fidgets with the lapels of his robe, his expression saying that this news is anything but excellent.

"Hello, Yuko," I say, smiling. "It is nice to meet you."

"And you. At least, I think so. I've never met a Nazco that I liked. That said, there's the possibility that you could be an exception. There are always exceptions to—"

"Yuko," Ami interrupts. "Bring me the Channeler Ring Entry Scroll."

"Yes, your brilliance." He bows a few more times.

Ami's face darkens. His eyes go wide in fear.

"Right away." He rushes off to one of the tall shelves lining the far wall.

While he searches through the shelves, we settle on a bamboo mat. Will she really be able to help me in the Ring? After facing the Dragon Seer in Slovakia and then the Reflector here in Japan, I feel like I'm only uncovering more problems than solutions. I try to relax and let the scent of sandalwood calm my nerves.

"Found it!" he exclaims, pulling it out and running to us. He hesitates handing it to Ami. "But is it okay? You know… because…" He clears his throat and gives me a furtive glance as if I'm an evil villain.

Who knows? I think, smiling. *Maybe I am.*

She takes it from his hands and unfurls the scroll. It's written in ink, the lines faded. Ami runs her fingers across the letters and they brighten as if remembering their form.

"It looks Japanese, but I can't read it," I say.

"Since it's one of our oldest Channeler manuals, it's written in man'yōgana. Old Japanese. You were likely not taught it at the Midnight Academy. It explains how to bolster a Channeler's powers to survive the Ring. Here it writes about different training methods to strengthen our powers."

Her finger continues down the scroll, the letters sparkling as she touches them.

"Do you really think any of these methods can help me?" I ask, trying not to get my hopes up.

"This one." She taps the ancient silk. "The energy tethers test."

"It sounds like I'm supposed to attach myself to something."

"Exactly." She reads a little of the text, nodding. "To become attuned to the elements, you must tether yourself to one of those forces and then draw power from it until you can't anymore. The key is to push yourself to the limit without being consumed by the power."

I try to imagine her as a young child, learning the ways of a Channeler. "Have you ever done this before?"

"I never really needed little exercises like this." She shrugs and begins rolling up the scroll. "Power came naturally to me."

Of course it did. This land, the dedication of her people, the way she handles everything with such purpose. She's a natural.

"How old are you?" I study her smooth skin, the sharp cut of her muscles, the silky smoothness of her hair. It's always impossible to tell since immortals stop aging in their thirties. She could be thirty or five hundred years old.

"A woman never tells her age." She tilts her chin down, flashing me a demure smile. "But let's just say for an immortal, I'm old."

Okay, so maybe five hundred was a bit on the low side. "Translation: you're more powerful than most."

"Come." She pats my knee and rises. "It's time we rip you inside out and then stitch you back together once again."

"Sounds lovely," I say sarcastically.

And yet, as torturous as it sounds, I'm eager to get started. My friends' faces haunt me.

Lexi's wink and bounce.

Jamie's strength and support.

Zayla's mischievous smile.

Mara's stoic determination.

If I'm going to help them, I need to be as strong as possible. The pain of not knowing who I was and the frustration of feeling like my body is locked behind bars lingers at the edges of my mind. That need to escape and be free.

They were there for me when I needed them. Now it's time to stand strong for them.

8

BEFORE: ARE YOU AN ANGEL?
LEXI

Florida

Someone is using a jackhammer in my brain. So loud. So annoying.

"Lexi," a voice whispers. It's deep and rumbly.

I blink my eyes open in confusion. A ruggedly handsome guy leans over me. Chestnut colored hair and honey eyes. No, not a guy, he's my angel who rushed into the bathroom at school with a sword. He rescued me from that gross and horrible creature.

The world is white around us. I'm even wearing white.

"Am I in Heaven?" I ask. My words come out dry and cracked like I haven't used them in a long time.

"There you are," my angel says. He's smiling, but he looks worried. It's a weird combination. Plus my angel has a scruff of a beard and looks just a little older than me. "Listen carefully. Nadia is about to come in. She doesn't know about Estrella or how you nearly died from the Wraith's blade."

Estrella.

Nadia.

Wraiths.

I try to put those words together like a puzzle but none of the pieces fit.

"Tell her that you were in the girls' bathroom and some kids jumped you. You got hurt. That's all you remember. Got it?"

The urgency in his tone warns me something bad is about to happen.

"Got it," I say.

My angel smiles and I reach for him, but he vanishes from the white room.

Probably flew away to do whatever angels do. Flutter around on the clouds. Or do they play harps? Can't remember.

My eyes shut only to wake back up to a too-familiar grating voice.

"Oh, Lexi, dear," the voice half-wails. "The doctor told us you've been hurt."

Gah. I hate that voice. It scrapes on my skin like sandpaper. I open my eyes to find Nadia. Her brown hair is yanked back into a harsh bun and her eyes glitter hard as stone. She's not as pretty as my angel.

"What happened?" Nadia holds my hand. Her grip is firm. "Can you tell us what happened?"

Val is standing behind her like he's her bodyguard or something. Wait. Maybe he is.

The pieces of the puzzle start to snap in place. Estrella

and I had gone into the bathroom during play practice. Tiffany was there and wanted information from us and when we didn't give it to her, she had those horrible things attack us. The betrayal stings.

Tears spring to my eyes. "It was so painful," I tell Nadia.

"What do you remember, Lexi?" Her hard eyes don't soften. She's as cold as Tiffany was, maybe more so.

I lick my cracked lips. "Estrella and I went to the girls' bathroom," I say. "Some kids jumped us or something. One of them stabbed me and I must have hit my head on a toilet. So gross. I don't remember anything else."

A sharp blade stabbing my side. Estrella screaming, trying to help me. So much blood on her hands. Then my angel showed up. His hot palms pushing away the agony.

"Well." Nadia lets out a long breath. "This has been such a scare. When the hospital called, I was absolutely distraught. I came as fast as I could, but apparently your injuries weren't as bad as I first thought."

I want to smash something on her head. Claw at her face. Scream in her ears. Yeah, I might be wicked, but she's pure evil.

And I want my angel back.

"I talked to the doctor," Nadia continues. "Great news. You can come home with us right now. He said that you're cleared to go. Isn't that wonderful?"

Nope, not wonderful at all. "Yay," I mutter.

Nadia pushes me to sitting. The room spins a little. I search for my angel. He's not here. I probably imagined him.

Great. I'm finally losing it just like the other girls.

"Don't you think it's too early to go back to school?" Nadia asks me when I enter the kitchen. Jamie, Mara, and Flora are sitting around the table eating breakfast. "You just got out of the hospital last night."

Mara peers up from her bowl of cereal. Her lips purse like she just ate something sour. "You look awful."

"Thanks!" I say brightly. "And I feel great. I don't want to miss any of my classes. Plus, if I miss another play practice, I'm going to lose my role."

"Just use the I-got-stabbed card," Mara mutters. "You'll get any role you want."

"Don't say such things, Mara," Nadia says, looking unusually frazzled.

Flora is weaving flowers into a vine. "I'm making you a crown," she says, perking up from across the table. "Then you'll be pretty."

"Excellent!" I flash Flora a smile as I grab a box of cereal and pour myself a bowl. "I'll look so great once I put Flora's crown on, my drama teacher won't have the heart to kick me out."

Nadia argues with me over the whole school thing while Jamie secretly slips a spoon in my pocket with a wink. It's a true testament to my acting ability because I leave the property with the crown of flowers firmly on my head and the secret of the attack in my heart. My side still aches. But what's really bothering me is that Estrella's and Tiffany's rooms are empty and no one is talking about it.

It's creepy and terrifying.

When we get on the bus, Mara and Jamie pull me to the back and confront me.

"Where's Estrella?" Mara demands. "And were you really in the hospital?"

I stare at them, wondering how much I should say. Can I trust them? I trusted Tiffany and it almost got me killed. It might have killed Estrella.

"I have no idea where Estrella is or even if she's alive," I say. "I thought she would be back at Nadia's."

"She never came home and neither did Tiffany," Mara says darkly. "The last time I saw either one was two days ago. I thought you got killed too but then Nadia brought you home."

"Tiffany is dead," I say sourly. "She betrayed Estrella and me."

The girls gasp, horror seeping over their faces. Then I tell them everything I know. Well, everything except for my angel. Because I'm still not sure if he really exists.

It's him. My angel. He's real.

He's sitting just two rows away in the cafeteria. Jamie is trying to convince us that we should escape Nadia's while Mara refutes each idea one by one. We are a hopeless trio. But when I see the guy, the burger I'm eating falls onto my plate with a thud. Maybe it wasn't a burger but a hockey puck.

"What is it?" Mara asks. "You look like you saw a ghost."

"Is it Estrella?" Jamie asks hopefully.

"No," I whisper. "It's him."

"Who?" Mara looks around. "Please tell me it's not that Tristan guy. He's scary."

"It's my angel," I say reverently.

"What?" Mara asks, and then follows my line of sight. "Just fabulous. Another guy here to ruin our lives. Please don't tell me that you named this one angel."

"We're supposed to pick a name out *together*," Jamie grumbles, crossing her arms.

He's looking at me, the corner of his mouth quirked like he wants to smile. He's as big as the football players, all muscle packed into that large frame. His hair is neatly combed back unlike how I remember it at the hospital. Also, he's smoking hot.

Which means I need to be cool. Except my heart is racing.

Because he's real.

I rise to my feet, toss my hair, and throw on my brightest smile, reminding myself that I'm Lexi Santos. I can do anything.

"Uh-oh, she has that look," Mara says.

"She's going to go talk to him," Jamie agrees.

"Don't bring him back here," Mara calls after me as I take off to talk to him.

"Hiya," I say brightly and plop myself across from the brown-haired guy. He's too bright and shiny to belong in this very dull, boring place. "Do I know you? Because you look familiar."

"I'm new here. But we've met before."

Light up my toes! It wasn't a dream. "You saved me, didn't you?"

"It's what I do," he says, shrugging.

"Then thank you." I feel a little breathless. "So battling

scary creatures and putting hot hands on girls is normal for you then?"

He laughs. "When you put it like that, it does sound strange."

"Why are you really here?"

"You get right to the point, don't you, Lexi? I'm here because Estrella made me promise to protect you."

My heart freefalls. "Tell me she's okay."

"She's safe. That's all I can tell you right now."

"You know my name but I don't know yours. Who are you?" And why do you look like you belong on the cover of a magazine?

"I'm Conrad, a friend of Tristan's, and I'm going to do everything I can to keep you safe."

I smile. I think I'm going to like this guy.

9
THE TETHERING TRIAL
ESTRELLA

Kakurezato, Japan

"Are you ready?" Ami asks me.

Ami, Yoku, and I all stand safely outside of the circular area sectioned off by a low stone wall. Her expression is eager, eyes bright, while Yoku's is crinkled in worry as he holds a wooden box strapped with metal clasps.

"As ready as I can be," I say.

"You may enter the Tethering Nexus," Ami instructs, and I move to position myself in the center of the walled area.

"Are you sure this is a good idea?" Yuko asks Ami in a whisper, but it carries easily on the wind. "She's a Nazco. And not just any Nazco, an ex-Conduit!"

"Silence," Ami says.

"Yes, your majesty." He quivers.

Stone dragon heads loom up on either side of the Tethering Nexus's entrance as if guarding the exit. The ground beneath my feet suddenly feels too hard. The air too thin. A wind shivers across my tunic, tugging on the edges not strapped down with the rope at my waist.

Yuko opens the small chest. Inside four spheres glow bright, stars of colors ready to be plucked from the sky.

"Blue for water." Ami points to the first and then moves down the line. "Green for earth, red for fire, and yellow for air."

I swallow and nod. "Let's start with water."

"If she tries to kill you," Yuko tells Ami warily, "I'll throw myself in front of your body to give you warning."

Ami rolls her eyes at Yuko's dramatics and scoops up the blue sphere. Carefully, she rolls it across the engraved stone toward me. As it comes my way, the sphere appears to melt. Water pools across the ground, spreading out. Wider and wider it grows.

"Feel the water," Ami says. I bend to reach down for it, but Ami stops me, saying, "Do not go to the water."

I jerk my hand away. "Then how do I get the water?"

"Make it come to you. As Conduits, our bodies yearn to pull powers to us. It's instinctual so let your instincts take over."

Taking a deep breath, I focus on the element. There's something oddly familiar about this moment. Like I've done this before. A memory snaps across my vision. I'm standing in a room, its stone walls streaked with ice. I'm practicing with the water element, running my finger through a bowl of liquid, turning it into ice.

Splash! Water hits my face, jerking me back to the

moment. I sputter, coughing and blinking.

"That's one way to get it to come to you," Yuko says, a little too gleefully.

"You must control it!" Ami throws her hands up in frustration. "Harness it. Try to remember your training from the Nazco academy."

I got distracted by the memory. I need to get a grip on my mind.

"Do they really experiment on their prisoners at the Midnight Academy?" Yuko asks. "I've also heard a popular Nazco tradition at their Winter Solstice is they entomb their enemies in ice and set them around their city as statues."

"Considering I don't even remember my closest friends and family," I say, frustrated, "I am hardly an expert on Nazco traditions."

With the back of my hand, I rub my eyes dry and refocus. The water now has seeped across the stone, trickling through the cracks as if trying to escape. If I don't gather it up soon, it will be gone.

"It's leaving," Ami says, cutting through my thoughts. "Think of the element like a person's powers. Take a hold of it. No. Not like that. You're failing."

Frustration wells inside my chest because she's right. The water is elusive, slipping out of my grasp.

I will not fail.

Gritting my teeth, I close my eyes and focus on the pulse of the element. I call forth the water again and hold out my hands. A rushing roar fills my ears. I open my eyes to find the liquid has gathered up and is swirling around me. It starts to move, faster and faster.

My heart stutters in shock. Did I create this force? It

tumbles around my body, on the edge of chaos. It's strong, so strong like it wants to either rip away or smack me in the face. Then it begins to slip from my frail grasp. My heart hammers against my chest.

As if sensing my fear, the water draws up over me, a wave of power. With a crash, it dumps over my head. I cry out at the sudden force. The deluge of water shoves me to my knees. Water is everywhere. In my eyes, in my throat. My hair and clothes are soaked. I sputter.

"Estrella!" a voice calls out.

I lift up my head to spy Dion running down the path. He's wearing black pants and a sleeveless black V-neck vest. Lightning swirls along his arms like tattoos. He's swift and fierce as death. Just seeing the power of him racing up to me takes my breath away.

"Fates alive!" Yuko recoils in horror. "Is that another Nazco?"

Dion's about to race into the circle, but Ami steps in his way, arms crossed.

"Do not enter the Tethering Nexus," she orders. "It is a sacred area for Channelers."

Dion halts, glaring at Ami before focusing back on me. "Are you alright?" His chiseled jaw clenches in anger.

I choke on the water a few more times but manage to nod and rise to my feet. His presence calms me.

"How are you feeling?" I ask. "You look much better."

Actually, he looks gorgeous. Tall and lithe with chiseled muscles ready to spring to action. The stubble of a five o'clock shadow hints that he hasn't shaved. Seeing him again reminds me of the first day we met at school when our paths crossed in the hallway. It caused so much pain that it made me pass out. I bit my lip, suddenly realizing that wasn't the first time I'd met him, was it? And the pain had been a result of my mind screaming at me to remember him. That feels like a lifetime ago now.

"Much better," he says, and the worry lines of his forehead smooth out. "The poison is nearly gone. I'm glad to see you're training. Can I do anything to help?"

"She needs to focus," Ami says, "and you're a distraction. The most helpful thing you can do is leave."

"Yes, very good idea, your perfectness." Yuko nods. "Two Nazco in one place is rather unsettling."

"No," I say. "Stay. Please."

"Of course," Dion says, sidestepping warily from Ami.

She tosses him a seductive smile, fingering her necklace, which right away draws the eyes to her breasts. Jealousy slithers into my chest. What was that look about? How old is she? She looks like she's in her thirties like all immortals, but I bet there's a pretty big age gap.

Does she want his powers or does she like him? I mean, what's not to like? He's magnificent. His powers practically spill out of his body, potent and tempting.

Calling to me.

Was that what attracted me to him? His powers? Is this bonding all my fault? I frown as I plant my feet and study the water.

"This is what I was talking about," Ami says, tossing a waving hand my way. "You're distracting her from connecting herself to the water."

"You once told me that you would search for the source," Dion tells me, ignoring Ami. "That's what you'd grab a hold of."

"I told you that?"

Ami snorts. "Such romantic pillow talk."

"We used to practice your skills on me." A hint of a grin. "You said you found it useful."

"I bet she did," Ami says, eyeing him appreciatively.

My face burns. I get the feeling that we did more than just practice my powers.

"Right." I clear my throat. "I'll see if that helps."

I close my eyes and refocus on the water puddled at my feet. *Search for the source.* Where is it? Then I hear it. It's almost like a heartbeat, pulsing, calling for me. Mentally, I grasp ahold of it. In a burst, the water shoots up. It tries to escape, slip through my hold, but I grasp it harder.

You are mine.

It softens as if hearing my voice. I decide to test it, waving my hand like a conductor leading an orchestra.

Turn right. Turn left. Up and down.

It's a dance with me and the element. Spinning and twirling. It molds to my call, follows my voice. A thrill rushes through me as the power flows through my core, in and out.

"Nicely done!" Dion's voice cuts through my focus. He starts clapping.

My eyes fly open. Pillars of water are circling me. They move up and down like a fountain. A smile bursts across my face and I release the water. It splashes back to the ground.

"I did it!" I exclaim. "I was able to control water!"

The air smells crisp and fresh. A world washed clean after a rainstorm.

"You did well," Ami admits, but she looks pleased. "I think we are done for the day."

She holds out her hand, and the water slips back into the sphere. It rolls across the ground into her palm and she places it back into the chest. I'm soaking wet as I practically skip out of the Tethering Nexus, but I don't care. Elation fills me. I'm floating on the rush of victory and power.

"You were incredible." Dion grins down at me proudly, and my heart blooms at the praise.

"It was rather terrifying," Yuko admits.

"This is very promising," Ami says and turns to Dion. "She has the abilities locked away in her mind. We just need to find a way to continue to help her remember."

"She is strong. Always has been." He rubs his chin thoughtfully. "I knew you could help her."

My smile slips as my eyes dart between the two of them. It's almost like they have a plan for me. A plan that I'm not privy to.

My stomach growls, yanking everyone's attention back to me.

Dion chuckles. "You always were starving after training," he says, his eyes sparkling with joy.

"I could eat," I say, rubbing my stomach.

"We should head back," Ami says. "Get cleaned up. I'll have dinner prepared."

"That would be wonderful," I say, squeezing out the water from my tunic as I join Dion on the path back to the main building.

His step is light beside me and that brooding mood of his from earlier has vanished. Is he excited because I'm becoming more attuned to my powers or is it because he cares for me? Regardless, tonight, I plan on cornering him. It's time to find out who I was and if there's any part of the old me still left.

10
YES, I'M ASKING THE HARD QUESTIONS
ESTRELLA

Kakurezato, Japan

Aservant leads me down the wooden-floored hallway to where the evening meal is held. My muscles scream with each step, reminding me how out of shape I am. The dress I'm wearing is so foreign compared to my Sabian gowns or even the jeans I wore in Florida. It's silky soft with wide sleeves. A white bodice decorated with orchids crisscrosses over my chest and my pendant glows fire red, reminding me that even here, I'm not safe. A long black skirt billows down to my ankles and a large sash ties at my waist.

I hardly feel like myself, but as much as I'm suspicious of whatever deal Ami and Dion made, I'm also grateful. Ami has not only protected me here, but provided shelter, food, and training. They aren't small gestures, which makes me suspect Dion is risking a lot more for me than he's letting on.

I step into the large dining room. The smells of rice and grilled meat waft through the air. Wood beams run across the ceiling and geometric patterned screens are pulled back to reveal the gardens outside, lit by hanging lanterns. Two long, low tables stretch across the large room where Ami's people all are sitting on cushions and talking softly. Lilting music fills the room, adding to the calming atmosphere.

"Please," the servant says, "have a seat."

Everyone stops eating and talking to stare at me. I stiffen until I spy Dion rising from one of the cushions, a faint smile tipping his lips. His skin glows golden in the lamplight, and his dark hair shines like it's been freshly washed. He's wearing a dark blue kimono-style tunic over his pants, cinched tight, showing off a fit frame. Basically, a makeshift outfit, half-his, half-Japanese.

I swallow, determined to not focus on how striking he is as I hurry to him. Based on other girls' appreciative glances turned his way, it's obvious I'm not the only one to notice his good looks. When I reach him, he goes to take my hand but stops. Instantly, everything feels awkward between us.

He clears his throat. "I saved you a seat." He waves to the cushion next to his.

"Thank you," I say, and as I sit, my dress billows out around me like a flower. "Ami provided me with a full wardrobe while I am here. I see you've been given clothing, too."

"You look beautiful," he says, and I can't help but flush happily.

"Thank you." Have I always wanted his approval or just now? It shouldn't matter what I think about him, I remind myself as a servant places a bowl of soup before me. He betrayed me. Lied to me. I won't forget that.

"How are you holding up?" Dion asks. "Ami said you did some sword fighting today as well?"

I'm glad for the small talk, but that's not my purpose. Tonight I need answers, but as I look around the table, I realize everyone sitting here is holding onto our every word.

"It was rigorous, but oddly, I was able to fight her. It's like my muscles and a part of my mind remembered what to do. It reminded me of how I was able to read Latin and other foreign languages while I was with the Sabians."

He stiffens when I say Sabians. "You were an excellent fighter. You practiced your martial arts, sword fighting, and channeling daily."

"Daily?"

"You were very dedicated to becoming the best you could possibly be. So driven. Nothing was stopping you." He stares at his soup as if remembering and then gives me a side glance, his mouth tilting up. "You haven't changed in that account. Watching you train today reminded me how determined you always were."

"You might be right." I chuckle. "I've been wondering about how much of me is still the same and how much is different."

"I'd like to believe you're still the same you. You just need time to remember that."

"Maybe, but a part of me knows deep down that I'll never be the same. Not after being rejected and treated the way I was." My stomach growls, reminding me to eat. I take a sip of my soup. Its rich flavor slides down my throat, warming me up inside. "I've got to admit, immortal food is so much better than what we ate at Nadia's or my old school."

"The cafeteria food may have been the greatest form of punishment," he agrees, chuckling.

I laugh with him, and for a moment, it's like we're back to being the two of us, hanging out and having fun back in Florida.

"What do you think was the driving force behind me training so hard?"

"You wanted to reach your full potential," Dion says, but he pauses as if he's holding something back. A servant places various bowls of food before us. Rice, noodles, grilled meats, vegetables, and other sides I don't recognize. "How much do you really want to know?"

"Everything," I say in a desperate whisper, clutching his arm, feeling his power. Quickly, I take my hand back. "Sorry. I keep forgetting I shouldn't touch people without their permission."

"You always have my permission." His eyes are soft, warm as honey. My defenses start breaking down.

I stiffen and focus on scooping food onto my plate. I can't let him get too close to my heart again. I won't let him hurt me. Quickly, I lock up those feelings, reminding myself that I'm here to train so I can save my friends.

There's a shift in the room and everyone rises and bows.

Ami is here, sweeping inside looking stunning in a pale-blue gown scattered with white flowers. Her sharp eyes scan the room once and then she glides to our table. Her face is unreadable, smooth, and clear of expression. She nods to Dion and me before settling onto a cushion at the head of our table.

"I see you've found your new clothing," she says. "How is the food?"

"Wonderful." I adjust my grip on the chopsticks. "You've given me so much—shelter, food, clothes, training. I'm not sure I'll ever be able to repay you."

"I'm glad you think so," Ami replies. Her eyes gleam with a knowing look. "Because there will come a time when I'll be counting on both of you to remember those words."

A sinking stone plunks hard in my stomach, an anchor weighing me down. So, I was right about her expecting something of me. I turn to Dion. "What is she talking about?"

He takes a sip of his drink, but he doesn't look at me. Like guilt is keeping him from facing me. "Not here," he says under his breath. "We'll talk later."

Musicians come out to play for Ami. Their talent takes my breath away. I'm not sure if I've ever heard anything so beautiful. Once I've eaten and all the entertainment is done, Dion asks Ami if the two of us could take a stroll through the gardens. Thankfully, she agrees with the condition that we are escorted by a guard.

As we step outside into the cool night, my heart thumps against my chest as I realize that Dion and I are alone for the first time since he kissed me at the end of our date in Florida. Patterned lanterns sway in the evening breeze from tree boughs, lighting our way to the gardens. The hum of Dion's electrical power snaps and crackles around my skin, enticing me. I squeeze my eyes shut tight, trying to push away the memory of his lips against mine, sizzling hot. Tempting me to never stop.

Back then, I thought I was falling for him, but after talking to Ami, maybe I was only attracted to his powers. Or perhaps he'd been my escape from the terrible situation of living at Nadia's? I study him in the moonlight and search deep within myself for answers. But the truth feels elusive.

Another reason why I need to get answers.

"What's going on between you and Ami?" I ask. "She keeps alluding that you two made a deal. And you heard her in there just now. She is expecting payment for everything she's done for me."

He heaves in a long breath, staring at the sky. "It's true. We made a deal."

My heart stutters like a flickering candle caught in the wind. "What did you agree to?"

"I was desperate to help you. Desperate to get you back. So I began to retrace your steps before the Empress excommunicated you. When your friends, Lexi and Jamie, had been wiped of their memories and sent away—"

"Wait." I stop him in his tracks. "I knew Lexi and Jamie before I went to Nadia's?"

"They were your best friends."

My legs feel weak. "Lexi always said she felt like we could be best friends."

"You were determined to do anything to rescue them and find a way to recover their memories. Every night you pored over ancient texts in the library, searching for a cure. The night of your test to enter the Ring of Eternity, you told me that you had found a secret that had either been forgotten or purposely hidden. You were going to tell me about it after your test."

"Except I never had the chance to do so."

He nods. "So I retraced your steps to where you studied. In that room behind a bookshelf, I discovered a hidden section of the library full of ancient books and scrolls."

My mind whirls with this information. "You think I knew about this secret room?"

"I know you had because inside, I found books I'd seen you studying."

"What kind of books?" I press.

"*The Lost Temple, The Fates of the Immortals,* and *Origins of Our Kind.*"

"It sounds like I was looking for the Fate's temple." I stop in my tracks, rubbing my forehead. "Do you think the cure to the memory loss is there?"

"I do. Does anything I'm saying sound familiar?"

"No." I sigh in frustration. "Nothing other than the vague teachings that my Sabian tutor gave me."

"I figured that might be the case, which is why I thought if we could build up your powers then it might be enough to recall some of your memories."

"And remember where the cure is located."

"Exactly."

We continue on and cross a bridge that curls over a small gurgling stream and sit on a wooden bench. The grass shimmers as if it's been sprayed with glitter, only visible in the lantern light.

I stare at the stream, considering his words. "So Ami is

helping me to regain my memories. What did you agree to give her in return?"

His face looks pained. "That you also tell her the location of this cure."

"That would give her a lot of power." I glance over at the guard, suddenly worried he overheard us. I scooch closer to Dion and switch to a whisper. "She already is incredibly powerful. Have you seen this place? She's gathering people around her and strengthening her powers. She's planning something."

"I know." He runs a hand through his hair. "I didn't know what else to do. The Empress has the two Nazco Channelers under close watch. Besides, neither of them are even close to your current abilities. I don't trust the Sabians, and we Nazco have no working relationships with the Caladrians as they are allies with the Sabians. Ami was my only choice."

I press my lips together, running through the options. Finally, I say, "You're right. It was the best choice."

He nods sharply, but I can't help but wonder if there's something else he's not telling me. I don't know why I feel it. It's not like I really know him. Or maybe I do.

A ring cuts through the air from my dress. I jump in surprise.

"What's that?" Dion frowns at my skirt.

"My phone," I say in realization. I slipped it inside my skirt because I've been so worried about Tristan and have been hoping he'd call. Quickly, I dig it out of my pocket.

"You have a phone?"

"Yes," I say without explanation. Something tells me he

wouldn't be happy to know it's Tristan's. "Let me take this really quickly."

I step over to the water's edge, heart beating.

"Tristan," I say breathlessly. "Did you make it to Nadia's? Are my friends safe?"

11
SECRETS OF THE FLAME IS NOT A GAME
ESTRELLA

Kakurezato, Japan

"Estrella." It's Katka. My heart sinks. I had been hoping it was Tristan. "There's something we need to talk about."

"What's wrong?" I ask her, clutching the phone like it's my lifeline. The last time I spoke to her was after she discovered me and Tristan kissing. To say she was unhappy is an understatement.

"No, nothing is fine," she snaps, "but that's beside the point. Tristan told me you sent him off on a wild goose chase back to Florida to watch over some Nazco convicts."

"I wouldn't frame it like that."

"Whatever. Tristan wanted me to tell you that he's in Florida, and he's going to your old high school tomorrow."

"That's great news."

"Let me get this straight. He's our prince and not some lapdog that can be run around to check up on your mindless friends who can't even remember what they ate for breakfast."

Fury rises up inside of me. I'm so mad I can't even see straight. But I have to be careful what I say to her. She isn't someone I want to alienate. She's my only connection to Tristan right now. Plus, I need to keep my voice down.

I glance over to see that both the guard and Dion are listening very carefully, so I turn around and whisper, "He offered to help my friends. What would you do to help those you care about? How far will you go to help Conrad out of prison now? Or to help Tristan if he was captured?" I press. She's silent, which may be the first time I can remember. "If I can find a way to get my powers back, I'm going to do everything I can to rescue both Lexi and Conrad. But first, I need to save my friends who need my help. I don't know how much time they have left."

She's so quiet I wonder if the connection is lost.

"I also have another message," she continues tightly as if I didn't just spill my heart out. "It's from Queen Kelli. She says to not tell anyone about your ability to use Sabian fire."

"Sabian fire?" My head snaps back and I stare at the phone for a moment. "What are you talking about? That's not possible."

"That day you practiced with the fire on the pedestal with Tristan. It wasn't fake. She was testing you. It was the real Numinous Flame, the power all our races need to survive and refuel our visik and immortality. Only a Conduit can access it."

The impact of her words slam into me, and I lean against a tree, remembering Ami's words: *As a Nazco, she will only be able to manipulate Nazcoian fire.*

"What does this mean?" I whisper.

"It means I want to help you because our people are going to need to replenish their powers soon. And yeah, I want to get Conrad out of that rat-infested Nazco prison. This must be a secret between the Queen, you, and I. The Queen explicitly told me to tell you that. Don't even tell Tristan."

My eyes travel to Dion, who is now pacing in front of the bench. "Why?"

"The less people who know the truth, the safer you are. The Queen asked me to do some research on Conduits who have had this ability, so I'm starting there. If the Eien Conduit or Emperor find out what you can do, they will kill you. Got it?"

"Just add them to the waiting list."

She hangs up without saying goodbye. I stare at the phone and the full impact of her words hit me.

I can manipulate Sabian fire. According to Ami, that's not possible. Tristan said the same thing when he was training me. Is this good? Bad? Could this be why the Empress excommunicated me? Perhaps she worried I'd betray them. I shake my head. Everything is too complicated.

Dion hurries to my side, holding my arms to steady me. "Everything alright? What was that call about?"

This must be a secret.

"It was a friend," I say vaguely, slipping the phone back

into the folds of my skirt. "She said Tristan is going to check on my friends at Nadia's. Make sure they're safe."

"Nadia's? Are you sure sending a Sabian is a good idea? If word gets out a Sabian—a Sabian Prince—is snooping around the home, that could put all of them in jeopardy."

"You may be right, but I think it's worth the risk." A raging headache storms against my thoughts. "I need to rest. I've got the worst headache."

"What can I do?"

Make the world less confusing. Give me back my powers, my friends, my life. I let out a long breath and say, "Nothing right now. But tomorrow, will you come with me to training? I don't trust Ami."

"Of course. Anything you need."

"Thank you." A desperate need to step into his arms and let him comfort me threatens against my barriers. Somehow, I wrench myself away to step further from him. "Good night."

Dawn comes too soon. I slept fitfully, haunted by dreams of ice and snow and a fire that was too bright for me to hide from. Dion and I head out to Ami's training pagoda to find her with Sensei Haruki. Morning sun filters through the paper doors, illuminating the polished wood floor. He bows to us, and we bow in return.

"Haruki will be leading us through our warm-up today," Ami explains. Her eyes drift to Dion and she lifts her eyebrows as if expecting him to leave.

"Dion will be staying." I turn to him and ask, "Would

you like to warm up with us?"

He's eyeing Ami warily but when his gaze focuses on me, it warms. "Of course."

Sensei Haruki nods and claps his hands together. "Follow my moves. Breathe in and out from deep within."

He begins a set of movements, and I follow along, lifting my arms up, bending my knees, stretching. The movements relax me and release the tension I was feeling earlier.

"Control your breathing," he reminds us as we lunge and reach for the sky, "for it's the breath that controls the body."

Once we finish, Ami leads me through a full day of training using different weapons and then ends the day at the Tethering Nexus for me to practice my channeling. Once we finish, my muscles are screaming and begging for a rest. As we drink some water and pack up, my mind goes back to the secret Katka told me. Is it really true that I can wield Sabian fire? And if so, could I also wield Eien fire? We head back down the path but when we reach the lake, Yuto comes running up, his robes tangled around him, and I worry he may trip. He drops to his knees, bowing his head to the dirt.

"We have an emergency, your wonderfulness," he says. "You must come."

"Apparently there are needs I must attend to," Ami says, annoyance tinging her voice. "I will see you at dinner tonight."

She follows Yuko to her Channeler pagoda in the center of the lake. I watch her go, but my mind can't help but wonder what would happen if I touched the Eien fire within that pagoda. Would it consume me like Ami said or make me stronger? Dion and I continue down the path but halfway back, I stop him.

"I appreciate you helping me and being here for me. But there's something I need to know about us."

He stiffens but nods as if he's preparing himself. "Of course. Whatever you want to know."

"On our date, which I guess was the last time we were really together, it would've been the perfect opportunity for you to tell me the truth about who I was. We were alone without Nadia or the Wraiths. Why didn't you tell me who I really was then?"

"I wanted to tell you everything." He frowns, his face pained. "You have no idea how much I wanted to, but we've been told that sparking an immortal whose memory has been wiped can permanently damage the brain. Also, I knew the moment you started remembering, the Wraiths would kill you. I couldn't risk a chance that I'd lose you again."

"Except I had already started to remember and the Wraiths knew when they tried to kill me at school. If Tristan hadn't been there, they'd have succeeded."

His face jerks as if he'd been slapped. "I know that now, and I'm sorry. Those had obviously been lies, and now, I feel foolish for believing them. The Empress sent me specifically to watch over you. At first, I'd hoped I could be there to keep you safe. But when it became clear other Nazco wanted you dead, I began to set up a plan to run away with you. That's why I went back home to Brazil. To get money and that necklace for you."

I touch the pendant hanging at my neck, now burning ruby red. "It's been various shades of red ever since you gave it to me."

"I can only imagine." He lets out a dark chuckle, running a hand through his short hair. "I was going to leave everything behind. My family, my name, my inheritance. Everything for you."

"But why? What did we have together that was so special?"

His eyes search mine as if begging me to remember. "I think that's been the hardest part. You not remembering us. I'm not going to lie. It's been a bit of an obsession to bring back what we once had. I threw everything else aside to search for you. I gave up everything to be here with you. But now that we're finally together, I'm beginning to wonder if hoping for what we had is even possible and if it's truly lost."

Pain etches in his face, wrinkling the lines on his brow and darkening those brown eyes. My heart hurts for the pain he must be feeling.

"I wish I could remember us," I say. "Every day I wake up frustrated, but you have to understand that right now this is me. Ever since I woke up in that hospital with no memory, I've created new memories with new feelings. I'm not the same person I was before. Sometimes I wonder if you're in love with the old me. What if you don't like the person I am now?"

He nods slowly and lets out a long breath. "Perhaps we can start over. Find each other again."

Can I do that? Do I even want that?

"I don't know," I finally say. "It's going to take a lot for me to trust you again after what happened, but I do feel like we've made progress. I mean, we are talking again."

"We are." He smiles, but there's sadness in his eyes. "I'm going to remain hopeful that we can find our way back to each other again."

12
THE TRIALS OF MORTAL EXISTENCE
TRISTAN

Florida

I can't believe I'm about to do this. Voluntarily. Of my own free will.

I glower at the front of Olympia High School as students enter through the main entrance and climb out of buses, beginning their day of drudgery. Why did I promise Estrella I'd do this again?

My eyes press close as memories of her rush to me like a flame hunts dry kindling, and it devours my every thought. Her scent is an intoxicating concoction of lavender and berries and always entices me to pull her in closer for another kiss. And those kisses! I groan. Every time her lips press against mine, my world slips into hers, a firestorm of heat I never want to escape.

This is bad. I can't torture myself. We both agreed our relationship is impossible. She's a Nazco and I'm a Sabian. And yet...my heart tortures me of the what ifs.

What if we could make it work?

What if we are destined for each other?

What if my people accepted her?

I can't deal with these debilitating thoughts, so I take another swig of the bitter coffee. My phone rings, and I frown. The only person who knows this number is Katka, and she has yet to answer any of my texts or calls. Probably still pissed at me for kissing Estrella.

"Katka, thanks for finally calling me back," I say, trying to mask my annoyance. Also, now I have an image of kissing Estrella, and I can't get it out of my head.

"I'm only calling because I want to help Conrad."

"Of course. I'm about to head to classes so I can't talk for long." I get out of my rental car, promising myself to get a better mode of transportation soon. "You don't happen to remember my schedule, do you?"

"Are you serious? Why are you going to a mortal high school?"

"Apparently, I'm a senior trying to get into university. Or is it college? I can't remember what they call it here."

When I pass by a group of girls, they giggle and bat their eyes at me, which is severely awkward. *Right. I can do this.* I try to give myself a pep talk. *I really can.*

"I'll text your schedule," Katka grumbles, "but I don't see how going to that school is helping get Conrad back."

The coffee tastes bitter as I scan the hallway until my eyes latch onto a pale-skinned girl with blonde hair that sticks out like a porcupine, dark-rimmed eyes, and tight black clothes. She's talking to another girl with short black hair, brown skin, and clothes that look like they're about to fall off her. I remember both of them as Estrella's friends. Something about these two Nazco girls tells me they're not only trouble—they were once very dangerous.

"I think Estrella was onto something when she sent me here," I tell Katka, squeezing my way through the school hallway.

"I still don't understand why you're doing this." She huffs. "It's a waste of your time. You need to be gathering up an expert team who can get us into the Midnight Kingdom and prisonbreak Conrad."

"I've got a feeling that's exactly why I'm here."

I hang up and pocket my phone before one of the school wardens spots me with it and sends me to their version of prison. Detention. I've almost reached them when I spy Shondra—or is it Chandra? —just on their other side, flirting with two boys who seem to have forgotten how to close their mouths. Quickly, I duck into a stairwell before she spots me, debating what to do.

First off, Chandra will recognize me right away after our battle in the alleyway, not to mention trying to kill Estrella and me again on our ride to the castle gates. I need to get a disguise. Eyeing the students passing by, I step into the path of a guy wearing a baseball hat.

"Nice hat," I say, infusing all of my powers of persuasion into each word. "You wouldn't mind if I borrowed that, would you?"

"You want to borrow my hat?" the guy asks, touching the bill like he's considering my words.

"Just until the end of the day." I hold out some cash because I can't promise it won't be charred when I return it.

"Sure, man. Thanks!"

We exchange goods, and he grins happily as if I'm doing him a favor. Then I push the hat on my head and tug the bill over my face before reentering the hall. Chandra is still there, making an effort to keep the two Nazco girls in her line of sight. Concerning.

Keeping my head down, I swagger to the locker next to Estrella's friends and pretend to twist the lock.

"Don't look in my direction," I tell them. "You're being watched."

The blonde digging through her backpack snaps her head up to stare at the brown-haired girl, whose jaw clenches. Neither glances at me, but it's clear they heard me.

"Estrella sent me," I continue. "She wants to help you escape from Nadia's."

"Remember that guy that used to stalk Estrella?" the brown-haired girl says. "He was so untrustworthy."

The blonde nods and pulls out a protractor, gripping it like a weapon.

"Oh, yeah, you could totally stab him in the eye with that," the brown-haired girl continues, nodding to her friend. "You know, in case he showed up."

I roll my eyes as they take off. *Message received.* The bell rings and I still don't know where my first torture chamber, I mean class, is located.

This isn't going well.

By lunchtime, I get my schedule at the office, do a little reconnaissance work, and discover the girls' names are Mara and Jamie. If I can get photos of these girls, Katka might be able to find them in our system and learn something about them.

I enter the cafeteria, keeping the bill of my hat low. I grab a tray and let the cafeteria workers load it with mortal food of a lesser quality than my horse, Wildfire, eats back home. But considering my stomach is growling, I know I'm going to eat every bite. Once I'm through the line, I search the packed tables for Mara and Jamie. Finally, I spy them in the far corner of the room.

The sooner I can get them out of here, the faster this will all be over. Plus, if I'm being honest with myself, I'm eager to see Estrella again. And taking them to her would be a great excuse to see her again.

As inconspicuously as possible, I snap a few photos of them, but based on the glances and looks I'm getting around the cafeteria, it's clear I'm not meant for espionage because it feels like everyone is staring at me. It doesn't help that I'm taller and wider than most. When I set my tray on the girls' table, they both freeze and stare up at me. I smile at them and then sit on the long bench. They glare back at me.

"Hello," I say, "I'm not sure if you heard me earlier, but I'm a—"

"We heard," Mara says tonelessly, "you're Estrella's friend. Where is she? What have you done to her?"

"She's safe. That's all I can tell you."

"That tells me nothing other than you're trouble."

She might be true on that account. Technically, I'm her enemy number one, but informing her of that detail won't help the situation. "What if I told you I can offer you a better life than this?" I point to what I think is meatloaf and potatoes.

"What if I told *you* that I never want to see your face again?"

"I wouldn't mind so much," Jamie says, winking.

"If you know where Estrella is, bring her back home to safety."

I shoot them a skeptical look. "I wouldn't exactly call where you live home nor safe."

"Never speak to us again," Mara says and then flashes me the middle finger.

Jamie smashes her tray over my head. Green beans and French fries rain over me like a food storm. The two girls march away, leaving me coated with food and rubbing my head. A few students glance my way, chuckling as if I'm an idiot.

"Maybe I am," I mutter and stab my lunch with fury, swallowing the bland meat.

This mission might be harder than it seems, but I'm not about to let Estrella down. I just need to find another way to get those girls' attention.

13
FATE HAS A SHARP EDGE
ESTRELLA

Kakurezato, Japan

"We will work until the moon sets," Ami tells me at dinner before heading back out of the main room.

I've been training all day, but Ami is relentless. And I get it. There's an urgency that tugs and pulls at me, too. When I was in Slovakia, it had been because I worried I'd continue to lose my memories. Now that I've made zero ground on remembering anything from before, I need to develop and keep any of the powers I still have left.

The immortal mark on my shoulder seems to burn against my skin, a reminder that time is valuable. Quickly, I stuff the last chunk of grilled meat into my mouth and rise from my cushion on the floor.

"If you have time," I tell Dion, "stop by her training pagoda later and make sure she hasn't killed me."

Dion chuckles. "I will. I need to check in with my father and then I'll head your way."

I'm about to turn to leave but pause. "Have I met your family before?"

"No." His face closes as if he doesn't want to tell me more. "They live in Brazil, far from the Midnight Kingdom."

There is more to the story here, but I don't have time right now to dive into this conversation.

"I'll see you later," I say and hurry back to my room to change into my gi. As I shove my legs into the loose-fitting pants, my thoughts linger on Dion.

Why does it always feel like he's keeping things from me? This is why it's hard to trust him, I think as I slip on my white jacket and wrap the cloth belt around my waist. I step outside in the cool evening. The floral breeze washes over my face, tugging at my ponytail. Night has settled over the land like a thick blanket, allowing only the glow of the moon and lanterns to provide any light.

The pagoda glows with soft honey light. When I step inside, I'm alone, having arrived first. I slip off my shoes and pad barefoot across the smooth wooden floor to the far wall where all her weapons hang like medals on display. Staves, poles, daggers, swords, bows... Her repertoire is impressive. Power trickles out of each, carrying with them a song of the elements. I've practiced with a few of her lesser-crafted weapons, but she's asked me not to touch anything that she hasn't approved of.

I've always respected her wishes while here, except one

sword catches my eye tonight. Its steel glitters almost as if it's winking at me. It's not Japanese. European, I'm guessing. Ornate carvings are engraved in the hilt and the hand guard curves outward with scrollwork. The blade is long and sharp and far heavier than my sea dagger.

Curious, I step closer to it, but I don't feel any power seeping from its metal. Unlike the others, it's still and quiet like it's holding a secret. My hand trembles as I take it off the wall. The steel shimmers where my fingers swipe across the blade.

"I should've known you'd eventually find her," Ami says from behind me.

I spin around, guilt burning my face. She's wearing her gi, white as a lily, and her black belt is cinched tight across her slim waist. Her long, shining black hair is pulled up in a ponytail. She's ready to practice.

"This weapon is different from the others," I say.

"How is it different?" she pushes.

"It doesn't have powers coming off it like the others. But there's something about it."

"It's a Channeler blade. It was found in the ice in Sweden recently and I received it as a…gift, if you will."

I smirk, betting she totally forced someone to give it to her. "It's stunning. Does it have a name?"

"If it did, the name is lost. Channelers don't share their weapon names with others or allow them to go into the history books."

"We sound like a paranoid bunch."

She snorts. "To put it mildly. Conduits are even worse."

"It's also heavy."

I'm able to lift it and thankfully, it's not as heavy or large as Tristan's sword, but as I swoop the blade in front of me, my arm is already getting tired. She goes to the corner of the room and opens a long box set against the wall and plucks a katana out of the silk wrap. The curved steel shines. She swishes it through the air, quick and effortlessly.

"This is my Channeler blade. In ancient times, Channelers held their own weapon to help channel their powers. But as you can imagine, these weapons were very powerful. All other immortals feared them more than anything else."

"Why?" I twist the handle in my hand, studying the weapon. "It doesn't hold any power."

She grins, her blue eyes glimmering. "The purpose of the weapon is to focus powers that you take and amplify them."

She dips into a graceful bend, swishing the katana through the air with precise movement. The blade catches the lantern light, glimmering. She pivots on her toes, elegant and yet powerful, and swipes the blade in swooping quick arcs and slices. It's a beautiful dance of death.

"Immortal artifacts are so incredibly rare that only the most powerful immortals have them," she says. "I saw you have a dagger and you wear the pendant."

"I found the dagger at Nadia's." I touch the pendant that hangs against my chest. "Dion gave this to me."

"That is quite the gift." She slashes at an invisible enemy and I'm glad it's not me. "Most artifacts are lost or owned by only the most powerful immortals as they're rarely being made anymore. It takes so much power to create an artifact and our powers aren't as strong as they once were."

"Which is why most of the artifacts are old." I ease to Ami's side and start to mimic her movements.

She nods as I join her. A hint of a smile tilts at the

corners of her mouth. If I didn't know better, I'd think she actually was enjoying this.

"When you take another immortal's powers," she explains, "you push all that power into this blade. It holds the power and allows you to release it all in one hit or you can slowly ease it out, giving you greater control than if you were to release the power without it."

"Interesting. When I took a guard's power from him while at the Sabian castle, it spilled out of me quickly, so you're saying this weapon would help hold it?"

"It depends on the power source of course and your ability to maintain focus, but the simple answer is yes. Come, practice some moves with me."

We arc our swords, cutting the air. Our knees bend and our bodies twist. Silence rules the pagoda, only disrupted by the hiss of our blades. My arm burns from holding the sword and sweat drips down my face. I sag to the floor and set the sword across my knees.

"My arm is killing me," I say. "I thought I was starting to get in good shape with your exercises, but this is eye-opening."

"You should start training with the sword each day for one hour. That will help you build up endurance."

"But it's not like I'll be carrying your sword around with me," I point out.

"It's always best to be prepared. You never know what tomorrow will bring you. Master your craft or someone will become the master of you."

She models a series of movements and then tells me to practice them. She turns over an hourglass and points to it.

"Continue practicing until the sand has reached the

bottom," she instructs. "Then you can rest. I will see you at dawn."

We give each other a tight bow as she had instructed me to do and then she leaves. I let out a long breath and start up my moves once again, envisioning a hot bath afterward to soothe my muscles.

I'm startled when Dion steps into the room. I'd forgotten that I invited him. He's wearing his black training outfit that shows off his toned arms. My pulse ticks up a notch.

"She gave you a sword?" Dion asks, his brow raised teasingly.

"Shocking." I shoot him a smile. "I know I offered for you to come, but I changed my mind. I'm so bad at these moves that I can't promise I won't wound you."

"You've got moves, huh?" He crosses his arms, his lips twitching. "This I've got to see."

I roll my eyes but after his insistence, I start the sequence of my new moves.

"So what's the deal with me and your family?" I ask, bending and pointing my blade in his direction before pivoting and cutting the air. "You seemed cagey when I asked if I'd met your family."

"I didn't want to get into it at dinner, but yeah, my father has always been wary of you. He didn't approve."

"Of us dating?"

"Technically, we never dated since it's not allowed until graduation. But he knew that my trips to the Midnight Kingdom weren't to hang out with friends. It was to see you. He worried you were the Empress's little pet and that you might use me for my powers."

I lower my sword. "Was that the kind of person I was?"

"I'd like to believe you weren't." He steps closer to me, his eyes intense. "But he didn't know you other than that the Empress had big plans for your future. She and my father were always at odds. He has been trying to secretly overthrow her, and I think she suspects. As long as she had a powerful Conduit under her control, she was unstoppable."

"Except she didn't feel like she could control me, did she?"

He shakes his head and his hand reaches out to push back a flyaway hair that has fallen over my face. "No. It didn't help that she excommunicated your two best friends, Lexi and Jamie. I don't think she knew how close you were to them."

"I don't know what kind of person I was before, but I don't want to ever abuse your powers."

I feel our bodies pushing together like two magnets trying to find their mate. Quickly, I spin away, breaking that pull. Even though my arm burns, I start up my exercises once again, needing to get my focus off him.

"You're holding the hilt wrong," he says.

I put one fist on my hip. "Since when did you become a sword expert?"

"Here." He comes in behind me. "Place your index finger in the hilt over the outside arm of it like this."

He takes my hand and adjusts my fingers. His chest presses against my back. His breath whispers across my bare neck. I can barely focus on my fingers when he's so close to me.

"Your thumb goes here," he continues and moves it to the other side. "Now close the rest of the fingers tightly around the grip. Yeah, like that."

The pommel is now firmly in my grasp. Sparks from his power flutter over our palms. "That feels better," I reluctantly admit. "Thanks."

"Try a few thrusts now. I'll help hold up your arm."

"Are you insinuating I'm not strong enough to hold the blade?" I quirk my eyebrows up and glance over my shoulder at him only to find his lips so close to mine. My face burns and I quickly focus back on my blade.

"Do you want to be able to protect yourself?" he shoots back.

"Fine." I shake my head to clear my thoughts of his scent and body and start up the sequence of moves once again.

It's easier this time with Dion's hand supporting mine. It keeps the weight of the blade off my muscles. It allows me to focus on each move and my grip. He moves with me perfectly as if he's attuned to each step I'll take and how my body will shift and turn. Sparks fly around us. It's like we're dancing and I wonder if we've ever danced together before.

When I finish the sequence of movements, I glance at my timer. The sand has completed its way to the bottom of the hourglass, probably a long time ago. I lower my arm and he steps away from me, his chest rising and falling as if he's out of breath. His eyes burn bright, silver and white like lightning streaking across the sky.

"I should go." He backs away as if being near me is dangerous. "Good night."

He vanishes out the door before I even have a chance to respond. This is good because I'm scared that if he'd stayed, I would've grabbed his vest and yanked him closer. Wrapped my hands behind his neck and pressed him against me.

Tasted his power on my lips.
And I don't know if I could've stopped.

14
BEFORE: THE BAD IDEA I CAN'T RESIST
LEXI

Florida

I used to guzzle Mountain Dew to wake me up. Now I just drink in the sight of Conrad. Yeah, it's super cheesy, but it's not like I'm actually going to tell someone that out loud.

I look for him every day the moment I step on the school grounds. I usually find him outside on one of the benches or leaning against a pillar reading a book. He said that we can't be seen actually talking to each other so when we do talk, I face one direction and he the other. Or I pretend I'm talking on my phone, but I'm really talking to him.

Since he doesn't attend our school, we have only a few minutes to chat each day, a situation that is starting to get really annoying. So today when I stride up to where he's sitting on a bench, I've got a plan.

"This whole secretly talking to you for five minutes while pretending not to talk to you is starting to really get annoying," I tell him.

"Good morning to you," Conrad says softly. "I'm sorry I'm annoying. We don't have to talk. Maybe you can give me a gesture to let me know that you're okay."

This is another thing about him. He's like everything I'm not. Big and warm and soft and gentle. While I'm a bit scrappy, wild, loud, and okay, sometimes I can be obnoxious. Anyway, I may or may not dream of curling up in those arms when I go to sleep at night.

"We need a better plan," I say.

He sits straighter. "I'm all ears. What do you need?"

I smile. "I want to talk more about this whole hot hands thing you did and those horrible creatures and what everything means."

"That's a lot. I don't think we have time for all of that."

The bell rings as if agreeing with him.

"Meet me at the downtown library," I say. "Today after school. Nadia thinks I'm at play practice and it's close enough for me to walk there."

"That could be risky," he says, glancing around as if one of those horrid creatures might jump off the roof and attack us. "But I'm willing to give it a try."

"Excellent," I say, walking backward and flashing him my biggest smile. "Then I'll see you later."

And that's how it all began. Us meeting in secret at the library. It's where I learned all about the immortals, that I was an immortal with powers—gosh, I still haven't gotten over that—and that my own people, maybe my own family, kicked me out to live with Nadia. It should make me sad, but the fact that I can't even remember them makes me feel more hollow than sad. Like I'm a jack-o-lantern and I've been hollowed out and now I'm just trying to light a flame in the darkness.

But it's also where he kissed me for the first time. Maybe it was even my first kiss. I don't know nor do I care. All I know is that right now my life is split into two parts. Before Conrad and after him. And I never want to go back to before.

A truck screeches to a halt on the side of the street and a group of people jump out, wearing black suits and sunglasses. Conrad pulls out what looks like a full sword, which okay, is bizarre. But it doesn't matter because the group attacks Conrad and me with such precision and quickness.

One of the men holds out his hand and sends a bolt of light, blinding toward both of us. I cover my eyes and then hands grab me, locking my arms behind my back and snapping my wrists into what feels like handcuffs.

"Fight, Lexi!" Conrad screams.

I dig deep for my fire power that Conrad's been working with me to develop, but it's too weak. It sputters inside of me like the usual useless flame. Furious, I twist and writhe in the arms of my attacker. I find some solace when I manage to bite him in the arm.

The dude cries out. "The girl bit me!" he whines like a baby, but unfortunately his grip on me tightens.

A woman with black hair woven with silver streaks appears before me, a smirk on her blue lips.

"Sleep," she says and blows a long breath over my face.

"Let me go!" I cough and fight to pull away from the strange blue cloud settling over my face, but within moments, my knees buckle beneath me. My eyes close and the world falls into darkness.

I shiver awake on a hard surface and sit up. Where am I? This place is freaking cold. My whole body trembles in the semi-darkness. It takes a moment for my eyes to adjust. I'm sitting on a stone floor with stone walls around me. Veins of ice run through the walls, glowing in a really creepy blue color. Across the small space are shimmering blue bars.

This is a prison cell.

I tremble in fear.

"Are you kidding me?" My voice crackles like firewood. "I've been imprisoned?"

I climb to my feet, but grimace. My legs tingle with numbness like when I've sat too long on them. It must be whatever that blue-lip woman did to me. Pain shoots from the back of my head. I don't remember hitting anything so it must have happened when I passed out.

"Lexi!" Conrad's voice calls to me.

"Conrad?" I stumble to the glowing bars, closer to the sound of his voice.

"Lexi!" he says again, his face filling with relief when our eyes land on each other. "You're alive. I was so worried when you didn't get up."

He's across a narrow hall, standing tall behind another set of bars. His brown hair hangs over his eyes and a five o'clock shadow has formed along his jaw. The guy looks fierce as a captive bear, but seeing him settles me a little. Ever since the attack in the bathroom at school and Estrella left, he's been my rock. Not only did he heal my wound, but over the past few weeks, he's also been telling me the truth about who I am and trying to help me revitalize my powers.

"Why are we here?" My heart slams against my chest as panic starts to set in. "The last thing I remember was these creepy people jumping out of a van and attacking us."

"Don't touch the bars," he warns, which is a good thing because I was just about to do that. "They'll stun you. They act like inhibitors and suck away an immortal's powers."

"What's going on?" My voice quivers. "What is this place? Conrad...I'm scared."

"I know. I'm so sorry, Lexi. I could be wrong, but based on the ice walls and the blue bars, I think we're at the Reckoning Hall in the Midnight Kingdom."

"That makes a lot of sense. You basically told me gibberish."

"The Reckoning Hall is a Nazco prison. It holds the Empress's worst enemies. The ones she fears, or hates, the most. It's located in the Nazco capital in Antarctica."

"Antarctica? As in the continent?" When he nods, I grab the hair on top of my head and start to pace my cell. "Are you freaking serious?"

"I could be wrong." He looks around, and for the first time, fear etches lines on his face. "But I'm probably not."

"So what I hear you saying is that we're prisoners on the

most remote continent on earth by a group of people who *clearly* are our enemy. Basically, we're screwed."

He grimaces and rubs the back of his neck. The fact he's not denying my statement shoots another wave of fear through me.

"This is just great. I'm in a prison cell, but I've never even committed a crime. What did we do wrong?"

"I hate to break it to you, but in the eyes of the Empress, we broke a lot of rules. Committed a long list of crimes. At least you're Nazco. I'm just Sabian scum in their eyes."

"Well, this is just fabulous. You've got a plan, right?" Because he's always had a plan before. When Nadia came into my hospital room, I pretended not to remember anything just like he told me to. And it worked. And when I started to get my powers back, he gave me these cool gloves that looked fashionable. And that worked, too.

"No, not even close," he mutters.

A slam of a door, a jangle of keys, and then footsteps echo down the stone hall.

"Someone is coming," I whisper.

Four guards with faces straight and expressionless as stone march up. They're suited in blue uniforms with a snowflake emblem and their boots and belt buckles glimmer in this bizarre light. Each of them holds some sort of baton. I eye them nervously. There's something oddly familiar and deeply disturbing about those sticks. I shudder. Somehow I get the feeling I've felt them before.

"You've been granted a great honor," the one wearing an eye patch says. "Her Majesty wishes to speak to you both."

"Wow. Yay us!" I snap sarcastically, shooting him a glare. "What if I don't want to speak to the majesty?"

"You don't get a choice," Eye Patch says with a snarl.

One of the men presses a card to a panel on the wall, and with a click, the blue bars of my cell transform to hard metal. The door groans open and then they come at me with surprising speed, handcuffing me with strange glowing blue bands.

Next, they turn to face Conrad, eyeing him nervously. Even though Conrad looks completely harmless, shoulders sagging as he leans against the wall, the guards tense and they hold out their wands in preparation as the one unlocks the cell. The moment the cell clicks open, Conrad springs to life, a lion set loose. He sweeps a foot out and knocks one of the guards to the ground. He manages to snatch up the guy's wand and stab the second guy. Meanwhile, I twist and knee the guy holding me.

But with a swift movement, my guard stabs me in the arm with his wand. I scream in pain and my legs buckle beneath me. I drop to the ground. The hallway swims as my whole body convulses. The guard yanks me up and holds me in front of him, a knife to my throat.

Conrad is standing before me, free. The guards wallow on the ground in pain.

"Put down your weapon or she dies," he tells Conrad.

"Fine, I will." Conrad holds his arms up and drops the wand. "Just don't hurt her."

The guards climb to their feet and handcuff Conrad. Tears sting my eyes, but I blink them away. I was never a crier before. I'm not going to start now.

"That's the best you've got?" I lift my eyebrows at my captors, chuckling. "Next time you should send five guards.

Seriously, Conrad nearly incapacitated all of you without any weapons or powers."

"Are you always this difficult?" Eye Patch asks, clearly annoyed.

"Only when I haven't had my Mountain Dew," I say as my guard shoves me forward. "It puts me in a bad mood."

The passageway winds around and then up a long set of steps. Soon we enter a massive, grand hallway lined with statues of men and women bound or chained up. It's quite disturbing if you ask me. They seem to be frowning at us as our footsteps clack against the marble floor. The only relief is that the arched glass ceiling allows sunlight to flood the room, a hint of freedom.

Once we step outside, a sharp gust of cold air swooshes around me and I gasp in shock. My hair snaps against my face, red against a world of white.

"Snap, this place is cold," I say, shivering. I take in the snow-laden path and glistening silver trees lining it. "But it's also kind of pretty."

Except then my eyes land on a tall black spire, rising out of the snowy ground just ahead of us. Mist cloaks the top in a swath of gray. It's a splotch of darkness in a world of white, oddly reminding me of Estrella's painting in art class. A band of fear clenches around my throat.

The guards push me forward, but I can't shake the feeling that I've been here before. And that scares me more than the prison.

I glance over at Conrad. His eyes are focused on me as if assessing how hurt I am. I can almost hear him ask me if I'm okay. He's a Healer so even though he's limping, I know his body has probably already healed itself and now he's pretending. If we survive this, I'm going to tell him how impressed I am by his skills.

The path turns and my guard pushes me forward onto a long icy bridge that stretches across a chasm, so deep I can't even see the bottom. On the other side of the bridge is a palace that looks like something carved out of a fairy tale. Spires of ice, turrets the color of midnight stars, and walls sparking like freshly fallen snow.

"What is this place?" I ask, unable to hide my awe.

"That is the Empress's palace," Eye Patch tells us, a sinister grin creeping across his face. "Most who enter don't leave."

15
TIME IS TICKING
ESTRELLA

Kakurezato, Japan

After another long day of training, I managed to drag my sore and beaten-up body to my room. I strip off my clothes and take a long shower, letting the sweat and grime of the day wash off me. The scent of sandalwood fills the air, soothing away the fears that I'll never be good or strong enough. When I get out and wrap the towel around me, I pause to stare at the immortal tattoo on my shoulder blade. It's now almost completely visible, brighter than it's ever been. Does that mean I'm getting my powers back again?

My thoughts fly back to the day at the beach when Tristan showed me his immortal branding and explained how every immortal was born with one. My eyes fly open. I forgot to check Tristan's phone today. What if he called?

Maybe he has news of my friends. I hurry to the chest where I keep it. Sure enough, an unknown call has come through along with a text.

> Call me at this number. Your fellow Roach Killer.

I grin at Tristan's method of keeping his identity a secret just in case someone saw this text. Quickly, I call him back.

"Estrella," Tristan answers, "is everything going well?"

"You're okay." I sink into the low bed and close my eyes, soaking in his deep voice. It calms me because I know I can trust him. Ever since I've arrived in Ami's land, I've been tense from all the training, trying to understand the dynamics between Dion and myself, and worrying about Ami and her secret schemes. But with Tristan, I know where I stand.

"I started getting worried when you didn't call back."

"I've been good. I spend every waking minute training with either Ami or Sensei Haruki. It's exhausting, but I think it's paying off. I was just checking my tattoo after I got out of the shower and it's brighter than ever."

"That's uh, great. But now you've got me thinking about you and showers. Not exactly great for my mental zone right now with us breaking up."

I smile as I sag onto my bed. Leave it to Tristan to find a way to ease my worries.

"I'm making progress and starting to build off the training you and I did at your house," I say, but I'm also reminded of what Katka told me about the Sabian Numinous fire. It's on the tip of my tongue to tell him, but Katka's warning keeps me in check. "But what about you? Are you in Florida? Have you seen any of my friends?"

"I made contact with Jamie and Mara."

"What?" I leap to my feet. Just hearing him say their names makes my heart tumble around like a kite caught in a storm. "How are they? Are they okay? Where did you see them?"

"Woah! Slow down with the questions. They seem well. I saw them at your old school and we chatted in the cafeteria."

"That's wonderful!" I start pacing the room, trying to imagine my friends meeting up with him. "What did they say? Did you work out a way to get them out of there?"

"I didn't get to say much." He clears his throat. "Truth is Jamie took my tray and smashed it over my head. And Mara flicked me off before they left."

I smile, imagining them both. "Yeah, that sounds like something they would do."

"But I'm going back to purgatory—I mean your old school—tomorrow. How do those humans handle that place day after day?"

"You're asking the girl who has no memory?"

He chuckles. "It's good to hear your voice. I miss you."

My heart flips, but I tamper it down in place. "I should go. Text or call me if there are any updates, okay?"

After I hang up, I stand at the floor-to-ceiling window and stare into the valley below, trying to understand and rationalize my feelings for Tristan. The sun hugs the horizon, spilling crimsons and pinks like a tapestry.

But all I can think about is Tristan's startling blue eyes.

His calloused hand cupping my chin as he leans in for a... I shake my head. *Stop this*, I order myself. If I continue down this path, I'm only headed for trouble. It's been a week since the mob outside of his castle came to kill me. And they aren't the only ones who are against me working with the Sabians. Imagine how they'd feel if Tristan and I were together.

We can't work. We're not meant for each other.

But...ugh.

It's so hard because my heart screams that we are meant to be together. What I need is to focus my thoughts and efforts on helping my friends. And that's all that this is between Tristan and me.

Yesterday, I asked Ami for paper, pens, and paints because drawing and painting helped me at Nadia's. My fingers itch to put my thoughts to paper. I go to the stack of paper and pull out a pen. Sitting on the floor, I write down the names of the girls from Nadia's.

Lexi
Jamie
Mara
Zayla (aka Sneaky)
Izzy
Flora
Min (aka Piano girl)
Gaia (aka Bread girl)

My pen hovers in the air as I try to remember the last two girls' names but I can't. Sally maybe? I trace each curve of the letters. There were twelve of us, minus Traitor Tiffany. My stomach clenches at her betrayal.

A knock on the door yanks me from my dark mood.

"Come in," I say, not bothering to get up.

Dion steps into the room just as I'm slipping the phone secretly into my pocket. "Hey," he says. "You didn't come to dinner so I thought I'd check on you."

He smiles down at me but it's strained. Guilt tugs at me and the phone burns against my side, evidence of my secrets. He knows I'm keeping things from him, and it worries him. Once again, it shocks me how much I can read his mood, his expressions. Even though my mind doesn't remember him, a part of my heart does.

"I got distracted." I stare at my list. "Started thinking about my friends back at Nadia's. I wanted to write their names down and remind myself why I'm doing all this. But as I was writing their names down, I realized there are two that I don't remember. Isn't that awful?"

"That's not your fault. You were barely holding yourself together."

"I should've tried harder. I just sat there for so long and believed the lies. Followed along." Frustration builds in my chest. "I don't want to be that person anymore."

"Estrella," he hunches down to be eye level with me, "you were never that person. You've overcome the impossible and did what no one who was sent to those facilities had ever done before. Not only did you escape, but you're recovering your powers. This is a big deal."

"I appreciate you saying that." I stand up and prop the list of names on the low table by my bed. "Thank you again for everything you've done so far. It means a lot to me."

His eyes are warm as chocolate, and he takes my hand. I should pull away, but I'm captivated by the intensity of his gaze. He lifts my palm to his lips and kisses it, eyes never leaving mine. I suck in a breath, shocked as a spark flutters across my skin. It's tantalizing. He lets my hand go, and I can almost believe that didn't happen.

Except it did and now I'm more confused than ever.

Wordlessly, we head out into the hall as if neither of us dares to talk about what that was or what it could mean. When we enter the dining hall, it's nearly empty other than a few stragglers, a musician strumming the zither, and a few servants cleaning up from the meal. Ami is still there, leaning close to Sensei Haruki in deep conversation. As Dion and I settle onto one of the soft cushions, a servant hurries to bring us food and I dig into the grilled meat and fluffy rice with relish.

Dion's phone rings, interrupting the quiet room as it echoes off the rafters.

"Hey, BJ," he answers. "Still alive?"

I frown. That name is familiar. A face pops into my mind. A kind face with dark, wild hair and a scruffy beard. Sharp brown eyes, almost black. A spear of pain stabs at my temple, and I drop my chopsticks to press my fingers against my head.

"Right," Dion says. "You sure? Like one hundred percent? Okay. I need you to head over there ASAP. Monitor only, got it? Keep an eye out for Chandra. They might bring her in for this."

He hangs up and runs a palm over his face. My headache has subsided somewhat but my hands still shake a little as I pick up my chopsticks.

"What is it?" I ask. "Is something wrong?"

"That was BJ, a friend of mine. He says an order was just sent out. They're moving Nadia's facility and all its occupants."

"What do you mean moving?" My pulse throbs against my temples.

"Transferring them to another facility is my guess. They feel Nadia's current location has been compromised so they're taking the girls to another place."

My thoughts flicker to Tristan. Was he spotted? Or are they transferring them because they know I escaped with a Sabian?

"Can we find out where they're relocating them?" I ask.

"Considering it was impossible for me to find your location when they took you away, no, it will be nearly impossible. The Empress will make sure of that."

"I need to get them out of there before they're moved." A cold fear slips over me. "I'm out of time."

Dion nods, his face grim. Ami rises from her cushion and hurries over to us.

"What do you mean you're out of time?" she asks. "What happened?"

"They're moving my friends to another location," I explain.

Ami's eyes widen. "How soon?"

"We don't know." Dion shrugs. "I imagine within the week."

Understanding settles into my chest as I know what I must do next. "Which means I need to go into the World of Between."

"That's a bad idea," Dion says. "You're not ready. You've only just started training with Ami."

"It's a ridiculous idea," Ami says, crossing her arms.

"I also trained with Tristan," I remind him. His face darkens and his lips press together. "I can't rescue them without my powers."

"Then I will help you," Dion says.

"You and I both know we can't do this alone," I point out. "Think about that fight we had in the alley against Quadril and Chandra. We had Tristan then and we still almost didn't make it out of there alive."

"They will have a guard escort," Ami agrees.

"How soon can we go into the World of Between?" I ask Ami.

"We need starlight to enter the Ring," she says. "I will need to make preparations, but if tomorrow night is clear, we will try. Are you sure about this?"

Even though every fiber in my body screams, *No, you're not*, I say, "Absolutely."

16

DO YOU THINK SHE'D BE JEALOUS?

DION

Kakurezato, Japan

Stars on fire, I don't know if I can handle this. The last time Estrella went into her test, I couldn't sleep for days beforehand. There are too many stories of those who've been annihilated by the Ring's power, and then others about Channelers entering, only to never return.

The Ring of Eternity is dangerous.

Deadly.

After a restless night of pacing, the morning brings me new resolve. I need to find a way to stop this. There has to be another way for Estrella to regain her memories enough to recall where the Temple of Fates is located. Entering the Ring is extreme.

Even my father who has been hounding me for results is against the option when I spoke to him about it.

My phone rings.

"Dion," a cool voice greets me. My heart stills. "Remember me?"

Unfortunately. How did she get my number? "Of course, your Highness. You are unforgettable."

"How is our little agreement shaping up?" the Empress asks. "You were supposed to give me updates."

"I apologize." My heart pounds. It takes effort to keep my voice steady. "I thought BJ discussed my latest update."

"BJ is not you. My sources tell me that you were able to extract Estrella from the Sabian's castle. Excellent work."

"Thank you," I croak. *Blistering stars, she knows.* I start pacing. *This is not good.*

"But I expected you to have brought her back to me by now." She sighs dramatically. "I'm not a patient person, Dion."

"Of course, your Highness. We were hunted by the Sabians. We have been hiding out until it's safe."

"Do not keep me waiting, Dion. There will be consequences otherwise. Remember, if you bring her to me, I'll let her keep the memories of you, but if I have to come get her, I'll make sure she never remembers you again."

She hangs up. I swear under my breath, throwing the phone across the room.

I join Estrella and Sensei Haruki at Ami's training pagoda and go through the morning warm-ups. I try to allow the movements to focus my mind as a cool morning breeze wafts through the room, but all I can think about is the Empress's threats. Why did I ever pretend to work with her? But then what choice did I have?

Estrella practices beside me, moving with lethal precision. Her arms and legs execute the kata forms to perfection. Her brow pinches in the center just as I remember, the only sign of her fierce determination. Her long blonde braid trails down her back, snapping back and forth with each move. The thought of losing her again is debilitating.

If the Empress finds her everything I've worked for will be for nothing.

Once we finish and Haruki leaves, I broach my idea to her while she settles on the floor to stretch.

"Are you sure entering the World of Between is the only way to help your friends?" I ask and sit across from her. "In the last few days, you've made huge progress. Think about the person you are now compared to who you were at Nadia's."

"I know you don't want me to go into the Ring of Eternity, but it's something I have to do."

"There must be something else we can do to spark your memories."

"I've had moments where small memories sparked to life, but most of my ability to use my powers is based on intuition and muscle memory. While training in the Tethering Nexus, it felt like there was a wall I couldn't get past. The Dragon Seer said I'd find the answers I seek in the World of Between. It's my best hope right now."

"Do you trust this Dragon Seer? She is a Sabian, you know."

She chuckles as she bends her arm over her head and stretches to the left. "What's up with the Sabians and Nazco hatred and mistrust? While I was there, they made sure to constantly remind me I was the enemy. It was like any other possibility couldn't be imagined."

"Which is why I worry if you can trust this Dragon Seer."

She stares at her palm as if remembering something and then swallows hard before looking back at me. "She spoke the truth. I'm sure of that. But you're right to not trust her. She would've killed me if she could've."

This startles me, and I reach for her hand, squeezing it tight. "You're not alone in this. I'm here now. It's hard for me to see you trusting the Sabians more than me. You used to hate them, too. It's what drove you to become so powerful. It was almost an obsession."

"What do you mean?"

I hesitate, unsure if dredging up a past that haunted her is a good thing.

"You promised you'd help me remember my past," she presses. "What aren't you telling me?"

I let out a long breath. "Do you remember your parents?"

"You know my parents?" Her whole body tightens and she leans closer to me. "Where are they? I want to talk to them."

"Knew," I reiterate, and dread pools into my stomach knowing what I'm about to tell her. "I knew your parents before their death."

"No." Her blue eyes widen, and she rises to her feet as if to run away from my words. "What happened?"

"The Empress sent them on a mission. Paris." I stand, but I don't go to her, instead giving her space. "They were sent to retrieve some ancient documents from the catacombs. Of course the Sabians showed up. It's their territory, but technically, your parents weren't breaking any of the laws of our Immortal Code. Something happened. I'm not privy to the details, but apparently, there was a battle. Their heads were sent back to the Empress by order of King Julian."

She stifles a cry, pressing a palm to her mouth. I go to her and wrap my arms around her body, pulling her close.

"I hate that I'm causing you so much pain all over again," I say.

"How could King Julian do that?" she asks, pulling away to look up at me. Tears spill down her cheeks. She quickly brushes them away with the back of her hand. "That's brutal."

"It was in retaliation for the Empress's own severe killings. She started the practice that has become quite common among the Sabians and Nazco. Your parents were merely pawns in a ruler's game."

"I can't believe he did that. He's Tristan's father."

"I know. Tristan's family doesn't really get along with my family either. We have history."

"Do you think Tristan knows what his father did?"

"I doubt Tristan knows anything about it, but the king? He might know they were your parents. The Empress kept you secret from the other immortal groups for as long as she could. King Julian may not have made the connection or maybe he didn't tell you so you wouldn't lose trust in them. I don't know. But now don't you see why trusting the Sabians with your life isn't smart?"

"And trusting the Nazco are?" she snaps. The fire of

betrayal burns in her eyes. "They're the ones that kicked me out, wiped my memory, took my powers from me, and even tried to kill me."

"You're right. I just—"

"I don't know who to trust right now. That's the hardest part. I think of you as a friend, but is that foolish of me knowing that you didn't tell me everything last time?"

"You can trust me," I say, and yet the secret blood contract I made with Ami claws at my throat. Not to mention how heavy the agreement with the Empress weighs on me.

"I do know my friends at Nadia's feel the same way as I do, that constant torture of not knowing who you are and desperation to become whole again. You know what, I can't have this conversation. I need to enter the Ring or die trying."

She marches out the door just as Ami slips inside.

"Lover's quarrel?" Ami asks sarcastically.

I glower at her. "I was trying to stop her from entering the Ring. You know how dangerous it is. Her odds of survival are what?"

"Not good," Ami says far too casually for my comfort.

"What do you mean? You don't think she can do it?"

"I don't think her powers are strong enough," she confesses. "Or ever will be. I have been training Channelers for four hundred years. I know their limits. She's a strong Channeler, but she will never be a Conduit."

"Blistering stars, then tell her that!"

"There's a chance I'm wrong. She might be *just* powerful enough to enter through the Ring."

"You're threatened by her," I say in realization. "And

because of that, you decided to let the Ring get rid of her for you so you won't have to break our agreement."

Fury rages through me and I lash out. My electricity bursts from my palms. It courses through the air, streaks of white aiming for Ami's heart. But she's ready. Her hand snaps out and she grabs a hold of my arm in a vice grip. She reaches for my visik.

Her intent is clear. She plans to drain me of my powers and take them for herself.

A sudden searing pain strikes my chest. My electrical powers vibrate around us, neither going to Ami nor hurting her. Her body shudders, too, and she screams. I'm not sure if it's in anger or agony, but it's instantly clear to me that our blood contract is being enforced.

I release my powers and rip myself free of her. My breath comes out in heavy gasps as my chest screams like I'm on fire. I rip off my shirt, desperate to be free of the burn. The tattoo of the bird, the symbol of Ami, flames red as if it's been branded on my skin. Ami pulls back the V-neck of her shirt, exposing the top curve of her breast where my lightning bolt is also burning.

I lean against the wall, dizziness from the pain washing over me in waves.

Her eyes meet mine, and a devious smile curls on her lips. If she's four hundred years old, she's powerful. Far more powerful than me, barely in my twenties. She closes the gap between us, and her fingers skim along her mark on me. Her scent is heady and her touch is oddly intoxicating. I want to pull away, but I'm still panting, so weak I can hardly move. Plus, the burning of the tattoo connecting us eases the closer she is.

Her chest presses against my bare torso. My heart pounds in confusion. I need to push her away.

"I guess we're going to have to get along," she whispers into my ear. "The contract seems to want us to keep from hurting the other. Just remember, Estrella might not appreciate you for who you are, but trust me, I find you absolutely riveting."

Her lips brush against mine, a hint of a kiss. I shove her off me and stumble away.

"Never do that again," I growl.

"This conversation is to remain between us. If you decide to tell Estrella about our little exchange, including our contract, I'll be sure to tell her about our kiss. It was delicious. Do you think she'd be jealous?"

"Now you're blackmailing me?"

"That said, she might not be jealous." She taps her chin as if in thought. "She did seem quite taken by the Sabian Prince."

I glower at her and storm out of the pagoda, determined to never get within ten feet of Ami again. She's poisonous. She may think she's got me cornered, but she doesn't know Estrella like I do or the lengths I will go to help her.

17
THE RING OF ETERNITY MIGHT KILL YOU
ESTRELLA

Kakurezato, Japan

The gown is so stunning that for a heartbeat I forget I might die tonight. It's spun of ethereal silk with a full skirt beneath that makes the starlight-blue material billow out like a flower. I spin in a circle, watching it swirl like an endless night. The dark blue bodice is tight and smooth as glass with long, tight sleeves threaded with silver strands, making it look almost irides-cent in the lantern light.

The two servants helping me dress both nod approv-ingly and then carefully braid my long hair into two parts, one braid curling over my head like a crown and another falling down my back.

"The Ring is powerful," one of the ladies explains,

patting me on the shoulder as if to comfort me. "The braid should help keep your hair off your face but still look pretty."

"This dress is as close to making you look like a Nazco as we could," the other says. "As perfect as we can make it."

"Thank you for your help," I say, wondering what exactly makes a dress look Nazcoian. If I survive this test, I'll have to find out.

"Do your best," the other lady says, but when I go to grab the necklace Dion gave me, she pushes it away. "Ami says no jewelry. Too dangerous."

Another reminder of what I'm about to get myself into. Doubt creeps up my chest. What if this is the wrong choice and the Dragon Seer is tricking me into going into the Ring? Could Dion be right and this isn't the best way?

But then another, stronger thought overcomes all others. What if I *can* get through the Ring and find the answers I seek?

I clench my fists and rise to my feet. The two give me a slight nod and then lead me down the corridor and out into the cool evening where Dion is waiting. He's wearing a dark fitted tunic edged in the same silver thread on my dress. His hair is combed back neatly and his face is freshly shaved. He looks magnificent, sharp jawline and dark eyes soaking me in like I'm dessert.

"You're all dressed up," I say, joining him on the path.

"You look like a star," he says.

He takes my forearms and pulls me closer to him. I should resist, but right now my nerves are too wound up to stop him. He leans in close and I breathe in his spicy scent. He kisses my forehead. Now is the time to pull away, but he feels so good and safe. His lips lightly brush the side of my face and then hover over my lips as if waiting for me to lift up on my toes and close the distance.

The sparks of his power skitter across my skin, tantalizing, but I step away. This is not the time to explore whatever this is between us.

"Thank you for being here for me," I tell him.

"I want to go into the arena with you," he whispers, side-glancing at the servant waiting to escort us.

"Ami said it's forbidden," I say.

"Tell her it's a Nazco tradition that you can have an escort or whatever you want to say. The Ring is powerful, but I don't want her using it against you."

"You think this is a trap?"

"I think if you need more power," Dion says, "reach for me. I'll give you mine."

I stare into his dark eyes, suddenly unreadable. "There's something you're not telling me."

"Promise me you'll survive and return."

"I will do everything in my power," I say. "But I don't want to drag you into this. If I die, I'm not bringing you with me."

The servant clears his throat as if to get our attention. It's time. Tonight the moon is absent, perfect for entering the Ring, according to Ami. The lanterns light our way down the path until we reach a large stone building with tiered rooflines along its edges. A long stairway leads us through intricately designed pillars holding up a swooping tiled roof.

We enter a large gateway. Inside, colored stone pavers are placed geometrically across a wide circular area ringed by dragon torches. The walls are lined with ornate screens and red pillars. But what takes my breath away is the Ring, which rises higher all the way to the arched roof.

This afternoon, Ami explained the process and how the Ring works. It's a portal between our world and the World of Between, which is the home of the Fates. Each of the four immortal groups has its own Ring created by our ancestors. It's the place where each of the immortal groups' Numinous Flames burn and where the Conduit goes to bring that power back to their people.

Ami stands before us in front of the Ring. She's decked out in a traditional Japanese emerald gown that glows in the firelight. Six other men and women wearing pale green robes are with her.

"Dion is not allowed in here," she says, frowning.

"It's a Nazco tradition that the Channeler brings an escort." I lie because as much as I'm wary of Dion, I trust her less.

Her lips press closed but she doesn't disagree. "This will be the first time a Nazco has entered through our Ring," she explains and waves for me to join her by a set of stairs at its base. "It shouldn't matter as long as you can survive its power. Each of us will be chained at our ankles because sometimes Channelers get lost inside of the World of Between."

I stand beside her and a servant hurries to shackle my ankle to a long chain. The clicking sound sends a chill scraping through me and my heart starts to pound, a drum beating the death march. My eyes find Dion's, who stands off to the side, arms crossed, stone-faced. He looks fierce and ready to take down anyone who comes in his way.

"You can still change your mind," he tells me. "We can find another way."

My eyes drift from his up to the massive stone Ring above. A spear of pain shoots through my head and I stumble from the unexpected shock.

A memory. Me standing in a similar place, a cold cuff snaked around my ankle, fear pumping through my blood.

"Are you ready?" Ami asks, clearly unfazed by my pain.

I bite my lip and nod. I'm tired of these headaches and the not knowing. This is my chance to change everything, and I'm not going to let fear take the opportunity away from me.

Ami and I climb the steps, but dread makes my feet feel like they're filled with lead. When I reach the platform at the center of the Ring, I glance down below at Dion once again. He's looking up at me, brow pinched with worry, body tense as if preparing to use his powers.

The other green-cloaked Eien surround the Ring to prepare for the ceremony. With a jolt, the roof rumbles and then it splits in half, opening up and exposing the star-riddled sky above. Spring air blows against my cheeks, smelling of lilies and cherry blossoms. One of the Eien below begins to play a three-stringed instrument that Ami told me earlier was called a biwa. It's supposed to call forth the Ring's power. As Ami and I stand before the Ring's center, the biwa's sharp, rhythmic strumming echoes across the hall, melodic and yet haunting.

The glittering Ring begins to glow, shimmering like stardust. It's magnificent and ageless. Then, the Ring begins to turn inch by inch. Soon, it becomes faster, spinning from whatever magic we're creating here. It glows brighter and stronger. The skirts of my dress snap at my feet. My braid whips behind me. My heart tumbles around in my chest as if begging to escape. I clench my fists and take deep breaths, forcing my legs to not run.

You can do this, I tell myself.

"I'll go first," Ami yells to me over the whirlwind. "That way you can see what I do. I'll be there to greet you on the other side."

I nod, too terrified to utter a single word. The whirlwind intensifies, if that's even possible. Starlight blazes around Ami and myself. The pain in my head is back, screaming at me to stop what I'm doing. It takes every muscle in my body to keep myself from collapsing.

The center streaks with a kaleidoscope of colors. And then I see it.

The World of Between shimmering just behind a thin veil inside the Ring.

Ami steps confidently to the center and touches the surface. It bends slightly, resisting, but she doesn't waver. Rainbow light encases her body. In a blink, she's sucked into the Ring, vanishing from the spot she stood. I'm startled to find her on the other side. It's hard to see her through the wavering light, but she's definitely there.

Boosted by the ease of Ami's transition, I shove my legs forward to where she just stood. The Ring latches onto my chest and yanks me closer. Its power surges around me, a maelstrom. Suddenly, I'm second-guessing my decision. Pain lances at my chest. My muscles feel like I ran a marathon. My head burns.

This is it. My chance. With a trembling hand, I reach out and touch the surface.

A jolt snaps my whole body rigid. I'm lifted off the ground as if the Ring is holding me tight, trying to decide if I'm strong enough, powerful enough. A wave of energy floods my body. All I see is starlight. A white-blazing fire races through my veins, sucking up my power with a relentless need.

It's a hungry beast raging through me.

Consuming my body, burning my mind, eating at my soul.

A curdling scream erupts from my core. Then a bolt of electrical power bursts into my body. I know that power. It's Dion's.

I look over my shoulder to spot him touching my ankle. I was right. He's given me his power. Except, if it's not enough, the Ring will not just consume me, but also him. Desperately, I try to channel his power through me and make it stronger.

Because if I don't, not just my life is on the line. His is, too.

"Let go!" I scream at him.

"Not until you're through," he yells back.

I grit my teeth. Determination to survive pushes me to channel his power faster, deeper, stronger. I rage against the Ring, my scream melding with the storm. I'm lifted into the air. Bolts of electricity spark over my skin. Lightning strikes out of me. I'm nearly tapped out.

"No!" I scream, refusing for this to be the end.

I won't let it be.

I dive headfirst through the rainbow surface just as the Ring strikes my heart.

18

BETWEEN WORLDS

ESTRELLA

Kakurezato, Japan

My chest burns. My muscles are on fire. My mind aches.

But there's soft grass beneath my fingers. I blink against the once-starry blaze of the Ring to take in the golden light pooling around me, glittering with the breath of magic. Slowly, I ease to my knees and take in the open meadow, dotted with periwinkle flowers, surrounded by swaying pines. Jagged mountains jut up in the distance topped with snow the color of diamonds.

The World of Between.

"You sure know how to make an entrance," Ami says, her teasing voice cutting through my awe.

"It's beautiful," I say, taking her hand and climbing to

my feet like a newborn deer. The chain clasped to my ankle bites at my skin as if it knows it doesn't belong in this world. The Ring rises beside us, our chains disappearing into its center that wavers like a murky pool. Vaguely, I see the others on the other side.

"It is rather nice." Ami smiles. It's full and soft, and it lights up her eyes. A true smile. "A place only a few privileged dare or can enter. You seem to have tricked your way in, but you're here nevertheless."

"There's something familiar about it," I say, scanning the tree line. A memory niggles at the corner of my mind but it's just out of reach. I shrug off the usual frustration at my mind's incompetence and suck in a breath of the air. It fills my lungs, soothing every ounce of pain I felt upon entering. "Does this place have healing qualities? I already feel better."

"I suppose so. I hadn't thought of it like that."

"So do the other three Conduits enter from other Rings?" I ask, needing to understand this place.

"Each of the four Conduits enters from their Ring and exits through this very same meadow. Our pedestals that hold the four flames are located in each of the four directions: north, south, east, and west. Now that you're here, do you have any idea of what the Dragon Seer wished for you to see?"

"No." I bite my lip, frowning. "She said I'd find my answers here. Do you have any idea what she might have been speaking of?"

Ami's startling blue eyes study me warily as if searching for a lie. "Maybe. Come with me."

We set off across the meadow and enter a path cutting through the forest. My chain rattles, resisting each step I take. I breathe in the heady scent of pine and scrape my fingers across the bark of the trees just to feel their realness because, with the golden light and the perfect temperature, this place feels more dreamlike than reality.

"How far can we go with these chains?" I ask, skeptically.

"Far enough for us to do what we must. There are three of us, you know."

I frown. "Three?"

"Conduits. Myself, you, and Zola."

"Zola. The Caladrian Conduit."

"Yes. Tristan's sister, Ivana, was the fourth until she was killed by the Nazco. It wasn't long after they excommunicated you, which seems too coincidental if you ask me. We never got along well, but we tolerated each other."

"You knew Ivana?"

"But of course. We Conduits have our own little secret society if you will. Unfortunately, you didn't last long enough to join."

"A secret society? What do you mean?"

"Patience."

I glare at her back as we hike, but bite my tongue. I need her and getting angry won't help me find answers or my powers. The path spits us into an open space that falls off into a cliff. Beyond, mountains rise up as if this land goes on for eternity. How big is this World of Between? Stone pavers are set on the ground to create a circular platform with an ornately carved pedestal rising in its center. The most impressive part is the ice-blue flame that flares from the pedestal's center.

"The Numinous of the Nazco," I whisper and move as close as I dare to touch the flicking fire.

"Indeed. The source of the Nazco power."

"It's beautiful."

"But smaller than I remember it last time," Ami says, her head tilting as she studies it with a frown.

A trickle of worry nips at me. Usually Ami is so confident and composed, so seeing her look worried concerns me.

"What do you mean?"

"For thousands of years the Numinous Flames have burned bright, a massive torch erupting from their pedestals. But in the last decade, they have slowly been depleting. We have no idea why. Dion told me that you might know the location of the Temple of Fates. While you are hoping it will heal your mind, I'm hoping it has answers to what is happening here with the flames."

"So that's the real reason you agreed to train me." Finally, I know her true intentions. It's not what I was expecting. My mind thinks back to that dream—or maybe it was a vision—when I spoke to Future's Fate. Her words still ring in my ears.

The power of the immortals is failing. Our gifts of water, earth, fire, and air are fading because of corruption and greed. There is great power in you, but it is lost. And because of that, so are you.

But the words, *You are not worthy*, still haunt me.

I stare back at the flame. Could this be what the Fate had been talking about?

"What is it?" Ami asks, stepping closer to me. "Do you remember something?"

I jerk at her voice. I certainly don't trust her enough to tell her what Future's Fate said. Instead, I say, "I was just wondering if it's safe for me to touch it."

"Maybe. I wouldn't take the whole flame. It might be too much for you."

I swipe my finger through it, pulling out a tiny blue ball. A spike of power surges through my body, sending a shiver up and down my spine. It awakens something inside me. The world brightens and my skin tingles like I dove into a cool lake.

"Be careful," Ami warns.

The flame starts to burn my skin, cold and biting. Fear spikes at my chest. It's going to consume me if I don't let it go. Desperately, I roll it back onto the pedestal with the rest of the fire. I step back, grasping my palm, which still burns. Tears of pain prick at my eyes.

"Don't worry," she says, "it will only sting for a short period of time. You aren't strong enough to wield the Numinous in its purest form."

The skin on my palm mends itself quicker than it ever did before, solidifying my theory that there's something special about this place.

"I feel sharper, stronger," I say, "but I still don't remember my past. The blockage in my mind is still there. I wish I knew what Zmeya wanted me to find here."

"Zmeya?"

"The Dragon Seer."

"I didn't realize you were on a first name basis with the dreaded dragon."

Annoyed with my body, I march to the edge of the cliff. My chain jerks tight.

"Our chains are only long enough to take us to our pedestals," Ami explains, coming to my side.

Interesting. Something about that irks me.

"So I take it you've never been down there?" I point below where a narrow chasm runs. It looks as if the Fates had sliced out a section of the land. There's actually an entrance to it. Two crumbling statues and half an arch.

"That is the Whispering Chasm," she says. "It's a place where past Conduits left words of wisdom or their last thoughts. If we are able to, we bring the bodies of the Conduits who have been killed there as a final resting place."

"So it's a burial ground."

"I suppose you could call it that," Ami says. Her eyes darken and her shoulders dip as if the thought of whatever is down there weighs on her. "I like to think of it as a place where Conduits lay to rest but never truly leave us."

"You buried someone there, didn't you?"

Her eyes dart to mine. "My mentor."

"But if this is as far as our chains take us, how did you get...oh...you took the chain off."

She smiles wickedly. "You're catching on." She bends down and unlatches her chain and drags it over to a hook on the pedestal, clipping it to it. "This is another of our Conduit secrets."

"Does this mean I'm a part of your secret society now?" I follow her lead in clipping my chain to the pedestal. I have to admit that I feel naked and vulnerable without it.

"We will have to ask Zola what she thinks."

"The other Conduit? Are you saying she's here?"

"I let her know we would be here and to meet us."

My heart skips in excitement at the thought of meeting another Conduit. Ami starts off down a different path that runs along the edge of the cliff. I hurry after her, making sure to keep a hand on the rock ledge as we curve around the side of the mountain. The rock face opens up to another section of the forest. These trees though are a sparkling silver. The branches drape with moss glittering as if dusted with sugar. A breeze sifts through the trees, bending the boughs so they create a lilting sound, almost like a pan flute.

"It sounds like you and Zola are friends," I say. "That you trust her."

"I trust no one as you would be wise to practice, too. But she's been the Caladrian's Conduit for a hundred years. We've known each other for a while."

A series of stones leads us across a gurgling stream that sparkles an aquamarine color like it gushed straight out of a glacier. I try to process the idea of someone being a hundred years old.

"How old are you?" I dare ask. "You keep mentioning hundreds of years like it's some normal thing."

"Four hundred and twenty."

I gulp down my shock. Wow. This girl has been around a long time. And she's had time to gain power.

Ami stops and waves ahead to what looks like the ruins of an old temple. Vines curl up the sides of ancient stone and trees arch over crumbled pillars. "We're here. What happens in this land must remain among only the three of us. Do you understand?"

"Absolutely." I'm unable to stop the grin on my face. My

heart pounds with excitement because, for the first time, I feel like I belong to something and a place.

Ami tilts her head, biting her bottom lip as if considering. "We will see what Zola thinks about you and if you're worth our precious time and energy."

19
STAGE MEETUP AND SPOTLIGHT MISCHIEF
TRISTAN

Florida

I pace the backstage area of the school auditorium, my patience flagging with each minute ticking down. Students rush around, setting up props and carrying costumes as they prepare for what Mara had called a dress rehearsal. They are in some sort of play and today is a practice performance. This was Mara's suggestion when I told her I needed to talk in private. Estrella texted that they were being moved to a new facility and wanted to warn them.

Now that I'm here, meeting backstage with a bunch of other teens doesn't exactly seem private to me. I eye the students, wondering if any of them are Nazco.

"Excuse me," a lady with purple glasses hanging off the

end of her nose says. "Are you supposed to be here? This practice area is for cast only."

"Ah, then you must not have heard," I say, trying to use my most persuasive voice, "I recently joined up. Heard you needed extra hands."

"Really? And your name is..." The lady pulls out her clipboard, inspecting it.

"Doubt you'll find it on that little sheet of yours. I'm new."

This woman is far too vigilant for my comfort. Annoyance irks me. Mara and Jamie were supposed to show up five minutes ago. I was surprised they agreed to meet me today after school. Maybe it was too good to be true.

A guy passes by us carrying a long ladder and stumbles. The perfect distraction.

"Hey," I say, rushing to him and escaping the drama teacher. "You all right? Here. Let me give you a hand."

I take the end of the ladder and nod for him to continue. Thankfully another student runs up to the teacher with some sort of emergency so I'm quickly forgotten. Where in the blazes are Mara and Jamie? Maybe they couldn't get away from their evil stepmother-wanna-be, Nadia. Could they already be in evacuation mode?

The real reason I'm annoyed though has nothing to do with Mara and Jamie not showing up. It's the fact that I feel so helpless here while Estrella is about to face one of her biggest challenges yet. Apparently, she's entering the Ring right now. I still remember Ivana's first entry into the Ring and how we all treated the hours beforehand as if they might be her last.

Give me a sword and a Wraith any day over sitting

around waiting and worrying. I wish I were at her side rather than carrying a ladder across the stage and waiting for two girls to show up. I finish helping the guy set up the ladder and then duck into the shadows of the stage area to check my phone. My eyes land once on that last text Estrella sent me. My stomach turns over all over again.

> Estrella: I'm going to try to go into the World of Between tonight. Wish me luck.

> Me: Why tonight?

> Estrella: I'm tired of waiting. Not knowing if I'll ever be good enough.

> Me: Please wait. We can try to find another way.

> Estrella: The Dragon Seer promised me that I'd find what I was seeking there. I have to go.

I tried calling but she never answered. I clench the phone as I stare at the time. It's past midnight in Japan, which means she's attempting to enter the Ring right now or already has. I rub a palm over my face realizing I never wished her the luck she'd asked for. The silence and not knowing is killing me.

I'm slightly mollified when Mara and Jamie finally enter the backstage area, both wearing all black. They check in with the teacher and then begin picking up props, but Mara's eyes shift around as if searching for me. I step out of the shadows, nodding for them to join me.

But the moment we step into the storage room and I

close the door, Jamie pulls out a knife and holds it to my throat.

"Quite the weapon you've got there," I say, holding up my hands.

"What's the big thing you wanted to tell us?" Mara asks. "Don't tell me you brought us here to murder us."

"Hardly," I scoff. "I'm trying to help you. We have gotten word that your facility, I mean home, is being relocated."

Jamie lowers her knife but keeps it inches from me. "Relocated?" she asks.

"Nadia would never move," Mara says. "She loves that old lighthouse."

"There's more to Nadia and her lighthouse than you know."

"Cryptic." Mara crosses her arms, face unimpressed. "Sorry, but if you're trying to get us to go with you, you're going to be disappointed. Come on, Jamie. Let's get back to practice."

"You're not normal humans," I blurt out.

They freeze and slowly turn back to me.

"Does the pretty boy have something worthy to say?" Jamie asks.

"What are you talking about?" Mara asks.

I'd been hesitant to tell Estrella the truth when we first met thinking it could hurt her, but now that I know that had been false information, I might as well get straight to the point. "You're immortals whose memories have been wiped."

"What?!" Mara exclaims.

"He lies," Jamie says.

"You were sent to Nadia's to help you acclimate to this

new life," I continue. "This is the truth that Estrella learned and nearly died because of it. She escaped and now she wants to help you—all of you at Nadia's—to also get free."

The two girls glance at each other as if trying to make sense of what I've just said.

"Do you have proof?" Mara asks.

"There should be a birthmark on your left shoulder blade." I start unbuttoning my shirt.

"What are you doing?" Mara's eyes narrow.

"I'm showing you my mark," I explain.

"Nice muscles." Jamie nods appreciatively as I pull back my shirt. "Very nice."

"Shut up," Mara grumbles.

I twist my body to show them my endless knot birthmark. "Does this look familiar?" Neither girl answers, which tells me they've seen this mark. "I don't know when Nadia is planning on moving you, but Estrella and I want to get you out of that place before they do."

"What if we don't want to leave?" Mara asks. "Others have tried and were killed."

"You don't belong there," I say, rebuttoning my shirt. "Both of you were once powerful immortals. You deserve to get those powers back and be free to choose what you do with your own life. Don't you want that, too?"

"Yes," Jamie says. There's a firmness to her voice and her jaw is set. "I want out."

"You're just impressed by those muscles." Mara rolls her eyes. "Listen, buddy. I don't know who you are, and I still don't trust you or your weird theories about who we are. If you say you're working with Estrella then why haven't we heard from her? Where is she?"

I run a hand through my hair in frustration. I've never been good at negotiations or persuading people. This conversation only proves that. Besides, a spark of warning flares inside of me. Why is she asking where Estrella is? Can these girls really be trusted? After all, that other friend from the home, Tiffany, betrayed Estrella and Lexi.

"I can't tell you where she is," I say, "but I know you're running out of time."

"We're not going anywhere with you, that's for sure," Mara says. I don't miss the disgust in her voice. "But we'll consider it after we talk to Estrella. Until then, don't speak to us again."

With that, the two leave. I sag onto one of the boxes in defeat. "That didn't go so well," I mumble.

I pull out my phone and stare at the text between Estrella and myself. Fear clutches my chest at the thought that she might not survive the Ring. What would that mean for me?

I wake thinking of her. I breathe each breath knowing it gives me a chance to be with her again. She is everything I've ever wanted or needed.

Fates, I'm stuck in this stuffy, hot closet because I want her friends to be free.

And if she doesn't survive, I don't know how I will either.

20

THE SECRET SOCIETY OF CONDUITS

ESTRELLA

The World of Between

"Before we go inside," Ami says, "don't tell Zola about the Temple of Fates. Let's keep that just between the two of us."

"Agreed," I say. "The fewer people who know about it the better."

My heart thuds against my chest, but this time it's not from fear, it's anticipation, hope. I've had such a hard time trusting Ami, but this place has brought us closer together. Sure, we may not be equals, but we have a common power.

Stone walls rise up on either side as I trail after Ami through a narrow corridor into a rotunda. The roof has crumbled, leaving behind a bright periwinkle sky. Vines crawl up the ancient stones, which are covered in hieroglyphics. A large bowl filled with water rests on a pedestal in the center of the rotunda. On the other side of it stands a woman who must be Zola.

She's wearing a burnt orange tunic that hangs all the way to her ankles. Her ebony skin glistens under the ethereal light of this land. Long braids are twisted into a tall bun on top of her head, studded with topaz gems. She has the look of a queen who has high expectations that must be fulfilled and never takes no for an answer. As we walk inside, her thin eyebrows lift as if she's surprised to see me.

"The lost Conduit made it," Zola says. Her voice is rich and deep with a strong lilting accent. "This is unexpected."

"She got help from Cabral," Ami says, going to Zola and kissing her on both cheeks.

"Cabral?" Zola says. "Fascinating. I've known they've wanted the Nazco throne for decades. Perhaps they are using her to finally get what they want."

I find myself bristling at the two of them speaking about me as if I'm not standing right beside them.

"Zola, yes?" I ask and step up to them. "I'm Estrella Cortez. Once a Nazco Conduit but now I have no allegiance since they excommunicated me. Dion Cabral has been helping me as well as the Sabians, but I assure you, no one is using me."

"I think I might like you," Zola says, her lips quirking. "What is it that brings you here to our Inner Sanctum?"

I explain what happened to me along with the Dragon Seer's words. "She said to find Ami and have her take me to the World of Between. Supposedly, I'll find what I seek here."

"So have you found what you seek?" Zola asks.

"No. Perhaps there's something in this place that can retrieve memories."

"Not to my knowledge," Zola says. "I'm more surprised by the fact that any Sabian would wish to help you, a Nazco."

"You're not the first to tell me that," I say.

I press my lips together, remembering the Fate's prophecy: *Caught between fire and lightning's might, your rule may be fierce, but it will also bring light.*

Could that have something to do with this place? As much as I want to tell them Zmeya's words, Tristan warned me to not share her words with anyone. Prophecies and destinies are apparently kept in secret. Even I don't know what destiny she gave to Tristan.

"Do you think the Scrying Basin would help?" Zola nods to the large bowl resting in the center of the room. The aqua water glistens like it's been mixed with diamond dust.

"Unlikely as it seems to have a mind of its own," Ami says. "But it can't hurt. Estrella, go and touch the water. We will see if it will show us anything."

I stand at the side of the stone basin, its edge carved with intricate designs. Perhaps I should be wary but after surviving the Ring, I feel like I can survive anything. I dip my finger into the water and peek into its depths, but nothing happens.

"All I see is water," I say.

"Perhaps its power is waning like so much of this land," Zola says, lines of worry puckering along her forehead.

"Speaking of which," Ami says. "We visited the Nazco Numinous Flame. It's smaller than the last time I was here."

"They all are," Zola says softly. "It is concerning."

"I wish we knew why," Ami says, pacing, and then to me, "If the flames burn out, so do our powers as immortals. We will all become mortals as we once were before the Fates blessed the Four Mothers."

"I think I know why," I dare say. If the world of the immortals is being threatened, we need to work together, not against each other. It's time to start telling the truth.

"*You* know?" Ami snorts and rolls her eyes, telling Zola, "The girl who doesn't even know herself?"

"Let her speak." Zola waves a hand as if to quiet Ami. "Tell us. What do you know?"

"I had this experience," I begin, unsure if I should tell them. But if anyone in this world could know what it meant, it would be these two. "Maybe it was a dream or a vision. I'm not sure. But I think I spoke to Future's Fate."

"Sounds like a dream." Ami crosses her arms. "No one speaks to the Fates."

But Zola's sharp blue gaze narrows on me. "What did she say?"

"She said the power of the immortals is failing. And that their gifts of water, earth, fire, and air are fading because of our corruption and greed."

Ami's eyes sharpen and Zola whistles as if she might actually believe me.

"Did the Fate say anything else?" Ami demands, leaning closer as if she wants to rip the information out of me.

"She said she was Future's Fate, and that she had spoken." I bite my lip, recalling the moment. Even now, it's still sharp in my mind. "I asked her what could be done, and I'd do it. She said to destroy the one who seeks to destroy the Fates."

Silence falls heavy on the three of us as Zola and Ami stare at me in shock.

"Why didn't you tell me this before?" Ami asks.

"We've been a little busy training me," I say. "Also, I wasn't sure if I could trust you. But now that you've brought me here, I realized I'd been wrong."

"Do you think she speaks the truth?" Ami asks Zola.

"If not, it is a peculiar lie," Zola says. "But who would wish to destroy the Fates? It is a foolish end game."

"And how?" Ami says. "I do not know of any immortal other than the Four Mothers who have seen or spoken to one. Perhaps it was just a dream or a hallucination. The Empress ruined her mind. She doesn't know what is what."

As the two debate over my experience, movement in the pool catches my attention. Two violet eyes stare up from its center, unblinking. As if listening.

Wariness trickles down my arms. *I know those eyes.*

"The Skyring Basin," I interrupt them in a whisper. "Future's Fate is watching us."

They stop arguing and turn to look into the water, but the eyes have vanished.

"Nothing is there." Ami studies me skeptically.

"Maybe I imagined it." I rub my forehead. "Maybe you're right. My mind isn't right."

Which is why I need to find the Temple of the Fates and get healed.

"We have been in the World of Between too long," Ami says. "It may be taking a toll on you. We should go."

"I will research possible enemies of the Fates," Zola says.

"Don't bother because I already know who that is," I

announce. "The Empress of the Nazco. She's the one we need to stop."

Ami tilts her head, considering this. "You may be right. She has been trying to usurp power from the Sabians over the last century, and she's been making ground. Once she has control over them, she will likely look our way."

"I have heard she has Wraith creatures that have risen her to power," Zola notes.

I shudder. "I've come across them. They're terrifying."

"We have kept out of conflict with the Nazco for centuries," Zola says. "I do not wish to start an unnecessary war."

"But why would the Empress destroy the Fates?" Ami muses. "They are her source of power."

"A question that must be considered," Zola notes. "I will focus my attention on learning what the Empress might be doing to anger the Fates."

"Our time here is long overdue for our own safety," Ami says, eyeing the walls as if they're going to close in on us. "We must leave."

She wishes Zola goodbye and hurries out through one of the narrow corridors. I cast one last look at the pool. Had I imagined the Fate's eyes or was she there all along, listening? I turn to leave, but Zola reaches out and pulls me back.

"I know Ami is helping you regain your powers," she says, "but be careful. She is powerful and dangerous. She is not your friend. And if it's true that the Fate has spoken to you rather than her, she will be very jealous."

Dread curls through me and I wonder if telling them about my experience with the Fate had been wise.

"Thank you for the warning," I say, and hurry after Ami

before I find myself getting lost here in the World of Between.

Zola is right. I allowed myself to be lulled into thinking I wasn't alone in this world. That I had friends who were fighting alongside me.

But I was wrong.

21

THE WHISPERING CHASM

ESTRELLA

The World of Between

I hurry down the path of the Conduits' secret meeting place, but nothing here looks familiar. I must have exited the ruins from a different way because Ami is nowhere in sight. Did she leave me purposely or did she not realize I wasn't behind her? I'm realizing those few moments with Zola were costly. My heart kicks up a notch with worry.

"Stay on the path," I tell myself. "It will take me back to my chain."

The gurgle of a stream catches my attention. Ami and I crossed a stream to get to the ruins. But when I hurry to it, I stop short. A man is sitting on a rock fishing. He's humming softly, a hauntingly familiar tune. His ragged clothes hang on him, and though this place is beautiful, I imagine being here alone would take a toll on a person.

Do I talk to him? Turn around? Sneak by? I clench my fists in indecision. Ami is long gone, which tells me she purposely left me. Zola was right.

"No need to be scared," the man says, shifting his body to face me. He smiles widely, but there's something strange about his eyes. They're almost clear like they've been washed out of nearly all their color, a sharp contrast to his bronze skin that glows in this world's golden light. "Are you hungry? I'm looking to catch myself some dinner."

Fear claws at my throat despite his words. Who is this guy and why is he here? Unless he's one of the Conduits who have been roaming these lands, forgetting who they are.

"No, thanks." I try to smile back. "I'm just passing through."

"Are you lost?" he asks. "I only ask because you're not wearing your chain."

"I'm headed back to get it now." I gingerly begin crossing the stream, balancing on the large rocks. "I'm assuming the path ahead will take me there."

He nods. "But you don't have to go back to your world. You can stay here as I did."

I should keep moving, not linger in this land, but curiosity overrules my fear. "Why did you stay?"

"Less stressful. The thought of returning...the pressure... the demands. Being a Conduit was something I never wanted."

"I was cast out after my trial. I understand what you mean about not meeting expectations. It's nice to meet you..."

I let my words fall off, hoping he will tell me who he is.

"Ralco. I once considered myself a Nazco, but now I am just Ralco." He chuckles lightly as if he just made a joke. "Rhymes, doesn't it?"

Yeah, he's a little unhinged. Keep moving, I warn myself. Except, I find myself lingering.

"I was once a Nazco, too." I bite my lip, realizing I said *was.* What am I now?

His line jerks and he rises, yanking back on his wooden pole and lifting it into the air. A silvery fish flaps about at the end of his line. "Victory!"

But the fish fights itself free, splashing onto a rock near my feet. Ralco cries out in distress. Quickly, I snatch it up, moments before it flops back into the stream. It's slippery and it fights against my hold. Carefully, I backtrack the way I came and hand it to Ralco.

"Much appreciated," he says and slips it into a pouch made of leaves. "You have a kind heart. Why are you here, Estrella? What is it you seek?"

My mouth dries up and my heart quickens. Did I tell him my name? "I'm trying to find a way to get my memories back. The Empress took them and by doing so, took away most of my powers."

"I cannot help you, but maybe another Conduit holds the answer you seek." His voice has turned serious and his eyes gleam even more translucent. It's definitely creepy. I take a step backward. "There are always two paths before you—the easy one or the hard one. The choice is yours, but it depends on how far you are willing to go."

"Thank you, Ralco. Perhaps we will chat again."

"Stay for dinner," he says, his voice suddenly light and

carefree again. "You will have to catch your own meal though because this one is all mine."

"Thanks for the offer, but I need to go."

I wave goodbye and scamper across the stream once again, needing to put space between the two of us. Ami had warned me that once you enter this land, over time, it can make you forget the outside world, but maybe that's not it. Maybe this place makes you realize all the reasons not to go back.

Relief washes over me as I step back onto the edge of the cliff where the pedestal stands holding the Numinous Flame, flicking with jagged spikes of blue. My chain is still here, clipped to the base. But Ami's chain is gone.

Cold numbness seeps through me. "She left me," I whisper.

I'm about to unclasp the chain, but my hands freeze as I remember Ralco's words.

Another Conduit holds the answer you seek.

I step away from the pedestal and let my gaze drift beyond the cliff's side, down into the valley below. Whispering Chasm, Ami had called it. Where Conduits leave messages. Could that be where my answer is? Two paths, Ralco had said. I could use my chain to lead me back to the Ring. Or...

Heart clattering against my ribcage, I scour the edge of the cliff, searching for a way down into the valley. And then I find it, hidden with overgrowth. A long, steep staircase of stone, clinging to the side of the cliff like a wild vine.

"The choice is yours, but it depends on how far you're willing to go."

"All the way," I whisper as if to answer Ralco's question.

I don't stop to consider the consequences because the possibility of success is too tempting. The wind whips at my hair and tugs at my dress as I descend. These steps have no railing and my long dress is one step away from tangling around my legs, sending me plummeting to the ground. I pause to rip off the bottom half of the material, freeing my legs to move easily.

"Forget the fancy dress," I grumble. "If I ever come back into this land, I'm wearing pants."

As I descend, the rock wall scraping against my palms becomes my security. In one section, the stairs have been eroded so heavily there's only a wide enough space for my foot to fit. I press my back against the rock face and shimmy myself sideways across the thin portion of the remaining step. My heart gallops in my chest, but I press on.

When my feet finally reach the ground, I sink to my knees. My body shakes from the journey, and I allow myself a moment to recover. Five deep calming breaths is all I give myself because time is not on my side. I climb back to my feet. The chasm stretches before me.

There are two towering weather-worn stone statues of the Fates, wearing chitons and wreaths of flowers ringing their long, flowing hair. One holds a book, the other a sword. They both bear the mark of time and weather. Hunks of stone have crumbled from the edges of their robes and limbs. Patches of lichen creep up their sides. Even still, these two statues that must be fifty feet tall loom from above look fierce and intimidating, guardians from another time.

Clenching my fists, I hurry forward, hoping these statues don't possess some sort of power to keep me from entering. Thankfully, I pass by them with no trouble.

The moment I enter the chasm, I'm met with graves scattered between the towering smooth rock walls on either side. There are no headstones. Instead, objects stand at the head of each mound of earth. Swords, spears, long poles with pendants wrapped around them...they're all stuck in the earth. My feet slow as I realize these aren't just any graves—they're the final resting place of Conduits before me.

These are my sisters and brothers, connected by a unified ability. My heart aches for them even though we have never met. As I study each mound, I wonder which one Ami dug and who was her mentor.

My thoughts are interrupted as I hear a voice to my right. I spin, searching for the source. No one is there. Just the wind sifting and whooshing across the dirt. Goosebumps rise on my skin as the feeling that someone is watching me pricks at the back of my neck. A chill scuttles down my spine.

The chasm stretches ahead, twisting to the right so I can't see beyond. Could someone be hiding up ahead?

"The future is unknown," a voice whispers, "but today is in your power."

I whirl around. No one is here. My pulse thumps, a bell clanging with warning.

Swallowing my fear, I continue deeper into the chasm, and as I do, the whispers intensify.

"Trust no one," a voice says. "You are alone in this world."

"The pursuit of power leads to destruction."

I'm passing by the last grave when I spy the inscriptions on the rock walls. I step up to the one on my right. The words shimmer as a voice speaks to me. Interestingly, the words are written in a language I don't recognize, but the spoken words must somehow translate so I can understand them.

"Live a simple life and gain a great reward," the voice says and then it's carried away by the wind.

I caress the letters. The voice whispers the message again. And again and again.

"Whispering Chasm," I say, chuckling at my discovery. "That's how this place got its name."

My steps quicken as I stride deeper into the chasm's wandering path, running my palm along the wall as I listen. These are all messages left by former Conduits. Some are angry and full of regret.

"Until death's bitter taste, I will stand against Ransley," one says.

"I will curse Lily until the end of time," another one spits out.

But then there are poetic ones and lines of great wisdom that I wish I could write down in my journal and sketch out the images they evoke.

I bite back a stifled cry when I stumble past a skeleton. Did someone actually die in this chasm? Or were they killed? The need for answers pushes me forward. I'm not sure how long I walk, but soon the whispers intensify, especially now that the walls are narrowing in tighter. They press on my mind in a desperate need to squeeze away all other thoughts I have. I should turn around, but what if the answer I seek is here?

I trip on a stick only to discover it's a bone. I scream with a jump and dart away, leaning against the stone wall for support as I take deep breaths.

My plan to find a message that may or may not exist suddenly seems stupid. There are hundreds of inscriptions. I don't have time to read them all. My head starts to pound. It's getting harder to think properly. I close my eyes and press my fingers to my temples.

What I need to do is focus on specific words. Like cure or Fates or temple.

I take a deep breath and continue my trek. The graves grow sparser, and the chasm narrows even further, closing in with each step. If I held out my arms, I'd almost be able to touch either side. It makes it easier to see the messages, but also harder because they're all whispering so closely to each other now.

An idea strikes me. Could I ask the chasm for an answer?

"Hello!" I call out. "I need help getting my powers back."

The whispering continues, oblivious to my voice.

"Well, now I just feel silly," I say, huffing.

I mean this place is amazing, but I've been away for a while. Can I even get back through the Ring? How long does it stay open?

My heart pounds as the realization that I have made a very, very poor choice slithers into my thoughts. Dion must be out of his mind with worry. If I miss the window, I could get stuck in this place.

"Do any of you know where the Temple of Fates is?" I ask again. I'm a fool, sending a last desperate plea before I turn around, but I don't care.

The whispers continue on like a wave crashing against the shore. Dizziness washes over me, so I turn to head back when a certain whisper drifts over me like it's tapping me on the shoulder. It's a little deeper than the others.

"The Temple of Fates," it says.

My heart stops. Was that a trick of my mind or is there really a message about the temple? I turn back around and dart ahead through the narrow rock walls, hope spurring me forward. It's so narrow now that I can barely run through it without turning sideways.

"Tell me about the temple!" I call out.

"The Temple of Fates," it whispers again.

There's a strong possibility that I've lost my mind. That I'm like those other Conduits who enter the World of Between and wander for eternity. It all makes sense now why. This place would drive anyone mad.

Suddenly, the tunnel opens into a large circular area the size of a small house surrounded by towering rock walls that rise steeply on all sides. Above, the sky shines a baby blue, teasing of escape. Bones and skeletons are scattered about. Dread hugs my chest. Did they come here seeking answers like I did and fail? The air feels cooler here and thick with the earthy scent of stone. Every whisper echoes deeper and richer, magnified by the curved rock.

I sidestep around a set of bones toward the words etched in stone straight ahead.

"I am Ulsa," the voice whispers. "My life is fading, and so I have created a haven where we Conduits may etch our final words. Now our spirits will last for all of time, immortalized in these stones."

"You were the first," I say in understanding. "You created this place."

I move to the next message and my heart skitters with excitement.

"Within the Acacus Peaks lies the Temple of Fates, forgotten by time and mankind. Its Sanctum guards the source of immortality and the power it holds. Beware for only the bold and foretold may seek the power."

"Acacus Peaks," I say. The whispering repeats the same message again. I kiss my fingers and press it against the words. It might be my mottled brain, but I think they sparkle beneath my palm. "Thank you. Thank you so much."

I back away but stumble. I'm a little dizzy and my head pounds from an intense headache. I need to get out of here. I hurry out of the stone chamber, but the tunnel wavers before me. My body crashes against the sides of the chasm as the dizziness disorientates me.

I grit my teeth and shove myself forward only to realize I'm back in the inner amphitheater once again. Confusion swirls through me along with panic. If I don't pull myself together, I really won't make it out—I'll be joining the other bodies here, decaying and forgotten.

I rip another part of my dress off and stuff my ears with it. It's not soundproof, but it does seem to muffle some of the sound. Then I press one hand to the side of the wall and close my eyes to keep myself from getting dizzy. I set off, walking once again as fast as I can.

Soon, I trip over something and I open my eyes. I'm back in the graveyard area and the entrance is straight ahead. Hope surges through me and I run as fast as I can out of the chasm.

Except I can't find the staircase. I'm still a little dizzy and confused. Did I pass by the stairs or are they still up ahead? I take off in a jog, fear spurring me ahead. Finally, I find the stairs, but the first few steps are missing. Was it that way before? Maybe? I'd been so excited that I hadn't been paying much attention.

I reach up to the sharp rock, and with a grunt, pull myself up onto the first step. Wearily, I begin the slow ascent up the side of the cliff. When I finally reach the last step and stumble onto the stone platform area of the Numinous Flame, I'm out of breath and my legs are on fire. The sky is turning to a deep purple. Night is falling. All I want to do is sag to the ground and curl into a ball, but I need to get out of here.

Except when I bend down to grab my chain, it's not there.

22
THE UNRAVELING OF SECRETS
ESTRELLA

The World of Between

Ami betrayed me. How could I have been so blind? She lured me into trusting her so she could leave me here, lost and forgotten. She's probably back in her land right now, telling Dion I didn't survive. Or maybe that she lost me.

She's obviously a master at lying and deception. Four hundred years' worth of learning the craft.

I rise to my feet, determined to find my way back to...

Where did I want to go? I can't seem to remember. Fear curdles in my stomach. I'm forgetting things. Desperately I swipe my hands through the flame once again. It burns but also replenishes my inner visik, sharpening my senses and strengthening my body.

But as the fire sinks into my skin, confusion washes over me. The Numinous Flame isn't blue anymore. It's red. How did that happen? Or am I now even imagining things here in this land? I'm losing it.

"Estrella!" a voice cries out.

I jerk in surprise. A beautiful Asian woman with a flowing green gown strides into the clearing, hefting a chain. "Ami? I thought..." *You left me*, but I bite back those words as I eye her suspiciously.

"I've been looking for you everywhere," she says, coming to my side and handing me my chain. I take it. It's cold and otherworldly, and yet, oddly comforting. A reminder of what lies beyond this place. "Where did you go?" Her words are sharp and worry fills her eyes as if she truly is upset. "Why didn't you follow me?"

"I thought you left me."

"You're too valuable to leave behind." Her mouth dips in skepticism. *She doesn't believe me.* "What happened to your dress and what are you doing here at this pedestal?"

"I was looking for my chain, but it was gone." I attach it once again to my ankle. "Did you take it?"

"Don't be ridiculous. This is the Sabian pedestal," Ami says, her voice clipped and wary. "That's why your chain wasn't here. You are lucky I thought to come to this spot to look for you. I was worried."

I blink at the flame. So that's why it's red. Then a new thought slams into me. Queen Kelli was right. I can touch Sabian fire. Before I can fully process this, Ami takes my hand, yanking me away from the Numinous dais.

"Come," she says. "We must hurry. Darkness is coming to this land, which means dawn is arriving in mine. We must hurry before the starlight in Japan fades and there won't be enough of its light to travel through. Otherwise, we'll have to wait another day."

"Have you ever had to wait another day before?"

"Of course not. I've never been foolish to do such a thing."

Our chains lead us back to the meadow where the Ring sits like a foreign object belonging to another world. Its center wavers with a translucent light as if calling for us, but it's softer and not quite as bright.

"We're almost out of time!" Ami cries out. "Hurry!"

We take off running. My chain hangs heavy against my ankle, dragging me down. I'm not used to seeing Ami panic. Her fear spurs my legs to run faster. When I get to the Ring's edge, I hesitate, oddly sad to leave this place. The World of Between pulls on my chest, begging me to say.

"Don't even think about it," Ami says.

She grabs my hand tightly as if sensing my reluctance and hauls me to her.

We leap through the wavering light.

The Ring's surface burns and tears at my skin. I cry out and stumble onto the hard stone of the platform on the other side. The air tastes and smells bitter and stale. The golden ethereal light has been replaced by the first dregs of dawn in Ami's land.

Strong arms scoop me up and wrap around me. I blink and look up to find Dion, supporting me, worry pulling his mouth into a frown.

"Estrella," he whispers, "I was so worried. You were gone too long."

I throw my arms around him and exhale a long breath. "You're not the only one who was worried," I say. "I couldn't have made it through the Ring without you or your powers. Thank you."

Despite both Zola's and Ami's skepticism of Dion and the Cabral family being trustworthy, today he proved them wrong. I want to tell him everything I discovered right away, but I need to wait to tell him in private.

"We're a team," he says. "No matter what happens."

A servant rushes up and unclips Ami's and my chains before taking them away. Ami leans down, her eyes running over my body, calculating as she assesses me for any possible injuries.

"Does anything hurt?" she asks. "Do you remember who you are?"

I nod. "I do, but if you hadn't found me, I don't know if I'd have returned before the starlight faded. I was getting confused."

"Thank the Fates you are safe," Dion says, and then to Ami, "Thank you for bringing her back."

"As much as I hate to admit it," Ami says, "she's grown on me."

And then she does something unexpected. She helps pull me to my feet and squeezes my hands. "For not having your full powers," she says, "you did well. Get some rest, and then let's talk and regroup."

My body shakes as I wobble down the steps. Thankfully, Dion supports me, his arm wrapped gently around my waist.

As we take the path back to the main building, my mind is flying with a million thoughts as I think about the information I discovered in the World of Between and what it could mean.

Back in my room, Dion wishes me goodnight, but I pull him inside and tell him we need to talk. His eyebrows lift, but he follows my lead. My body is screaming to sleep, but my heart is pounding too hard to even consider that. I close the door and wave for him to sit on a cushion in the sitting area.

"You need to know what happened in the World of Between, and I want to tell you while it's still fresh in my mind."

He listens patiently as I rehash everything about our secret Conduit meeting place and my belief it's the Empress's fault that our powers were failing.

"What do you mean powers failing?" Dion rises to his feet.

"There's so much I need to tell you," I say, rubbing my head. "While at the Sabian castle, I had a vision or some sort of experience with Future's Fate. She told me the immortal powers are fading because someone is misusing them. According to Ami and Zola—"

"Zola?" Dion questions.

"She's the Caladrians' Conduit. They both said the Numinous Flames are getting smaller every year. If this continues, all immortals will no longer have their powers."

"And become mortal," Dion finishes. He runs a hand through his hair and starts pacing. "This is bad. We need to tell someone."

"But who can we really trust? I think the Empress is the

one causing this. If we destroy her, we can save all the powers."

He heaves in a deep breath like the world sits on his shoulders and it's too heavy. "Overthrowing the Empress is no small feat."

"There's more," I say.

"More? Blistering stars."

"Ami and I got separated."

"You think she left you?"

"I thought she had, but maybe it was the World of Between messing with my head. It's a strange place, full of the Fates' powers. I wish you could see it."

His face softens. "So do I."

I pull him back to sitting down and then whisper, "I found it."

His eyes widen. "Found what?"

"The location of the Temple of Fates."

"This is wonderful!" He grabs my shoulders. "Now we can get your memory and powers back."

"It's located in the Acacus Peaks. Have you heard of this place?"

"No, but it's a name. We can work with a name."

The worry and stress on his face fall as I tell him about the Whispering Chasm and what happened.

"That was a big risk you took. You're lucky it paid off. I'll talk to Ami and we'll put a plan together for this."

"Do we have to tell Ami? I mean, I know that's the agreement, but I'm still not sure I can trust her."

His body stiffens. "I need to come straight with you about Ami. As you know, we made a deal. She helps get your powers back and you give her the location of the Temple of Fates."

"You made that deal with her, but I never did."

"I know, but I didn't have any other solutions. The thing is, our deal isn't just any deal, it's a binding agreement of powers. Should either of us fail to fulfill the agreement, their powers will be transferred to the other."

I gasp. "You didn't! How could you take such a risk?"

He unbuttons his shirt to reveal a tattoo of the bird in flight on his toned bronze chest. "Her mark is on me and mine is on her until the agreement is fulfilled."

Shock curls through me that he did this. It's strange to see her mark branded into his body. Like she owns him. I'm not sure how I feel about it.

"I'm so sorry," I whisper. "It's my fault you're in this mess. I'm not worth losing your powers."

"You are worth it." He takes my hand. "We may never have the relationship we once had, but I still remember how good we were together. I'd do anything for you. Also, now that we know what's happening with the Numinous Flames and that our powers might be dying, perhaps I wasn't such a fool after all putting so much trust in you and your abilities."

"Thank you for believing in me. There's no way I'm letting you lose your powers, which means we have to tell Ami the location of the temple. But I think we need to be smart about it. I suggest we wait and don't tell her the details but allow her to travel with us to the location. That way we stay in control."

"I like that plan." He clears his throat. "There's something else you need to know since we're telling secrets. Ami kissed me the other day. I think it was more for blackmail since she said that if I told you about our agreement, she'd tell you we kissed."

Anger flares up in me that she would treat him like that. I'm surprised I'm not jealous. She's a sly one and I have a feeling if she had her way, she'd keep him for herself like the others here in this land.

"I want you to know that you can tell me anything," I say. "Even the hard things. You need to be careful with Ami, though. She's the kind of woman who likes to get what she wants."

"I know." But his face clouds over as if something is bothering him. "I'm exhausted from staying up all night so I can't imagine how tired you must be. Get some rest. I'll talk to Ami and tell her the plan. Tomorrow we'll start our search for the Acacus Peaks."

"But before you go, let me try to replenish your powers. Mine were renewed when I touched the Numinous Flame and you must be weak after what you did for me at the Ring."

I take his hand and slip a stream of energy into him. It's the first time I've given someone powers when I haven't been in a battle or fighting for my life. Dion's bronze skin instantly brightens and his eyes regain their spark. He even seems to straighten taller. And as my powers blend with his, I feel his raw feelings for me.

A flash of a memory skitters through my mind. The two of us are sitting on the floor in what I think is a training room, me holding his hands, slipping power into him.

"We've done this before," I say in realization.

"Yes. A few times while you were at the academy. But always in secret. You said it wasn't allowed."

"Well, no one is here telling us what we can or can't do. It's the least I can do after what you did for me."

He leans closer and I sense he wants to kiss me. I quickly rise, pulling him to his feet, emotions roiling inside of me. In silence, we walk to the door.

"Thank you for everything," I say, breaking the awkwardness.

"Always." He leans down and kisses me on the forehead, sending sparks skittering over my skin. Then without another word, he leaves, closing the door behind him.

Heaviness settles over me and I sag onto my bed. It's obvious he wants more than my friendship, and after today, I'm starting to want more too. Being in the World of Between changed me in ways I didn't expect. Since we've been here, he's proven I can trust him, yet deep down I still feel his betrayal at the pond in Florida when I learned the truth of who he really was.

And who I was.

I don't know if my heart is willing to risk falling for him again.

23
THE TESTING OF LOYALTIES
DION

Kakurezato, Japan

It takes all my effort to drag myself down the hall away from Estrella. I'd been so worried about her surviving, and now that she has, I don't want to leave her side. Talking to her tonight was the first time it seemed like I was talking to her old self. Whether she realizes it or not, going into that land gained her some of herself once again.

We're finally regaining our trust in each other, but at the same time, I feel that deeper romantic bond we once shared slipping away. If we find the Temple of Fates, will she regain her memories? And if she does, will she still love me after everything that has happened?

But the bigger, more pressing problem is her news that the Numinous Flames are depleting. This could mean the end of immortality and the powers of all immortals. It could change everything.

My steps quicken down the hall and into the main room. Ami is standing in the opened doorway between two red pillars, watching the pink sunrise. She's changed into a pale pink kimono that hugs her body, showing off every perfect curve. Her long hair is unbound and trailing down her back. She is beautiful. Sensing my approach, she turns her head, eyes flickering over me.

"Come," she says, "let's go for a walk."

We step outside into the dawn. Dew sparkles across the bright green grass and birds chirp in the trees, waking up for the day.

"How is Estrella?" Ami asks.

"She's resting but well," I say. "I told her about our deal and your attempt to kiss me."

"Look at you," she shoots me a sly smile, "getting all honest. Are you sure that was the best choice?"

"It was the only choice. I'm tired of keeping things from her. She deserves to know everything that is going on. Which leads me to my next question, how long have you known about the Numinous Flames depleting?"

"Not long. Six months. Zola noticed it first when she went to retrieve more power for her people."

"That's why you were willing to meet me in Chichen Itza and made the blood contract."

"We didn't know why it was happening. I was so desperate for answers that I was even willing to work with a Nazco."

"We're not all villains, Ami," I say, chuckling.

"Perhaps not." She tilts her head and shoots me a mischievous smile.

We come to the center of an arched bridge, and I pause, leaning over the railing to stare down at the fish swimming along in the stream, trying to make sense of this new information.

"Did she tell you about her encounter with the Fates?" Ami asks.

I nod. "Do you think they really are communicating with her?"

"When she told us her vision about the Fates," Ami says, "it was unexpected, to put it mildly. If she is speaking the truth and they are talking to her, it means she's valuable. I wonder if the Empress knew this and that's why she went to such extremes to wipe Estrella's memory and deplete her of most of her powers. She didn't want Estrella standing in her way."

"I want to believe it's the Empress that's doing this. My family despises her, but I can't figure out what the Empress has to gain by angering the Fates."

"It's a moot point as we still don't know where the Temple of Fates is."

"That's what I wanted to talk to you about." I turn to face her. "Estrella found the name of the location while she was in there."

"Really?" Surprise lights her face and she lifts her eyebrows. And then she huffs and clenches her fists. "So that's what she was doing. She disappeared on me. I looked everywhere for her. She nearly got us both stuck in that land for another day, which is dangerous. Foolish girl."

"I wouldn't say foolish. I'd say brave, and it was worth the risk."

"Where is the temple?" Ami snaps. She has turned on me, cold as death.

"The contract between us doesn't stipulate when I tell you the temple's location. Only that I do."

"You conniving Nazco scum."

"I'm going to pretend you didn't say that. Once we find the location, you'll be invited to journey with us. You'll be with us every step of the way. As long as you cooperate, of course."

"You think you can manipulate *me*?"

"I'm not manipulating you, Ami. Just telling you how this is going to go down."

Ami glares, and by her clenched jaw, I can tell she's debating what to say next.

"There's something you need to know about Estrella," she finally says.

I roll my eyes. Ami has done everything possible to undermine Estrella, and I'm getting tired of it. "Now what?"

"When I finally found her in the World of Between, it wasn't at the Nazco Numinous pedestal like I expected. She was at the Sabian pedestal and she was touching the Sabian fire."

I frown. "But that's not possible, right?"

"No, except she did it and it didn't kill her. In fact, it revived her."

Dread seeps into my core. "What does that mean?"

"I don't know. I've never seen or heard of such a thing. I need to do some research. But if she didn't tell you, it means she is keeping secrets from you."

My heart sinks. Here I thought we'd finally had a breakthrough, no longer keeping secrets from each other. My phone rings, breaking the heated silence. I look at the caller ID.

"It's my friend BJ."

"Don't you dare answer that," Ami says. "We aren't finished discussing our terms."

"When you put it like that, I'm definitely answering." I grin and put my phone to my ear. "Hey, man, what's up?"

"You asked me to do some research on that rehabilitation center Estrella had been at," BJ says, getting right to the point. "Just got word that they're moving all the occupants tomorrow night."

"What?" I ask, aghast. "That soon?"

"If you wanted to get any of those girls out, you better hurry. Also, I saw the transfer request. They're sending in two additional Wraiths to add to the three already at the facility."

"Blistering stars, this is not good news. We don't have enough power to stand up to five Wraiths and Nadia's guards."

"You want me to come?" BJ says.

"No, I want you to stay safe. You're in too deep already."

"I'm taking that as a yes. I'm heading to the Traveling Pool this instant. Do you need me to bring anything?"

I rub my forehead in frustration. "If you can get your hands on any artifacts that would help."

"Sure, I'll fly to the moon and grab some rocks while I'm at it."

"You asked."

"I'll see what I can do, but you know those artifacts are rare. I'll be in touch."

"Watch your back. The Empress will have people trailing you." I hang up to find Ami looking at me like I'm crazy.

"You know the location of the temple and you're going to risk your life to save a bunch of brainless Nazco instead? You might not survive."

"They're not just a bunch of brainless Nazco. They're Estrella's and my friends. We need to do this. Will you help us?"

"All Eien Traveling Pools are heavily guarded," she says. "The moment they spot the two of you, you'll be arrested."

"That's not helping." I cross my arms. "Do you want us to come back here alive or not?"

"There is one pool you can try, but it's risky. You'll have to travel to Tokyo."

"I'll let Estrella know. We leave within the hour."

24

DRAMA AND DECEPTION IN THE CLASSROOM

TRISTAN

Florida

I stare at the text from Estrella. My heart thumps as I lean against the wall of the school hallway. Students wander past me, chatting about their day or listening to music. Lockers are slamming and even at this forsaken seventh hour in the morning two girls are already starting a fight.

But all I can think about is Estrella and if she's safe and alive. My last memory with her haunts me. The way a loose curl hung over her eyes like it was desperate to escape. Her soft skin, glowing in the ethereal light. Those plump lips slightly parted, begging me to kiss them one last time. I groan, tortured by the memory and desperate to find out if she's okay. Another text pops up. I jerk, the words practically blurring in my excitement.

> Estrella: I made it! Also I found the location.

I punch the air in silent victory. Pride swims through me. I knew she could do it. I knew it!

I text her back.

> I'm so happy for you. When do we go?

Dots show up, telling me she's typing. I wait for her to notice the *we* and tell me I can't come.

> Estrella: Just found out they're moving the girls tonight. Dion and I are on our way.
> Warn them.

Tonight? The Nazco must be suspicious of something. I rub my chin in thought.

> Me: Are you sure this isn't a trap?

The bell rings. I'm going to need to put my phone away soon if I don't want one of these wardens to confiscate it. Finally, Estrella answers.

> Estrella: Text me a meet-up point.

I send her the location of where I'm staying and then head to class, mind spinning. Something about this whole situation reeks of suspicion. I settle into a desk right beside Mara. When she sees me, her eyes darken.

"You aren't in this class," she says.

"I am now."

"I told you to leave us alone."

"Estrella wants to meet up with you." I pause as the teacher starts taking roll. "After school, meet me in the parking lot."

"Meet you or Estrella? Because I thought I'd already made it clear that I'm not going anywhere with you."

"Open your textbooks to page ninety-six," the teacher calls out. "You're going to do the warm-up questions on your own and then we'll review them together."

Everyone starts pulling out their textbooks and paper. I lean in closer to Mara. Her dark brown eyes assess me warily.

"Hopefully both of us. I heard they're transferring you tonight."

"Tonight?" She lifts her eyebrows skeptically and her mouth dips. "I don't know what Estrella ever saw in you, but your charm won't work on me."

I groan, out of patience. *You are impossible*, I want to yell back, but that wouldn't help the situation. Maybe I'm not using the right terminology. I switch tactics.

"Once they move you," I try again, "it's going to be very hard to find you again and rescue you. This is an opportunity we can't miss out on. Look, I'm going to show you the texts I got from Estrella. Then you'll see I'm telling the truth."

I pull out my phone and show her.

"How do I know it's really Estrella?" she points out, but I

spy a flicker of interest in her eyes. *Finally.* "That could be anyone on the other side."

"Do those messages seem like I'm trying to trick you? I'm literally the one worried about your safety."

"I'll think about it," she finally relents. "In the meantime, don't talk to me."

The classroom door opens and Chandra sashays into the classroom, her shiny dark hair swooping behind her like a swaying pendulum. She's wearing tight jeans and a frilly red shirt that shows off her chest. She holds a piece of paper in front of the teacher with the tips of her fingers and then drops it on his desk as if it's too disgusting to touch.

"My pass for being late," she tells the teacher and then turns to assess the room, not bothering to wait for his response. Her eyes land on me, her red lips twisting in disgust.

I glare at her, remembering how she literally tracked Estrella and me down to my castle's gate. I grip the sides of the desk to keep myself from launching at her. Unfortunately, I rip off the top section of the desk.

Oops.

Beside me, Mara sucks in a breath at the damage I did, but I merely set it back into place, hoping no one notices. My gaze lasers onto Chandra. The girl is dangerous. Lethal, and if I'm not careful, she'll find a way to kill Mara before anyone knows what's happening. She clips in her high heels down the aisle and stops at the desk in front of mine.

"Get out," she orders the guy sitting there. "This is my seat."

The guy doesn't even pause. He gathers his books and flies out of his chair like it's on fire. Chandra plops in her chair with a sigh while I grind my teeth, trying to decide if I need to leave the room or stay here with Mara.

"You should've gotten the first five questions done," the teacher says. "Find a partner and compare your findings and check your work."

Everyone begins pairing off while Chandra swivels to stare at me.

"I see you've found a new pet to take care of," she says, dark eyes flickering between me and Mara.

"Watch yourself," I growl and rise from my seat. "She's not a pet."

She slips out of her chair, skimming long nails down my shirt. I jerk away from her, backing into a guy.

"Watch where you're going, idiot," the guy mutters.

"You're going to let him talk to you like that, Sabian?" Chandra opens her hands and a tiny funnel of wind swirls on her palm. "I could always put him in his place for you."

"Hard pass." I plop into my seat. "You better not be planning on breaking any of the Code of Conduct laws."

"Don't tempt me, Sabian," she says darkly, eyes flashing. "Where is Estrella?"

"You really think I'm going to tell you?" I lean back, grinning, pretending that everything is chill and relaxed.

So I was right. They are after Estrella. Thankfully, they don't know where she is. If only she'd remain in Japan where it was safe and not put herself in danger again.

"You know he can't be trusted," Chandra says to Mara, switching her tactics. "He kidnapped Estrella and who knows what he did to her. Apparently, he's now after you."

"Estrella never liked you and I can't blame her." Mara's eyes narrow. "What makes you say he kidnapped her?"

"Can't wait to hear how you're going to spin this lie," I tell Chandra. "I'm surprised you haven't joined the drama club."

"What proof has he given you that he hasn't already killed Estrella?" Chandra presses. "Have you even seen her? Talked to her?"

"He showed me his text messages," Mara admits. "They looked pretty legit."

"Text messages?" Chandra's eyes sharpen, knives ready to stab. "What did they say?"

No! I scream inwardly. My heart slams against my ribcage. *Do not tell her anything.* Sweat beads on my forehead, but I try to naturally laugh it away.

"If she cared about Estrella at all," I interject, looking pointedly at Mara and then back to Chandra, "she wouldn't tell you where Estrella was. Especially since you already tried to kill her twice."

"What in the...?" Mara's eyes dart between the two of us in confusion. "You tried to..." She gulps as if she can't even say the word.

"Now who's the dramatic one?" Chandra pulls out a tube of lipstick and a mirror. She slowly slathers on another layer of red like a coat of armor. "I hope you make the right choices, Mara. It would be a shame to not have you as a classmate anymore."

"Are you threatening me?" Mara whispers, her face pale as a corpse.

"Speaking of death, this school is killing my mojo." Chandra pops her makeup back into her purse. "I don't know how you do it day after day. So dull."

She rises and blows me a kiss. She winds her way

through the desks, touching some of the guys on the shoulders and even stopping to give the guy who called me an idiot a long kiss that has some of the students making catcalls. The teacher tells her to sit down, but she ignores him and exits the room. I glare at the closed door.

"She's awful," Mara whispers. "Maybe worse than you."

"Something is off." I shake my head. "That went too well."

"Too well? She basically threatened to kill me."

"Meet me outside the front office at your next break and don't wander the hallways alone. I need to figure out what she's up to."

I skirt through the desks and ignore the teacher who calls after me to sit back down. When I step outside, I'm met with a shifting breeze and an empty hallway. I reach into my back pocket for my phone only to find it's gone. Desperate, I check every pocket and pat down my body. Fear crawls up my spine as I head back into the classroom.

"Young man," the teacher says, "I'm writing up a referral for disturbing instruction."

I'm too busy searching under the desk and chair I was sitting at to bother with the teacher and his referrals.

"What are you looking for?" Mara asks.

"My phone. Have you seen it?"

"Not since you showed me your texts from Estrella." Then her eyes widen and she glances around the room. "Do you think someone stole it?"

Kids are staring at me but most are too busy looking at their phones, whispering, and even sleeping. Everyone except the guy she kissed. He's unwrapping that same gum

Chandra was using and popping it into his mouth. I sag into my chair and I run my hands through my hair.

"How could I have been so stupid?" I'm tempted to throw the desk across the room.

"What?" Mara leans in closer to me. "What is it?"

"Remember that guy she kissed? He got my phone."

"How?"

"She distracted us while he must have slipped the phone from my back pocket. Then he gave it to her when she was kissing him."

Mara lets out a long breath. "That was my fault. I told her about the phone."

"Nothing here is your fault. These people who are controlling you and everyone at Nadia's are the ones to blame, and you are the victim. I'm going to do everything I can to get you to safety."

25
KYOTO EXPRESS
ESTRELLA

Kyoto, Japan

Tidebreaker feels cool in my hand as I tuck it into the sheath beneath my shirt. I slip on the boots that Ami gave me and then zip up the black jacket, which is supposed to have some resistance to elemental powers. Once finished, I stare at myself in the mirror. Since leaving Florida, I've gained some weight and muscle, making my cheeks fill out. My blonde hair, tied up in a ponytail, almost glows after my last visit to the World of Between. With my tight black pants, jacket, and boots, I hardly recognize the girl who left Nadia's.

With determined resolve, I set off to meet Dion in the Great Room. I find him speaking with Ami, their expressions tight and serious. As soon as I walk up though, they stop talking. The change in their expressions is so abrupt and startling that I wonder if they were discussing me. Dion's eyes snap to mine, a storm brewing behind him. I'm not sure if it's from nerves like mine or the fact that we're going back into danger before I've gotten my powers. Regardless, I'm glad he's coming with me.

"I'm ready," I say, expecting them to explain their conversation but they make no mention of it. "Are you sure we'll be safe exiting your land?"

"I've done what I can to clear the way," Ami says, her normally smooth features wrinkled with worry. "Haruki will guide you to the train, but after that, you're on your own. Just remember to only use the Water Channel I mentioned. All others will be heavily guarded and if you're captured, you'll be tortured or sent back to the Empress."

I swallow hard, but nod. "Hopefully we will return soon."

"Which reminds me," she begins and then snaps her fingers at Yuto.

"Are you sure this is a good idea, your excellence?" he asks with a grimace but at her glare, he goes over to a table and picks up a scabbard. He carries it to me. "Please don't behead me with this."

Frowning, I take it and pull out a sword. Not just any sword, it's the Swedish Channeler blade that I practiced with. "This is too much. I can't take this."

"Right," Yuto says. "I'll take it back then."

Ami pushes him away. "You must and you will," she says firmly. "You're going into enemy territory so you should go armed. Besides, I already have one and mine is better."

"This is the most wonderful gift," I say in awe. "I can't thank you enough."

"You can by staying alive and finishing your end of the bargain. I'm only doing it for selfish reasons." She says this, but there's a look of pride in her eyes and happiness as I take the sword. Then reaching behind her, she grabs a long black tube with a strap on it.

"I had this map tube specially designed to hold the sword so you can travel unnoticed with it. Only you can open it, Estrella, by putting your finger here." She points to the fingerprint scanner on the end.

"This is incredible." I take off my jacket and Dion helps me strap the tube to my back.

"You are coming back here after you are finished, yes?" she asks.

"Of course," Dion says. "We will remain true to our promise."

"Tell me you have a plan for what you're going to do with your ragtag friends," she says. "This place is not a refugee center."

"Dion's friend, BJ, is looking for a location for them to go into hiding," I say.

"Good luck with that," Ami says skeptically.

"We should set off." Dion zips up the same tight jacket as mine, a spark of electricity escaping his fingers. It hugs his fit frame perfectly. "With the Fate's luck, we will return in three days."

"I'd warn you of the cunningness and ruthlessness of the Nazco," Ami says curtly. "But then you both are one of them so I suppose you already know."

I resist rolling my eyes at her obvious jab and take my backpack of supplies one of the servants hands to Dion and me. Ami's helping us and I need to remember that. If it weren't for her, I'd still be on the run with no opportunity to train or hone my skills.

Haruki is waiting off to the side, arms behind his back, feet spread apart. But when we turn to him, he wordlessly springs to action, leading us back to the gate out of Ami's land.

As we walk out, Ami whispers to Dion, "You have my number, but don't call. Unless you have something good to say, of course."

I suppress a laugh and head down the now-familiar path to the gate. The memories of when we first entered this world worm fear through me. Dion catches up to me.

"She's obsessed with you," I tell him as I pull out Tide-breaker, my body tense.

"She just likes to collect things that she can't get," Dion says, and we follow Haruki through the strange wavy light of the doorway.

My gut twists with a hard yank, but then I stumble out onto the long bridge. A wave of dizziness swims through me as I take in my surroundings. We're back in the courtyard of the Emperor's castle in Kyoto. I almost expect to be faced once again with a full army, eager to slice off our heads, but instead, we're met with quiet, peaceful gardens. Birds chirp from the trees and lily pads drift through the pond, reflecting the last rays of the low-hanging sun.

"Quite a different experience from our last visit," Dion notes as we take off after Haruki at a light jog.

He leads us through the gardens and around a maze of twisted corridors until we're opening that same secret entrance we first came through. As I squeeze through the rough rock's entrance, I hardly recognize the girl I was when I first entered.

Haruki presses a finger to his lips, indicating we remain silent. We nod and follow his trail, crouching low and hugging the shadows of the tree line. The exit through the forest is much faster this time with a guide, who points out every trap and snare along the way. Before we know it, we're strolling along a bustling street. Unlike Ami's land, which feels like stepping back in time to ancient Japan, Kyoto is a mix of old and new.

"I will take you to Umekoji Station," Haruki tells us. "Then you will need to take the train to Tokyo. The important thing is to keep a low profile."

"That might be harder than it seems," I say, looking meaningfully at a group of school girls in uniform huddled together. They're staring at Dion and Haruki, giggling. "If we don't keep moving, you two might get a fan club."

"Yes," Haruki agrees, his sharp eyes assessing the area. "We are already attracting too much attention."

Tour buses and cars whiz down the road while we hurry past people strolling along the sidewalk, taking pictures of the gardens or staring at their maps. The noises of the city ring loud in my ears after being in Ami's peaceful land for so long. We clip past tables piled with colorful hats and cozy scarves, set alongside bustling food carts. My mouth waters as the air fills with the scent of sweet soy sauce and grilled meat from a man who is grilling yakitori and the nutty aroma of sesame oil from a woman frying golden tempura.

When we reach the long concrete steps leading up to the station, Haruki stops and hands us a transportation pass.

"This is where our paths part," he says. "Perhaps I will see you both again in this life or the next."

"I hope so," I say. "Thank you again for your help."

"It is appreciated," Dion says and holds out his hand. Haruki eyes it warily, but then the two grab each other's wrists in a handshake.

Dion and I head up the steps and enter the train station. It feels strange squeezing through the crowds, just the two of us. I edge myself closer to Dion to keep us from getting separated. His sizzling power so is potent amidst the sea of mortals, I bet I could sense him from a long ways away.

"You know, it's never too late to leave all this behind," Dion tells me. "I have a place in Indonesia we could escape to. We could forget about this madness and live out our days with a simple life without looking over our shoulders, worried the next breath will be our last."

"You know I can't do that."

"I do." He smiles at me, but it doesn't quite reach his eyes. "In that part, you haven't changed. You always fought for those you loved."

"Besides, there will always be someone searching for me. The Empress won't stop until I'm dead or she's got me in her clutches again."

"You're not wrong." His face grows serious as we push through the crowd.

"How long have we known each other, anyway?" I ask as we push through the turnstile and enter the train station area.

Dion cocks his head to the side in thought. "A little over

a year, I guess," he says. "We met on your final examination field trip."

"My what?"

"At the Midnight Academy where you went to school, and even the Shadowland Academy that I attended, every student has a final exam where they have to go out into mortal territory and do some sort of test."

"And that's when we met?"

"Yep. It was a field trip to the Met in New York City. I actually had been tasked to watch over you because they wanted to make sure you stayed safe. They already knew then that you'd likely be the next Conduit."

We continue talking as we follow the signs to our train, but as we step into the boarding area, a strange sensation ripples over me. I frown and my steps slow.

"Everything okay?" Dion asks.

"I felt something." I bite my lip and shove my feet forward. "I think it's the powers of another immortal."

"That's not good." Dion's body stiffens. "Still, it might be someone just taking the train to Tokyo. Or it could be a tracker. You're wearing your necklace, right?"

"Yes." My hand instinctively touches my chest where the necklace is safely tucked beneath my jacket. "I wasn't about to leave it at Ami's."

"Good. Take my hand. If it is a Tracker, they won't be expecting anyone to be holding hands with a Channeler. This way we'll look like we're people in love taking a trip to the city."

"You sure you want to hold my hand?" I ask, but all I can think about is his words *in love*.

He laughs and grabs my hand. "Of course not. What are you going to do? Drain me of my powers and kill me?"

His skin tingles against mine and a thrill shoots through me as if something in my body remembers him, remembers us. His power is there, sharp and crackling with energy. I could take it. That's how trusting he is of me, and I feel myself trusting him more.

We step up to the train platform and that same sensation swims through me.

"I feel it again," I whisper to Dion as the doors to the train open and a swarm of people exit. "It's like a cool wave of water lapping across my skin, but not in a good way."

"We just need to get on this train and we'll be fine," Dion says.

I glance over my shoulder, searching for the power source. I lock in on it—a man with dark cropped hair, wearing faded jeans and a gray T-shirt. He blends in seamlessly, except for the fact that his eyes are roaming. He's searching for someone.

Our eyes meet. My heart stutters and I quickly look away. Did he recognize me? It doesn't help that I'm the only blonde girl around here. Dion pulls me forward and I happily hurry onto the train.

"I saw him, the Tracker," I say as we slip into our seats. I tuck my scabbard at my feet. "I don't know if he recognized me, though."

"Maybe we should have worn disguises."

I dare peek out the window. The guy is still standing there. Maybe he won't get on the train. Maybe I'm overreacting. I clutch the edge of my seat, praying for the doors to close and the train to pull away.

But then I watch as the guy slowly inches toward the train. My breath catches as he pulls out his phone and talks to someone. He pockets the phone and makes a beeline straight in our direction.

"He's boarding," I whisper to Dion. "He suspects us."

26
LIGHTNING ON THE RAILS
ESTRELLA

Japan

The doors to the train hiss shut. I stiffen, peering over my shoulder to see if he's coming through the compartment doorway.

"Do you think he recognized us?" I ask.

"Hard to know," Dion replies, rubbing his palms. Blue streaks of light spark across his hands like they're itching to protect us. "He could be a Tracker who patrols the train station for unwanted immortals. Or he could merely be heading to Tokyo like the rest of us. The only ones who know we are traveling are Ami and her people. It's unlikely someone would be on the lookout for us."

"Unless she betrayed us."

"She won't."

The terseness in his voice reminds me of the contract the

two signed, and my eyes instinctively snap to his chest where her mark is hidden beneath his jacket. Another reminder of how closely tied the two are. I haven't decided if this is a good thing or not.

Probably not.

"Our best move is for us to pretend we're tourists," Dion says.

"Then we should make up a story about us. Are we college students?"

"Maybe we're on our honeymoon."

I laugh. "How did we go from tourists to being married?"

My laughter dies as the door between the train compartments swishes open. I dare give a sideways glance. The guy has his phone in front of him, and he's studying it and then each passenger as he strolls down the aisle. He's searching for someone.

"It's him!" I whisper. "He's coming this way. It's too convenient for him to just be traveling."

Dion does the unexpected. Just as the Tracker moves up to our row, he pulls me to him and kisses me. The impact of his soft lips against mine is startling. The last time I kissed him was back in Florida before I knew the truth of who I was. My body tenses as Dion cups the back of my head with his hand. Any moment the Tracker could swoop down and attack us. Sitting here, kissing, makes us targets, ready to be killed with one strike. Except, if I move or react, it will just call attention to us.

I just hope Dion knows what he's doing.

"He's moved on," Dion whispers against my mouth. "I think we tricked him."

His lips hover over mine, a brush of danger. I should

pull away, but a memory resurfaces. Us kissing in the library, my back pressed against the wall, his body pinning me close to his. My heartbeat kicks up as I remember the passion of our kiss. The way our bodies felt perfectly aligned.

And now it's like my body remembers and wants that moment back. It doesn't help that Dion hasn't pulled away. That he sucks in a tortured breath as if that kiss wasn't enough. I lean closer, testing the moment, knowing I shouldn't open this door.

And yet...

I kiss him again. Not a pretend one to deter the enemy. A tentative kiss, searching to see if there's still a spark there between us. A swirl of excitement curls through my stomach like I've let loose a butterfly. The power of him races across my skin, tingling like I dove into a cold pond.

I pull away, swallowing hard. My cheeks burn and my head spins a little.

"Do you think it worked?" I ask, pretending the moment we had was purely an act.

His dark eyes are molten like I've woken him from a deep sleep. "Maybe. The necklace must be working. And he'd hardly expect us to be kissing."

"He wouldn't attack us here though, would he?" I shift to lean back against my seat. "There are at least ten people in this compartment. Aren't there rules among the immortals to keep their powers a secret from mortals?"

"Yes, but if they were to find out who you were, they may think you're worth the trouble. Let's switch seats. I'd feel more comfortable with you by the window."

But before we move, the Tracker leaps up from his seat

and spins to face us. He holds up a metal sphere engraved with some sort of writing on it.

I gasp. "What's he holding?"

"Stars alive, an elemental lockstone," Dion mutters.

The Tracker unclips a lever, but Dion doesn't hesitate. He throws up a hand, unleashing a bolt of lightning at the Tracker. The man holds up the lockstone like a shield. The light beams directly into the trap, vanishing like it's been sucked into a void.

Screams fill the cabin as people dive for cover. All except for one girl who rises from across the aisle of the tracker, a fierce expression twisting her face. Long ash-colored hair hangs straight down her back. She's wearing a tight crimson vest lined with clawed black dragons and leather pants.

She holds up both palms, mist slithering out of them like dragon steam. Dion unleashes another bolt of lightning, aimed at her, but it veers left, sucked away into the lockstone.

"She's a mist elementalist," Dion says. "Once that mist hits our lungs we'll be fast asleep."

"Not waiting for that to happen," I say and pull out Tide-breaker from my hip, no time to grab my sword.

I rush down the aisle, but the mist shifts to make contact with me. I veer left and then vault over a seat, landing on the cushion.

"Sorry," I tell the man and woman huddled on the floor, covering their heads as they eye the gleaming blue dagger in my hand.

I use the cushion to catapult over the next two seats. The mist has separated Dion from me. As if realizing this, he continues to blast bolt after bolt of lightning in rapid-fire across the space. One finally misses the lockstone and hits the side of the train, puncturing a hole in the wall.

The entire compartment shudders. I topple sideways, smashing against the window. A gust of air swooshes through the cabin, sucking the mist outside. Mist Girl growls in frustration and sends out another wave. Now that the fog is gone, a path has opened for me to the Tracker. This is my chance.

The train barrels on, heedless of our battle.

I jump on top of the seat back and catapult through the air, hefting my dagger. I land just as the Tracker pulls out a blade of his own. He swipes it through the air, aimed at my neck. I duck, then execute a set of moves I practiced daily with Ami in her pagoda.

Turn, sidekick in the chest, and thrust.

My dagger plunges into the Tracker's arm. The lockstone tumbles from his grasp, clattering to the ground. I scramble to snatch it up, but a foot smashes into my jaw. I fly backward from the kick and land with a crash on the ground. My breath is sucked out of me.

Lightning zig zags around us as it continues to be sucked into the lockstone lying open on the ground.

Mist Girl reaches down to take Tidebreaker from me, but I clench it tighter.

"*Wield my power,*" a voice rumbles in my mind.

A storm of energy bursts through me.

Raging wind, crashing waves, a tempest unleashed.

It's like the dagger lifts me up and I'm riding the crest of its power. I stab Mist Girl in the shoulder. She cries out, stumbling backward. Fear fills her dark eyes. Mist flows from her shaking palms, but the wind sucks it away. I level

Tidebreaker at her chest while she leans against the window, blood coursing down her arm.

"Don't you dare move," I say.

Dion arrives at my side and scoops up the lockstone, slapping it shut and pocketing it.

"Thanks for the gift," he says with a wicked grin.

"That's not yours," the Tracker snaps, crawling on his knees to take it back.

A bolt of electricity paralyzes the guy, shaking him to his core. He collapses to the ground, wallowing on the floor.

"Think I'll take this, too." Dion snatches up his phone.

A quick glance around the cabin tells me that everyone is sleeping. Some are slumped on the seats, while others lie still on the floor.

"Maybe they'll think they had a bad dream," I offer.

"Until they see the hole in the train," Dion mutters.

"We know who you are," Mist Girl says. "You won't get far."

"You have a choice," I say. "You can either call in that you were wrong about us. Or die."

I'm totally bluffing. I'd never kill her, but she doesn't need to know that. I wave my dagger at the phone in her pocket. Eyeing us warily, she slowly reaches into her pocket and makes the call. I press the dagger against her throat.

"Hey," she says, her voice impressively steady considering she's suffering from a wound. "I was wrong about the couple. They're just random mortals. Yeah. Okay."

I snatch the phone from her before she can finish the conversation. I hang up and pocket the phone.

"We can't have them following us," Dion says. "Use her powers and put them to sleep."

I frown. "I hadn't thought of it like that."

"You've done that sort of thing before," he says, shrugging.

That's what I did with the guard in Slovakia and how I amplified Tristan's and Dion's powers back in Florida. It's one of the reasons why people have always been fearful of me. Not only can I take their powers, but I can channel them to use for myself. For some reason, it feels strange now. Maybe it's because I'm using her own powers against her. But Dion is right. We need to use every advantage we can to survive.

"I guess it's your bedtime," I tell her.

Mist Girl's eyes widen. "Don't you dare touch me," she says, snarling, and then lifts up a palm to put me to sleep.

But I'm ready. I snatch a hold of her wrist while Dion holds her tight. Her visik is heavy like a thick blanket. I yank on it and draw it to myself, soaking it in, inch my inch. Mist Girl screams like I'm torturing her, but everyone I've ever done it to before has hardly noticed.

"Stop being so dramatic," I say, rolling my eyes.

Once I've depleted her of her powers, I send a wave of mist over her. She drops to the ground, her eyes closing, head lulled to the side.

"Sweet dreams," I tell her and then do the same with the Tracker and throw an extra dose on the passengers. Then I turn to Dion. "What do we do now? Our cover is totally blown."

"Now it's time to get a little creative."

27
A COLD-BLOODED BARGAINING

LEXI

The Midnight Kingdom, Antarctica

The guy hauling me down the icy hallway is really getting on my nerves.

"You know I am quite capable of walking on my own," I tell him. "No dragging necessary."

"Shut up," the guard says.

Conrad shoots me a tired smile. "I think they forgot to have their coffee this morning," he says, and even though I know he's trying to relax me, worry snakes up my spine. His right eye is practically closed shut from when the guards beat him up and blood still trickles down from the corner of his brow.

I could punch the guy who did that to him. Will punch

him if I get a chance. I'd light the dude on fire if I had my powers. That would be cool.

The corridor we're walking along has arched beams, glittering white like diamonds. Paintings fill some sections of the walls, showing off brutal battles and rivers flowing with blood. Based on the weaponry and the dress in those paintings, I'm guessing these battles were fought hundreds of years ago.

Soon we come to an entrance, wide as a barn door. The imprint of a snowflake is etched into the surface. It glitters like it's winking at me, so of course I scowl back. I shiver, but not from the cold—there's something about this doorway that feels familiar.

Dangerous.

Wrong.

And my whole body starts screaming like it's telling me to get out of here as fast as I can run. Unfortunately, I never took up running. That might have been a better choice than acting.

Note to self: If you survive this, take up jogging.

The doors swing open and my guard ever so kindly shoves me forward. I stumble and fall onto the cold marble, smashing my chin since I can't catch myself.

I swear under my breath.

"What is wrong with you?" Conrad snaps. "She was cooperating."

"Just making sure she gets inside on time," my guard says.

Tears spring to my eyes, but I grit my teeth and shove aside the pain. A flicker of fire surges up inside of me, but it has nowhere to go thanks to the weird handcuffs they've put on me. I struggle into a standing position and then smile sweetly at my guard.

"For your sake," I tell him, "make sure you never uncuff me."

He grunts and tries to push me again, but I quickly twist away from his grasp and move further into the room. I take in my surroundings and I am slightly startled. A fire burns in the center, except it's oddly blue as the sea, snapping at the cold air. Icicles hang from the ceiling, their glow brightening the room.

It's all so beautiful that it's a little overwhelming. I mean, compared to Nadia's place, this is like something from a fairy tale. Zayla would love it. She'd steal every little icicle and stack them in the corner of her room, proud of her new collection. A pang shoots through me just remembering my friends. I hope they are safe.

My thoughts are disrupted when from the corner of the room, a woman wearing a billowing silver dress, studded with sapphires, swishes over to stand before us. She's holding a silver scepter caked in ice.

"Bow to the Empress," my guard demands and then smashes my back so hard that I drop to my knees.

"That's one way to build undying devotion," I grumble.

So this is the Empress. Conrad had told me a little about her and said everyone fears her because she's awful. But hearing about someone who's bad and being in their presence are two totally different things. She looks breathlessly ruthless. A chiseled jaw, blood-red lips, a swooping nose, and eyes that glitter deathly like the tips of her icicles.

If looks could kill, she'd win that battle every time.

Conrad's guard forces him to his knees beside me. I

glance over at him, wishing I could reach over and hold his hand. . His green eyes are stormy and his mouth is tight like it's taking every ounce of his energy not to leap up and stab her in the heart.

"Oh my." The Empress clucks her tongue and shakes her head, staring down at me in pity. "You look dreadful, Lexi. The last time I saw you, your hair was bright and shiny. Now it just looks pitifully dull. Mortal life definitely doesn't suit you."

Questions rapid-fire through my mind. She knows me? And is my hair really that different in color? And man, she should see how she looks after being beaten up and imprisoned. She's egging me on, but I'm not going to bite.

"I actually like my hair color," I say happily. "It's a nice auburn and totally in fashion."

"I sent you away so you could stay out of trouble," the Empress continues and starts pacing before us, "but here I find you consorting with foul dogs like this Sabian. You should know better."

"Considering you wiped my memories," I say, "no, I actually shouldn't. And since he's helped me recover while you took everything from me, I'd say you're the dog."

The guards gasp and one visibly cringes like he's preparing to dive for cover.

"How dare you?" The Empress's eyes flash and she holds up her scepter. A streak of ice shoots out of it, slamming against my shoulder. Pain sears through my body and a cry escapes my lips.

"You will pay for that!" Conrad says, rising to his feet.

But his guard zaps him in the side with his wand once

again, sending Conrad to the ground, grunting and groaning. Then they gag him so he can't speak.

"The only reason why you're here, you bottom feeder," the Empress tells Conrad, "is I'm hoping you will be useful. Otherwise, I'll be happy to behead you and send it packing back to your King Julian. He does seem to hate it when I send him those little packages."

I gasp in shock, my stomach souring. Who does that sort of thing these days? That's archaic. Except she does seem to be the sort of person who'd actually do such a thing.

"Why are we here?" I ask. "Don't tell me you brought me all the way here to talk about my hair."

"Insolent as ever." The Empress rolls her eyes. "I'd hoped the memory implant managed to get rid of some of that. But we can't have perfection, can we? We can only strive for it. I've brought you here because I'm hoping you can tell us the whereabouts of Estrella."

"This is about Estrella?" I laugh, which makes my head pound even more. "If you're so worried about her, why did you send her to Nadia's?"

"It was a necessary evil." She turns and waves her hand through the air. A man with dark hair and skin almost as pale as the Empress steps to her side, bowing. "My Truth Seeker here is going to help assist you in remembering anything you conveniently forgot. Put her in the chair so it's easier for him to access her memories."

This is bad, I think as I'm hauled across the floor and practically thrown into the chair by the strange fire. What if they discover something about Estrella that will hurt her? The thought of betraying my best friend makes me want to puke.

My guards strap me tightly to the chair. I squirm and kick, managing to hit the Truth Seeker in the shin. It's a small satisfaction, but it also encourages the guards to chain my legs to the chair as well. Bummer. The Truth Seeker grimaces at me like I'm one of those cockroaches Nadia sends me to the kitchen to kill.

"Here's your first truth," I say. "If I ever considered myself a Nazco before, I now realize what an idiot I was. You're all awful, and if that's what it means to be a Nazco, I don't want any part of it."

"I need you to remember," the Empress says, "that if you don't cooperate, this mutt will be missing his head soon." She points to Conrad.

"Don't tell them anything, Lexi," Conrad says. "They're going to kill me anyway. So your best move is to keep everyone else you can safe."

"Cover his mouth," the Empress says. "I can't stand that Sabian accent. It gives me hives."

My heart squeezes. This time, I can't keep my tears in check. They tumble down my face and pure panic takes over. The thought of Conrad dying is too much. Sure, I've been flirting with him lately and we even kissed once. But now that his life is in my hands and I could lose him forever it's too much. My breathing comes out in rasping gasps as I feel my body lose control.

My skin burns hot, fire flickering along my skin. My insides feel like they could combust, but thanks to the stupid handcuffs and ropes, I'm useless.

"Just settle down and relax," the Truth Seeker says and drags another chair closer to me, plopping his heavy frame into it. He touches my forehead, which is super creepy. "Why don't you tell me where Estrella is right now."

"I don't know," I say, twisting my head to get his slimy hand off me, but my guard takes my face and holds it firmly. "The last time I saw her was at school."

"That's a lie," the Truth Seeker says. "You talked to her another time. Later…"

The last time I talked to her was when she was at the Sabian Castle with Tristan. She hadn't told me that, but I suspected it and after pushing Conrad for answers, he admitted that's where she was. I'm definitely not telling this Truth Seeker where she's at. But then it's like a hand reaches inside my head and plucks that memory free, pulling it out. Before I can stop myself, I blurt out, "She was at the Sabian Castle."

No! How did he do that? More tears stream down my face.

"Stará?" the Truth Seeker asks.

"I don't know."

"Does she plan on coming back to Nadia's?"

"Yes," I blurt out even though I really want to say no. I try to clamp my lips shut, but instead, more words spill out like a rushing tide. "Conrad and I set up a plan to get the girls out of the facility. Conrad said she needed to get her powers back so we were thinking of waiting until then, but it seemed like every day we were at Nadia's we were slowly losing ourselves so we decided not to wait."

"How is Estrella planning on getting her powers back?" the Truth Seeker probes while the Empress moves in closer, clutching her scepter so tightly her knuckles look transparent.

"I don't know."

"Do you know when this rescue is happening?"

"I don't know," I say again, this time forcefully. Now I'm glad Estrella kept secrets from me. Secrets are dangerous, and it's obvious I'm more of a liability than a help. I just hope she'll forgive me for not being strong enough.

The Truth Seeker lets go of my forehead. He takes a towel and wipes his hands as if touching me soiled them.

"She doesn't know anything else," he tells the Empress.

"So getting these two was a waste of time and resources." The Empress sighs and taps her scepter with her sharp nails, turning to the head guard. "I suppose you can go ahead and exterminate them. They are no longer useful."

My heart dives. Exterminate? As in kill?

"But we didn't do anything wrong," I exclaim.

"Not do anything wrong?" the Empress asks. "You killed two of our Wraiths and one of our assets, plus you put Nadia's home and the rest of the girls there in jeopardy by trying to escape. Not to mention that you were sent there in the first place because you exposed your powers to other mortals. You have done plenty to deserve death."

"Or we could use them as bait," a man's voice says from the doorway behind me.

Everyone turns to face the man striding into the room. His dark hair is slicked back and tied into a ponytail at the nape of his neck. He's rubbing the goatee on his chin thoughtfully, his dark eyes assessing me like I'm lunch. A dark-blue tunic hangs over his body and he's wearing tight black pants with a belt that holds a wand like the other guards.

Instantly, I decide I do not like this dude.

"Viamire," the Empress greets him. "You're back early. I hope you have information for me."

"You will be pleased," he says, his voice smooth as glass. "Quadril sent me to tell you the news in person. We found Estrella. And she's on her way to Florida right now."

28
CHASING DOWN THE PAST
DION

Japan

"You were amazing fighting off these two," I tell Estrella. She looked fierce, leaping over the seats, dagger raised. I'm still not sure what she did with that dagger of hers, but it looked as if it fought with her, raising her into the air, her long golden ponytail swishing behind her like a trail of starlight. "That was pretty impressive. And hot."

She blushes and pushes a strand of hair out of her eyes. "Thanks. It was mainly fear that propelled me forward. I wasn't ready to die. But the training with Tristan and Ami helped."

I wince at Tristan's name. It still kills me that he was the one who was there for her when she needed help. I shove that thought aside. I'm here for her now and that's the important thing.

"My guess is this team wasn't trying to kill us since one of them is a Sleeper," I note. "With a pair with these powers, their mission must be to track down enemies or potential threats and put them to sleep. Since you're wearing your amulet and I've been fairly close to you, the Tracker couldn't have recognized our powers. So he must have either been on the lookout for us or waiting for us."

Estrella pulls out the woman's phone. It's still unlocked. She taps on it and shows me a picture of Tristan, herself, and me on the bridge of the Emperor's castle.

"Looks like you're right," she says. "They had our photo, which means they were looking for us."

I frown. "I should've known they'd have photos of us, but it's not good."

"They're probably still sour about us evading them at the castle," she says.

I groan. "They likely sent in a report to their commanding officer before they got on the train."

"The call the guy made."

"We need to alter our looks. That should help. We have about two hours or less until we arrive in Tokyo."

"Do you think these two will sleep the rest of the trip?"

I make a face. "I don't know how potent her powers are. But let's get as far from them as possible just in case."

We work together to tie up our hunters with ripped strips of clothing. I smash their phones on the ground, stomping on them for good measure. No need for them to be able to get in contact with their sources. Next, we dig through the other sleeping passengers' bags and luggage.

Estrella finds a scarf to wrap around her head while I scour up a hat with a brim that hides my face.

"Once we arrive," I say, shrugging into a long brown coat, "we should split up. They will be expecting us to travel together."

"I don't want to split up." She slips a large flowered dress over her jacket and pants. Her boots stick out. Hopefully no one will be looking at her feet. "Besides, we work better as a team. You know this."

"True, but with that amulet, you are practically invisible to a Tracker. They'll just think you're a mortal."

She comes over to me and my heart scatters as she takes my hand. "We stick together. You've stood with me through everything. I'm not going to abandon you now."

I swallow and manage a nod. She has no idea how much those words mean to me. Every fiber inside me wants to drag her into my arms and hold her tight. Maybe someday. It's a dangerous hope and I'm unsure my heart can handle it. Especially after Ami told me about the Sabian fire. Does Estrella love Tristan? If she can actually channel the Sabian Numinous, will she join the Sabians? The Nazco sure haven't done themselves any favors to keep her on their side.

Once we've disguised ourselves as best we can, I slip some of the cash Ami gave me into each person's bag that we took clothing from.

"To replace the things we took," I explain to Estrella.

She studies me. "Everyone keeps telling me how awful the Nazco are. I've felt so guilty sometimes knowing I'm one of them. Except I watch you and you're nothing like the person these horrible Nazco should act like."

I shoot her a grin. "Not all of us are complete scumbags. At least not all the time."

Outside the windows, darkness has settled and only the pinprick lights of the towns indicate how fast we are zooming through the countryside. We duck out of our compartment and start moving toward the back of the train, giving ourselves distance between our attackers.

I know I should be worried about our safety, but all I really can think about as I lead her down the aisle is that she kissed me back there on the seat. Not the fake let's-pretend-we're-lovers kiss. The one after that. The one where she leaned closer and our lips met, breaking the barrier of time and lost memories. What does that mean?

Should I let myself hope?

I find us a set of empty seats in a fairly full cabin and we settle into them.

"I feel more at ease with so many mortals around," I note as we tuck our backpacks at our feet and she places the case with her sword in reach. "It's a deterrent in case other immortals try to attack."

"Yet they tried already," Estrella points out.

True. And worrisome. "The Emperor must really want us captured."

"Which means we need to be extra careful." She scoots closer to me, and my heart skips a beat. She smells of flowers and sunshine. "We have at least an hour until we get there. Tell me more about the Midnight Academy. Was it like Olympia High in Florida?"

I laugh. It's deep and full, and I realize it's the first time in too long that I've laughed like this. I've been so caught up in worry and fear that I haven't enjoyed this time with her. I lean back against my seat and dare take her hand. She doesn't pull away. My fingers trail a path along her palms and let a trickle of electricity flicker along the lines in her skin.

"According to you, your professors were very strict," I begin, "but you didn't mind it. You were driven, far more than any other student. Your favorite place to study was the library. When I visited you, we would sneak away to meet outside the dome in an ice cave where no one could see us together."

"Sneak away?"

"Dating isn't allowed until after you graduate from the academy." I roll my eyes. "Stupid rule if you ask me. Also, the Empress doesn't get along with my father and we knew people might see us as a threat if we were together."

"Like a power couple?"

I smirk. "We were pretty awesome together."

A flush of pink blushes across her cheeks and she looks away for a second. Then she asks, "What about my friends?"

"Your best friend was Lexi, but you were also close to Jamie. Tanix also hung out with you three. Nice guy, brilliant, but also a bit clueless sometimes."

"I wish I remembered him. Sometimes it feels like I lost so much." She pulls her hand away from mine. "And it's so frustrating."

"I know." I suck in a deep breath. "I feel the same way. I wish I could bring you back to the Midnight Kingdom and take you for strolls through the ice garden and wander the halls of the library like the old days."

But deep down, I know that as long as the Empress is in power, we'll never have those moments again.

Her eyes flicker with sympathy. "But it also makes me appreciate what I have right now. Thank you for everything you've done for me. I've been thinking a lot about why you wanted to keep me from this world of the immortals. Now I get it, but at the same time, I can't stop being who I am. It's like something inside of me is trying to break free and it won't stop until it does."

"You're a strong woman. I have no doubt that you will find yourself completely again."

"Maybe." She doesn't look convinced. "But that doesn't stop the fact that since then, I've gained so many more memories and experiences."

"You're talking about Tristan," I say tightly.

He's the last person I want to talk about and yet, the only person I need to talk about.

"We broke up." She looks down at her hands, but I don't miss the pain in her eyes so it's hard to be happy about their breakup, but secretly I am. "His people hate me. Well, you saw it first hand. I'm the last person they want their Prince having anything to do with."

"Well, I'm here for you and am going to finish what we've started."

"Thank you for that. I know I've been tough on you at first, but you've proven yourself. First with bringing me to Ami, then helping me enter the Ring of Eternity, and now here on the train. Maybe we can't have the relationship we once had, but we still make a great team."

"Of course." I squeeze her hand, but I can't mask the disappointment I'm feeling at those words. "I'll always be your friend and ally."

"Speaking of allies, when you have those phone calls with your father, it's about me, isn't it? He doesn't trust me."

I take in a long breath. "Actually, I think I've convinced him that you could be helpful to our cause in overthrowing the Empress."

"Me?" She laughs. "I'm hardly ready to overthrow the Empress, no matter how much I hate her. Right now, I can barely fight off two immortals. Besides, I need to get Lexi out of the Empress's hands before I even think about taking her down."

"Rescuing Lexi is going to be harder than you think. We're going to need help, and my father can do that."

"He's going to demand something from me, isn't he?"

"Maybe." I sigh, feeling tired. Tired of this maze of lies, manipulation, and deceit that my father is a master of. And maybe I am, too. "Probably."

"Right." She looks out the window into the darkness and I wonder if we can ever be truly honest with each other.

I lean my head back against the seat, trying to hold in my emotions sparking like a summer storm. Yet, the Empress's promise and our agreement fingers its way into my mind, a poisonous plant desperate to take root. I tell myself I'm a better person and I'd never actually follow through with the agreement, but...

I shake my head. Right now I must focus on surviving the next twenty-four hours.

29

PURSUIT AT THE PLATFORM
ESTRELLA

Tokyo, Japan

hen the train pulls into Tokyo Station, my stomach twists and my emotions are all out of whack. Between the attack on the train and kissing Dion, I'm feeling like everything is a little off-kilter. It was another reminder that I don't really know who I am or what I want.

Ami gave Dion the information he would need for our contact at Tokyo Station who would direct us to a Traveling Pool that's supposedly unguarded. Right now, I feel like we're sitting ducks, just waiting to be captured. I glance over at Dion. His jaw is tight with worry and I don't blame him. We are one step from walking into our enemy's clutches.

As we exit the train, we keep our heads down, trying to stay as inconspicuous as possible. This time we don't hold hands or even pretend we know each other. I tuck the scarf closer around my head to hide my blonde hair and take off into the throngs of people hurrying through the train station while Dion trails behind me. The buzz of people scurrying around to their next destination works well for us trying to reach our contact before being discovered.

But still, when I come to an intersection my feet slow and my eyes dart left and right. I search for signage, but none of the places make any sense to me. It takes all of my effort to not look at Dion to see if he knows if we should go left or right. Then he strolls past me, heading left toward the escalators. Of course, up would be the right direction! I've been letting my fears overrule my thinking. I need to keep my mind under control.

The escalator stretches at least four stories up, seeming to go on forever, and it's packed full of people. As I ride up, I quickly text Tristan.

Me: Arrived in Tokyo. Headed your way.

I stare at my screen, waiting for him to answer but he doesn't. It's strange that he hasn't responded to my last two texts. I bite my lip in worry. Could something have happened to him? Did he get captured, too? A text pops up.

Tristan: Great. Where are you?

My heart swoops. He's okay!

Me: Tokyo Station. About to leave.

Higher and higher the escalator rises, but it doesn't feel fast enough. It moves at a tortoise pace. A tingle of energy flickers through the air, and the hair on my arms rises. My eyes sweep around me. An immortal with strong powers is nearby.

My eyes land on the man, riding on the escalator going down. He's staring right at me, clutching the railing, and his body is tight like his muscles are preparing to spring. Almost as if—my heart dives—he's planning on climbing over the barrier and leaping across the wide open space to my side. If he were to miss, he'd fall like seventy feet.

Unless his power allows him to jump that distance.

My body tenses as his escalator inches him closer to me and mine to him.

He reaches into his pocket and pulls out a pair of silver handcuffs. They look exactly like the ones General Sage had me wear when I first arrived at the Sabian castle. They will nullify my powers. My pulse thrums against my skin. I wish I knew what his power is.

This man's visik shifts and churns. I swallow. His power must come from the element of air. Could he control the wind like Chandra? Or fly? Maybe even levitate. All are very bad for me.

One thing I do know. If he has those shackles, he was waiting for me.

Our eyes are locked on each other. We grow closer and closer. I'm trapped, lodged in between people in front of me and behind. I don't dare glance at Dion. It's clear this guy knows about me and is focused only on me.

We are nearly side by side now. He moves, his hands

pressing against the escalator's railing. He vaults his body over the side like he's an Olympic athlete. He practically flies across the empty space between the escalators.

My heart slams against my chest. I shove myself forward, pushing past the person in front of me.

Squeezing and pushing and begging people to move.

Faster. I need to move faster!

A glance over my shoulder warns me the guy landed on my escalator with the ease of a jaguar. He pushes aside the person in his way. Screaming fills my ears as people cry out with shock.

I propel myself forward. Adrenaline shoots through my veins. Dion is just up ahead, his eyes silver as if he's ready to launch a bolt of lightning at my pursuer. He nods to me and starts pushing ahead as well, creating a path for us. Finally, we tumble off the escalator but two other immortals are waiting for us at the top.

Dion shoots out a bolt of electricity. They cry out and fall to the ground, their bodies shaking from the impact.

"Come on!" Dion says, grabbing my hand and pulling me right.

We take off in a full sprint, dodging around people and shoving our way through the thick crowds.

A man at a small stand selling flyers and magazines holds up a pamphlet and calls in English, "Right this way for the best deal of the day!"

My ears perk up at the language switch. "That must be our contact," I tell Dion, pulling him left.

We rush to the cart. Dion holds out the yen that Ami gave him.

"We'll have two, please," Dion says, reciting the phrase Ami told us to tell our contact. "Because the road less traveled is the road to opportunity."

I pray this guy is who we think he is. His gaze darts nervously behind us, but he pulls a flyer from a drawer and hands it to me.

"Behind me," the guy says.

"Arigatō," I thank him and we hurry around the cart to find a long hallway.

We break into a sprint. We head down the hall, turn left, and then up another set of stairs, but when we reach the door at the end and Dion tries the handle, it's locked.

"It has a key code." Dion points to the panel on the side with numbers. "Does the pamphlet have the code?"

My hands shake as I flip open the pamphlet and scour the Japanese text. Then I find a number at the bottom. It's supposed to be a phone number, but it only has four digits.

"Try four, eight, one, three," I say.

Voices and the pound of footsteps echo through the corridor. As Dion punches in the numbers, I glance over my shoulder to find three men hurtling up the steps toward us.

"Hurry!" I exclaim. "They're almost here."

The door clicks and Dion throws it open, shoving me through it first. I stumble out as Dion follows, slamming the door shut behind us.

My senses are on overdrive as I take in my surroundings, orienting myself. We're outside on a busy street. Neon signs glow and blink against the darkness, illuminating the slick streets with a rainbow of light. People rush along the sidewalk as if hurrying back home from a long day at work. The air smells like exhaust and grilled meat. The sky is cloaked by the myriad of lights and buildings scraping the skyline.

"Where do we go now?" I ask, spinning in a circle.

"There." Dion points to the entrance of a temple across the street guarded by two stone dragons. "The Traveling Pool is located there."

30
REBEL, RUN, REPEAT
TRISTAN

Florida

"Listen, Tristan, or whatever your real name is," Mara tells me as we exit the classroom once the bell rings. "You seem like a nice guy. Or at least you're nice to look at, but I still don't trust you."

"Good," I say, but my real focus is scanning the room, searching for Wraiths or Nazco lurking around. I find none, which means they aren't concerned about Mara nor myself. The only immortal they're really concerned with is Estrella.

"Good?" Mara huffs. "That's all you've got to say?"

She moves to take off, but I call after her, "Wait. We should get out of here."

"Like right now?" She glances around the hub of students laughing and talking as they go to class. She steps closer to me. "Third period hasn't even started."

"Did Jamie come to school today? We need to grab her and get out of here ASAP." She crosses her arms, assessing me like she isn't going to budge. I press my last argument, "Unless you like this life. You can say goodbye, carry on with your classes, and continue to lose your mind and powers until there's nothing left of you except a shell. What about the other girls at Nadia's? The ones who were there before you? How are they doing right now?"

She glares at me. "You have such a way with words. Come on. Jamie is in English this period."

A paper airplane zooms past me and a student catches it with a cheer. A trio of guys huddle around a phone, laughing at a picture while another group dances to music. This life is so foreign to me. Even being here the few days that I have, it's still disorientating. But, I've got to say, there's a sense of sureness to it all. Will my life become like theirs if we Sabians can't get another Conduit and lose our immortality?

Mother said it will take about a year, but during that time, our visik powers will slowly die out without being refueled. And when that happens, our connection to immortality will, too. In time, I'll be no different than any of these students wandering the halls—a sobering thought.

Of course, the Nazco are in the same situation as we are. But the Empress purposely excommunicated her Conduit, so she must have some sort of plan up her sleeve.

"You stay here," Mara says once we reach the English classroom. "I'll go talk to her."

"Of course," I say and lean against the wall opposite the classroom.

I reach for my phone, but of course, it's not there. Blazes, that Chandra is a sneaky one. Now that I have no contact with Estrella, how am I supposed to tell her about the meeting location? There are a number of Traveling Pools in this area.

Mara exits the classroom with Jamie. While Mara's brow is bunched up like a knot, Jamie looks absolutely delighted.

"Are you really getting us out of Nadia's Home, Muscle Boy?" Jamie asks, clenching the straps of her backpack.

"That's the plan." I push off the wall. "Let's go before something else goes wrong."

When we arrive at the small house Katka rented for me when I first came to Florida to find Estrella, I pause at the doorstep. There's something different about the place since I left it this morning. I scan the area. Palms shift gently in the salty breeze, a few cars rumble past on the winding road, and there are no other cars in the sandy driveway except for the beat-up junker Katka rented for me.

"What's the matter?" Mara asks.

"Something feels off." I go to reach the door handle but still hesitate.

"Want me to go first?" Jamie asks. She's pulled out two butter knives, clenching them furiously in her hands.

I'm rarely impressed, but this Nazco cast-off is obviously fierce. Who runs around offering to go first into a potentially dangerous situation with merely butter knives? I wouldn't want to cross paths with her should she have her full powers.

"Remind me never to get on your bad side," I tell Jamie.

"Oh, Muscle Boy," she says, slyly, "that will never happen."

Inwardly, I chuckle. I pull out my knife from the strap hidden under my shirt and prepare myself for what lies on the other side. Before I move, the door flies open. I'm about to strike when I come face to face with a freckled girl with bright green eyes, and burgundy hair.

"Tristan!" Katka flies into my arms, hugging me like I've risen from the dead. "You're alive. Thank the Fates."

I hug her back, surprised at her outburst. It's like she's back to her old self again before she told me she loved me and I told her I wasn't in love with her.

"What are you doing here?" I ask as she finally pulls away. I don't miss how her hands linger on my body. The fact that she's left the castle, much less Sabian territory, means she's worried. Ever since her mother was killed by a Nazco when they were on vacation in Rome, she hasn't left the castle grounds. That was ten years ago.

"Where have you been?" she demands, her tone back to its usual stiffness. "Why haven't you been answering my calls and texts?"

"You've been texting me?" I groan and run a hand through my hair. "That's not good. Chandra stole my phone. I'm sure she's managed to open it. She's likely read all of our communications."

Katka stills as if calculating the ramifications of this. Katka might not have high powers like me, but she's brilliant when it comes to tech or analyzing situations. "I never sent you details about this place on that phone, did I?"

"No, it was on the phone I gave Estrella."

The mere mention of Estrella sends a cold hardness

across Katka's face. "I have Estrella's number. I'll text her and let her know your phone was compromised. We'll have to send her a new Traveling Pool location as well."

She whips out her phone and starts tapping on the screen. "We should get inside," she says, and turns back to head through the doorway, still texting.

"Estrella is coming here?" Mara asks. There's hope in her voice.

"That's the plan," I say. "Come on in. Katka is right. It's better to not be out in the open. This is Nazco territory, and they have plenty of assassins who would love to cash in on your capture."

Once we're all inside, I wave to the couch. "Feel free to sit down and relax," I tell the two Nazco girls. "Katka, this is Mara and Jamie. They are both Estrella's friends we're protecting."

"We're protecting more Nazco?" Katka looks up from her phone with annoyance. "You're not serious."

"They're not evil. They've been mistreated by the Nazco just as much as we have."

Katka presses her lips together but nods. "You're right. Were you both wiped of your memories and powers as well?"

"We have amnesia," Mara says. "So I'm guessing yes?"

"If you've been sent to Nadia's it means you once were very dangerous to the Empress," Katka says as she heads to the refrigerator and pulls out two bottles of water. She passes them to the girls. "Which makes me assume you likely had high powers or something valuable to the wicked witch of the snow."

"If we were so dangerous," Mara says, "why keep us alive?"

"You might have parents or friends in high places in the Nazco Kingdom who requested you not be killed, but given a mortal life," Katka says. "Or you're insurance to keep those who care about you in check. If they misbehave, you're killed for good. I don't know, but I'm sorry you've been treated like this."

"Thanks," Mara says, "I think."

Jamie is muttering under her breath and has already dismantled the lamp into what resembles a long dagger. She'll be just fine, I decide.

Katka turns back to me and nods to the study. "Can I talk to you privately?"

We step inside. "Leave the door open," I say. "I'm not letting these girls out of my sight until I know they are safe."

"What is the plan once you've rescued all of these girls from Nadia's?" Katka asks. "This could start a war. Have you thought about that?"

"I have." I take a deep breath. "But I can't just leave these girls to rot in that place. It's wrong. Also, you still haven't told me why you're here. You never leave the castle. So what gives?"

Her usual grass-green eyes soften. "I know I've been tough on you. Cruel even. But when you didn't respond...I...I couldn't lose you, too. My mother, Conrad, and then you. It was too much."

Tears fall and I feel like a jerk because I can't give her what she wants. I pull her into my arms, rubbing the back of her head. She clutches my shirt like she doesn't want to let me go. My heart aches as the memories resurface.

She was only ten when her mom was killed. When she got the news, she locked herself into her mom's tech lab and wouldn't come out. The only people she'd open the door for were Conrad and me. She refused to speak to her father, saying that he was to blame for what happened.

So I was the one who brought her food each day. I'd sit with her as she ate and we'd talk about nothing, and yet everything. Like how long we could hold our breath under water, what foods we secretly pretended to like and yet hated, and we found out we both had a secret obsession to visit a mortal's movie theater.

After a month, I finally coaxed her to leave the room. Conrad and I introduced her to horseback riding and picnics on the mountainside. We had become her family. But now, everything is different. Conrad and I grew up and moved on but Katka still hunkered down in the castle like if she didn't leave, it would keep things exactly the same.

Except she's here, which feels strange and weird.

"Don't worry, I'm not dying anytime soon," I tell her even though I know it's something I can't promise. "I still have vengeance to pay for my sister and your mother. Somehow I know that rescuing these girls will make the Empress suffer. I know you hate Estrella, but we need her to get our powers renewed."

Katka finally pulls away, sniffing. "I don't hate Estrella. I hate that I actually like her and that you like her. And well, that she might..." Her voice drifts away, but I know she means that Estrella will replace her. "Anyway, I'm willing to put up with all of this as long as you stay safe. Of course, I'm not opposed to making the Empress pay."

"Oh, she's going to pay. And if I have my way, she will be dethroned."

"You think that's possible?" Katka asks in shock.

"Estrella can make it possible. She's the key to everything. And I think the Empress knows this."

"That is a bold statement."

"I never say things I don't mean."

31
A STOLEN KISS
ESTRELLA

Tokyo, Japan

The sounds of the city fade away like a breath on a cold night as Dion and I walk through the temple grounds. The attendant warned us the grounds were closing within the hour. We didn't bother to tell him we had another exit in mind. The path curls around the gardens and then juts through thick bamboo, spearing up into the blurred city-lit sky. I keep glancing over my shoulder, expecting pursuers, but we are alone here.

The path opens into a small garden area centered around a pool. The water glimmers, and I'm not sure if it's from the reflection of the clouds above or because of the magical Water Channels. Dion hurries us to the water's edge as if it's just normal to jump into random pools and travel the world in a blink of magic, but my feet halt at the shoreline. My heart patters at the thought of traveling this way again.

"What is it?" Dion asks, turning and wading back to me.

"After being chased and attacked, I should be an expert on overcoming scary things, but the Water Channels still frighten me."

"If it makes you feel any better," he takes my hand, "you never liked the Water Channels."

A spark flutters through me as he steps closer. The wind catches his scent and wraps it around me, spicy and decadently rich. Our bodies are nearly touching. I need to step away because being this close to him is confusing and complicated.

"I just need a moment before I experience another terrifying thing," I try to explain.

His finger traces the contours of my face like the brush of a feather. Heat blooms where his skin touches mine as if he's shooting electricity through me. A memory startles me. The two of us are standing beneath an arch of ice, snow swirling around us in a dusty storm. His lips are on mine, shocking me with his power.

Now, I look up into his face, at his lips, wondering if I should kiss him again—if that would pull that memory closer. So I lift up on my toes and brush my lips across his. He doesn't move away, but instead, tugs my body toward him so my chest is pressed against his. The kiss deepens, electrifying and startling with its shimmering essence that races through me like a summer night's storm.

My chest rises and falls as his kisses trail along my neck. I could get lost in his touch if I let myself.

"Estrella," his voice begs, "you're all I want."

But is he what I want? Or am I just chasing memories like sand sifting through my fingers?

A voice in the back of my mind warns me to stop. That it's Tristan I care about.

Yet another part urges me to explore our connection and discover if this kiss could awaken memories of my past. I'm a lost star, spinning through a universe of darkness, searching for my place and the one I love.

My skin prickles and then a sharp pain surges through my head. I push away, crying out, pressing fingers to my temples to stop the agony.

"Estrella." Dion's voice is thick with fear. "Are you okay? Please tell me I didn't hurt you. Take a deep breath. Stay calm."

The sudden pain makes my stomach queasy and I take deep breaths. The headache quickly subsides, except now I start shaking. Dion rubs my arms.

"Whatever implant the Empress put in you must be linked to your past memories," he says.

"That's what Tristan warned me about," I say. "I shouldn't have kissed you, but I had a memory of us in some sort of ice place and wanted to see if kissing you in real life was the same."

"Was it?" His lips twitch as if he's teasing me.

"Yes." I shoot him a wry smile. "It was exactly how I remembered."

"I'm glad. Kissing you is always perfect for me. And that place you were remembering? It was the ice cave I was talking to you about where we'd meet in secret."

"That makes sense." I stare down at my boots, guilt threading through me. I look back up at him, knowing I need to be one hundred percent honest. "But still, I shouldn't have taken advantage of that moment and kissed you. It's not fair to you. I don't know what I want because I still don't know who I am."

His jaw tightens, and a flicker of frustration and sadness flashes through his eyes. "This is the Empress's fault, not either of ours. I'm trying to be patient, but I'm also not going to say it hasn't been hard for me."

"And that's why I feel so awful. Sometimes I feel like our connection is so natural, like we understand each other. Fighting beside you on the train, talking to you, and even kissing you. But then other times, it's like you are still in love with the old me, waiting for that girl to be resurrected."

"And the new you has fallen for Tristan?" His words are tight as a tripwire.

"Maybe." The truth, but my heart is scared to fall for Tristan, which is why I broke up with him. It could leave me heartbroken and alone all over again. His people hate me, and the fact that he's to be their next ruler only makes our relationship even more impossible.

"But you've fallen for him?" My heart sags.

"I don't have the luxury to fall for anyone. The only thing that matters right now is getting my friends and powers back. Which is why kissing you was a selfish move on my part."

"Never say that. You've never done a selfish act from the moment I met you. Listen, you can kiss me anytime you need. It will be a tough job, helping you recover your memories, but I'm ready for it."

His tone has switched to be lighter and almost teasing. My body relaxes.

"You sure?"

His mouth twists into a smile, vanquishing the pain that was in his eyes. "When they took you away, I thought I'd lost my whole world. Then when I got to be with you in Florida, it was like a part of my world had been handed back to me. I don't know what our future looks like or even if we have a future, but let's see where it goes."

I nod, the tenseness in my chest relaxing. "Okay, let's do this Traveling Pool."

She takes off the flower dress from the train and sets it on a rock. We wade out into the chilly water. Bubbles begin to pop up around us, and that iridescent glow I spotted earlier grows brighter. It swirls around us, faster and faster, matching the beat of my heart.

In moments, it will rip me beneath the surface and drag me through a terrifying wormhole. But the need to get to my friends and help them roots me to the spot. I grab ahold of Dion's hand and step into the pool, letting its waters churn around us.

The bottom drops out and we plummet into the starry abyss. My scream is stolen by the roar of the channel.

32
ANSWER LIKE YOUR LIFE DEPENDS ON IT
LEXI

The Midnight Kingdom, Antarctica

I pace my cell, a true caged animal. My thoughts are a torrent of fear, anger, and panic. What are they doing with Conrad? Are they torturing him or just extracting information from him like they did to me with the Truth Seeker?

Conrad had tried to get me to leave Nadia's and escape with him. At the time, it seemed risky to leave everything behind: my friends, the only place I ever remember as being a home, and school. I had no money, no job experience, and without a high school education, it would make my job search harder.

Except now I realize he'd been right. None of that mattered in the world of these immortals. They follow their own set of rules and they're nothing like the ones I'm used to.

"Ugh!" I cry out, clenching my fist. "This is so messed up."

My voice echoes across the icy walls like it's laughing at my stupidity. A clang and the sound of voices jerk my attention back to the hallway. Hope sends my heart clattering inside my chest. Are they bringing Conrad back? Is he still alive? The Empress had said he might not be useful anymore.

The guards round the corner, dragging Conrad with them. Even in the pale-blue light, it's clear Conrad is injured. Blood cakes the side of his face, matting his beautiful brown hair flat against his skull. His left eye is now almost completely swollen shut. I cringe at how his right leg drags behind him like it's been broken.

These guards aren't the same ones that took us to the Empress. They look younger and less sure of themselves. One of them even looks like he could be in high school. Maybe I can manipulate them into doing what I want.

"What did you do to him?" I demand. "Are you barbarians? He's bleeding and hurt. You're just going to leave him like that? Put him in my cell. It's the least you can do so I can take care of him."

The darker-skinned guard with hair that sticks up like a porcupine looks hard at me, his face twisting strangely. "Lexi?" he asks. "Is that you?"

"Of course, it's me," I snap, but then understanding floods me. That look on his face. It's like he recognizes me. I have no clue who this idiot is other than I hate how he's treating Conrad, but I need to use this to my advantage. "Wait, do I know you?"

"Yeah." Confusion swims through his eyes. "I thought you were dead. We all did. What are you doing here? Are you with this Sabian?"

"We were friends, weren't we?" I press, choosing not to answer his question.

"I mean, yeah. Except for that time when you lit my hair on fire."

"I did that?" Wow. Right now, I can only manage to flicker a few sparks from my fingers if I'm really concentrating hard. And that's after Conrad started coaching me.

"Tanix, you know we're not supposed to talk to the prisoners," the other guard says, shooting me a wary look as he unlocks Conrad's cell.

"I'm sorry about that, Tanix," I say, using his name. I wipe the snarl from my face and smile. "Would you please put him in my cell? He helped me when a Wraith stabbed me and I nearly died. The least I can do is to take care of him."

"You were stabbed by a Wraith?" Tanix's eyes pop open. "That's rough."

"It was." Oh my gosh. This dude is killing me. "For our old friendship, could you put him in my cell then?"

"I suppose we could," he says and looks to his buddy, who rolls his eyes. "We're supposed to come back soon and take you out for transport. But this is only because you were once one of my closest friends. No more favors, got it?"

"You're the best." I flash him a smile.

They unlock my cell and the one guy tosses Conrad

inside with me. I dive for him, breaking his fall to the ground.

The cell bangs shut as the one guard mutters under his breath about crushes.

"Take care of yourself, Lexi," Tanix says. "And um...it's good to see you again. I'm glad you're still alive."

"It's great seeing you, too," I lie.

"Before I go," Tanix says, "let me get you some cleaner water."

He runs off and returns shortly with two clear bottles of water. I take them.

"Thank you," I say. "That's really kind of you."

I wait until both guards are gone before I focus back on Conrad.

"Here." I open one of the bottles for him, and he takes a sip. Then I drink from the other. The cool, fresh water soothes my dry mouth. "That tastes much better than that sludge they gave us in the bucket. Can you walk to the cot?"

"Those guys are your friends?" he asks, giving me a lifted-eyebrow look.

"I've no idea who they are," I say. "But let me tell you, they aren't my friends anymore. Friends don't lock friends in prison. At least we got some fresh water from it all."

"Don't be so hard on them. They're just trying to stay alive like the rest of us. You saw the Empress in action. She's not one to mess with."

"This is true." I help him stand. His weight leans on me and nearly knocks me over. "Watch it there, buddy. Those muscles of yours are heavier than you think."

He shoots me a lopsided grin and then hobbles over to

the thin cot, rolling onto it with a grunt of pain. I rip off a portion of my shirt and douse it in the bucket of water.

"How are you doing?" I ask, wiping the blood from his face. "I was so worried you wouldn't come back."

"I heal fast. But they got too much information from me. I tried to keep it from them, but their Truth Seeker was too good at his job."

"Who cares? You're alive and that's what matters."

Losing him scares me more than I'd like to admit. To see a guy as big and powerful as him bruised and injured like this tells me that we are way over our heads.

"The Empress is cunning," he says, reaching for my hand. "The fact that we're both still alive means she has a purpose for us. I think they're going to use us to trap our friends."

"All I can think about right now is that you're here with me. I took that for granted before."

Weariness curls through my body. I crawl up beside him on the cot. His eyes are already closed. He looks so peaceful. I've wanted to kiss him so many times before but it never felt right. Now, knowing that this might be our last moment, it feels like we were always meant to be.

I lean over and press my lips to his. His eyes pop open, staring at me. I pull back. Maybe that was too forward of me. But then he pulls me to him and kisses me again, this time with a gentle firmness like he wants it too.

He takes up most of the space on the cot, but I don't care. I lay beside him and he doesn't complain. He wraps an arm around me, holding me close. I press my cheek on his chest and listen to his heartbeat. It steadies my fears.

My eyes drift closed, and I fall into a dreamless sleep.

I wake up to darkness. The air is thick and warm, smelling of salt and sea. Confusion swirls through me. Where am I?

I reach for Conrad, but he's not here.

Now I'm panicking. Did they take him? Is he being tortured again?

Except the mattress beneath me isn't the hard cot, but an actual bed. My eyes adjust to the semi-darkness. There's something familiar about this place. I spy the outline of a lampshade and fumble to turn on the light.

I take in the worn patched blanket, the faded floors, the window overlooking the ocean, and pieces of costumes strewn across the desk.

This is my room at Nadia's Home for Girls. Slowly, I rise out of my bed, looking around me for clues of how I got here. The last thing I remembered was sleeping next to Conrad.

Had that all been a terrible nightmare or had it been real?

33
FRIENDS AS CLOSE AS FAMILY

ESTRELLA

Florida

I cling to Dion as we rise up out of the water. His firm arms wrap around me like cords, keeping me from getting lost in the endless twisting Water Channels. The sky above is periwinkle blue, and thick palms and oaks surround the pond that we rose out of. I let go of Dion and swim until my feet hit the sandy bottom of the pond. Lily pads float in the water and the air here is thick with humidity and sea salt.

"It's a little shocking going from Tokyo to this place," I note, shoving my wet hair from my face. "Watch out for gators. That's one of the things Lexi warned me of—that every water source in Florida has them."

"Noted," Dion says, sloshing along beside me. "I think

I'll take a gator any day over our enemies. You sure you trust this Sabian woman?"

"Katka? She hates my guts and trusts me less than I trust her. But she's in love with Tristan, and if he asks something of her, she'll do it."

"In love with Tristan, huh?" He chuckles as he helps me through the tall weeds of the shoreline. "Does she know about Tristan and you?"

"Yes, but she's probably thrilled that Tristan and I broke up."

"Sounds like this Katka and I have a lot in common."

The sound of a car engine cuts through the quiet chirping of birds and shifting breeze. Instantly, Dion readies his body, moving to stand in front of me, hands out. Meanwhile, I pull out my dagger. It shimmers sea blue as if ready to strike fear into my enemies' heart.

The car zooms into view, spinning to a stop and spewing dirt in its wake. Tristan pops out from one side and strides toward us, his blond curls blowing in the wind. I'm surprised to see Katka emerging from the other side. But then, considering how much she cares about Tristan, maybe I shouldn't be. She's holding a long stick, and there's a wary look in her eyes as she leans against the car.

"Tristan!" I lower my weapon and hurry to meet him. "Thank you for coming."

"You made it," Tristan says. "I'm glad you got Katka's text."

As we meet up in the center of the field, awkwardness hovers in the air. A part of me wants to run and fly into Tristan's arms and feel his heat warming me all the way to my heart, but I keep myself firmly in check, remaining at Dion's side. Tristan's sky-blue eyes flicker between Dion and myself, suspicion darkening them. Can he tell we kissed? Would he be upset? Guilt is a tug-of-war—my old and new self playing a dangerous game.

Tristan seemed to understand that we needed to break up back in Japan, but his eyes now look at me intensely as if he wants to drag me into his arms and never let me go.

I turn my attention to Katka and wave at her, smiling. She doesn't move, but her frown deepens.

"I'm surprised Katka is here," I say.

"That makes two of us, but she has offered to help and we can't afford to say no," Tristan says. He clears his throat as if he too can feel the awkwardness. "Did you have any issues?"

"We were attacked on the train," I say. "But we managed to survive. The biggest issue is they had a picture of the three of us when we were in the Emperor's fortress. They were looking for us specifically."

"That's not good." Tristan rubs his square jaw. "Right now we have other issues to deal with. Come on. We should get you both away from this Traveling Pool to somewhere safer. Hopefully, Chandra is waiting at the wrong location and not expecting us here."

The three of us head back to the car. Dion and I pile into the back. The air is tense and sharp as a dagger's tip.

"Thank you for texting me," I tell Katka, who still hasn't acknowledged my presence. "If you hadn't, we'd have been captured by the Nazco."

"I did it for our people, not you," she says.

I stiffen. *Yikes.* This girl really does hate me. But she knows the truth of my ability to touch Sabian fire, something no one else knows. This is the real reason she's here, not because she wants to be kind or nice.

Tristan shoots me a sympathetic look through the rear-view mirror as he starts up the car.

"I heard Chandra stole your phone," Dion says, cutting through the strained silence. "That girl is more dangerous than she looks."

"No kidding," Tristan says. "She's been a thorn in my side."

"Dion used to date her," I can't resist saying with a smirk. "At least that's what she told me."

Dion huffs. "It was before we met and before I knew what a horrible person she was."

Tristan pulls the car off the dirt road and turns onto a smooth paved highway, cranking up the speed. It reminds me of when it was just the two of us on the run from the assassins, speeding away to a whole new life. So much has changed since then.

"I've got a fun treat for you," Tristan tells me.

"A treat?" I laugh. "As long as it's not your version of mint chocolate chip ice cream."

He chuckles. "Don't remind me."

"What's wrong with mint chocolate chip?" Katka asks, glancing over her shoulder to study me, forehead wrinkling.

"It's a long story," I say, not wanting to get into how it felt like our first date until I nearly died. Katka's eyes harden and her head snaps back to face the front of the car.

"Perhaps you two should keep your inside stories to yourself for now," Katka says.

Dion shifts uneasily beside me. "I wouldn't be opposed to that."

I grimace, realizing I just made everything even more awkward. Tristan's eyes meet mine in the rear-view mirror once again. They are soft and understanding.

"You're about to see a few of your friends at the safe house," Tristan says.

"Seriously? That's incredible. Thank you." My heart skips happily as Tristan fills me in on what's been happening at school and with the girls.

Dion's phone pings. He pulls it out of his waterproof jacket and looks at the text.

"Everything okay?" I ask.

"It's BJ," Dion says. "He wants to meet us. He has the latest plans for the removal of the girls from Nadia's. Katka, can you send me the location of where we're going?"

Katka looks to Tristan. "Do you trust this guy?" She nods to Dion.

"Not really, but right now we all want the same things, so maybe?"

"Why can't you just give me a yes or no?" she asks. "Why does everything have to be vague?"

Okay, I get the feeling there's more to that conversation than I'm aware of. Tristan sighs and then says, "Yes, but don't make me regret those words, Cabral."

"What's your number, Nazco?" Katka ask.

As the two make the arrangements, my nerves and excitement intensify to the point where it's hard to sit still. In just a few minutes, I'm going to see my friends again. I just hope they don't resent me for leaving them. If only I had been able to get back here before they took Lexi. It still kills me that she's imprisoned.

Soon, Tristan pulls up to a tiny cottage tucked away

beneath large oaks and surrounded by palms. I climb out of the car just as two girls exit the house.

My heart stops.

It's Jamie and Mara. Jamie's short blonde hair still sticks up and her light skin looks even paler under the bright Florida sun. She's clenching sharp knives in both hands, but when she spies me, she slips them into her belt and runs to me. I race to meet her, throwing my arms around her thin frame.

"Estrella," she says. "It's you."

"I came back. Just like I said I would."

I squeeze her tight even though the moment her arms wrap around me, a fierce pain stabs my forehead. It must be coming from whatever the Empress did to my mind. I must be trying to connect with a memory from the past. When I break free, Mara walks hesitantly toward me. Her dark hair sways at chin-level and her dark eyes assess me warily.

"You look different," she says.

"Different good or different bad?" I ask.

"Different good. I'm glad you're here."

"Me too." I take her hand and squeeze it tight, infusing some of my visik power into her. Her power is hidden deep away and I can't quite figure out what it is, but regardless, now she's got more of it. I hope it helps her.

She sucks in a breath and yanks her hand from me, staring at her palm. "What did you just do?"

"Just a little gift," I say cryptically. I don't think they are quite ready for all of the new information I now know, but someday we'll get there. "I can't wait to hear everything that's happened at Nadia's."

We all head inside and settle around the tiny living

room. Katka orders pizza and drinks as Mara tells us how awful life has been and Jamie shows me her latest knife tricks. When the food arrives, I devour its hot, cheesy deliciousness, realizing how little I've eaten in the last day. The scent of sauce and warm bread fills the air and a bond begins to form between us as we talk. After I tell them a very vague version of what I've been up to, Katka starts sharing her ideas of how we're going to intercept the transport as the girls are being taken to the new location.

I look around at our small group and my heart tightens. My parents might have been killed and I might have nothing to my name, but these people have become the ones I care about. Somehow, they've become like family, even cranky Katka.

Will our strength and plans be enough to break through Nadia's defenses? I'm not sure, but whatever happens, I know I'll do anything to get my friends out of there and to safety.

34
GATHERING AN UNLIKELY TEAM
DION

Florida

My nerves are coiled tense, ready to strike. Sitting here eating pizza and drinking Coke with this group is a nightmare. Never in my wildest dreams did I think that I'd be working with the Sabians to free our own Nazco prisoners, but here we are. The worst part is watching Tristan looking at Estrella as if he wants to swoop her in his arms and kiss her.

I've already come up with twenty reasons why I should decapitate the prince, but I don't think Estrella would approve. She said they broke up, but I get the impression that it wasn't a mutual decision. Or maybe it wasn't their decision but a forced one.

I set my greasy slice of pizza on the plate and excuse

myself, escaping into the next room. It's a study with tall shelves full of beach-themed knick knacks, plump-cushioned chairs covered with shell designs, and a smooth white desk. I decide to call my father and give him an update. It's a call I've been avoiding.

I'm surprised he answers on the second ring. In the past, he usually lets it go to voicemail and I leave a message—his way to show me how unimpressed he is with me.

"About time you checked in," Father snaps. "Where've you been? Why haven't you checked in?"

"I've been busy training Estrella," I say, moving the focus off myself.

"Do you think she's a viable Conduit for us?"

"She can't wield the Numinous Flame right now, but if she were to get her full powers back, yes." If she doesn't decide to join the Sabians instead.

"So we're back to you finding the location of the temple and hoping it has the Fate's elixir."

I don't like his use of pronouns. Like he's in charge and overseeing this operation.

"Everything is progressing as planned." I move to the window and lean against its frame, debating how much information I'm going to give to my father. All my life I've tried to live up to his expectations. Now I have a chance to hand him ultimate power on a silver platter if we can find the temple that holds the elixir. Yet, a niggling fear holds me back. Do I want him to have that amount of power?

The bigger issue though is what he would think about Estrella's ability to wield the Sabian Numinous Flame. I'm not sure how he will react to that, which concerns me.

"And..."

"We have a lead on the temple," I begin, "but Estrella won't go until she rescues her friends from Nadia's Removal Facility."

"You aren't seriously going to try a rescue mission, are you? That's madness."

"Madness or not, we're about to extract them. Just making the final preparations."

"You don't know what you're getting yourself into. The Empress will retaliate."

I stare out at the shifting palm fronds that sway over the pool in the backyard and take a deep breath to hold back the fear and worry clawing inside of me. "Once we extract the girls, is there any place we can take them?"

"You're calling me asking for protection?" He laughs darkly. "Son, you can either do things your way or my way. I'm telling you to forget about those girls and focus on getting to the temple before the Empress gets wind of what you're up to. Those girls were sent there for a reason. They're bad seeds. They have been punished for unforgivable crimes, and bringing them out of that situation is only going to make things more difficult for you. I've done my own research on the girls at that facility. They're all dangerous. Compile that with severely lost memories and you've got a bunch of walking time bombs ready to explode."

I hate that he's right. Helping these girls isn't going to help us get free from the Empress's reign. Except this is explicitly what Estrella asked me to do.

"These girls are important to Estrella."

"It's always about Estrella, isn't it? You need to get over your obsession because with her it's never about the right or smart choice. She's holding you back from your full potential."

"Really? Because if I'm remembering correctly, she's the one who found the information about the temple."

"Can these mindless girls even take care of themselves?"

Anger rises up inside of me. "Don't talk about them like that. They are just as much Nazco as you and I. A simple turn of events and they could be us, victims of the Empress's wrath."

"Sounds like these girls are your problem," he says. "Call me when you've found the Temple of Fates location. Then we can start real work on destroying the Empress's reign."

The line goes dead. Someone clears their throat. It's Estrella at the doorway. I startle. I suppose I'd been so engrossed—and angered—by my conversation with my father that I hadn't been paying attention to make sure no one came in.

"I saw you leave," she says. "You looked upset so I followed. Was that your dad?"

How much did she overhear? By the look of shock on her face, a lot. I grimace. "You heard?"

"He gets loud when he's mad."

"My father is a tough man."

"I appreciate you fighting for my friends and trying to rescue them," she says, perching on a chair's edges. "But we never discussed you giving him the location of the temple."

"It was the only way for him to arrange a meeting with Ami," I try to explain. "I didn't have the connection on my own."

She nods, but doesn't look at me. "Any other secrets you want to tell me about?"

"What about you?" I push back, feeling guilt, anger, and frustration building up inside of me. "Are you keeping information from me?"

We're interrupted when BJ bursts through the doorway. His dark hair is still wet, so he must have just arrived from a Traveling Pool. Upon seeing me, his face lights up.

"You're alive." He holds out his hand and we shake. "With Chandra as lead on this operation, I wasn't sure if she was finally going to kill you this time."

"She's the lead, huh?" Interesting. She's moved up in ranks quickly. "Thanks for coming and helping out."

"I've got you, man," he says and then nods to Estrella. "Good to see you again. It's been a while."

"Estrella," I wave to BJ, "this is Barden Jasper, my closest and most trusted friend."

"You can call me BJ for short." He jams his hands in his pockets. "I'd shake your hand too, but...you know."

"I'm a Channeler, I get it." She smiles at him. "I think I remember you. You look familiar."

"Really?" His thick, dark eyebrows rise. "That's good, right?"

"I'd like to think so," she says.

"I just got off the phone with my father," I say, wanting to get us back on track. "As much as I hate to admit it, he had some viable points. After we extract your friends from Nadia's, not only will we need to prepare for the Empress's wrath, but we've got to find a place to take them afterward. My father won't help."

"BJ, did you find anything?" Estrella asks hopefully.

"I want you both to appreciate how awesome I am," BJ

says with a grin as he settles into the other armchair. "I found a place."

"Really?" Estrella clasps her hands. "That's fantastic!"

"I wouldn't go that far," BJ says, holding up a hand. "How capable are your friends at adjusting to new places and languages?"

"Not great." She bites her lips, enthusiasm waning. "Where is this place?"

"Madagascar."

"Madagascar?" both Estrella and I exclaim at once.

"It's just on the outskirts of the jungle," he continues. "Very remote, but there's a Traveling Pool right by the village. I secured a small house for us to use."

"That's not going to work," Estrella says. "They won't last a week in that situation."

"Then you better have another option quick," BJ says, "because according to my source, they're transferring the girls tonight at 8 p.m. There will be at least two Wraiths and four guards."

"Do we know anything about the guards' powers?" she asks.

"No, but I imagine the Empress is going to send ones with high powers," he says with a shrug.

"Only Tristan and I are the ones with fighting abilities," I point out as I calculate our odds. "That leaves us outnumbered."

"What am I? Chopped liver?" BJ scrunches up his face, pretending to be offended.

"I've got other plans for you," I say. His powers are getting information and acquiring resources. He's not a fighter and there's no way I'm making him face a Wraith. "I'm putting you in charge of overseeing the operation."

"Now we're talking!" He beams and rises to give me a high-five.

"But we still don't have a place for the girls once we rescue them," Estrella says. "The jungle isn't going to work."

"It's going to have to," I say. "It's our only option unless you want them to stay where they are."

"It's not ideal," BJ agrees sympathetically, "but it will be better than where they're at now."

"You're right, and I do appreciate all that you've done to prepare a place for them." Estrella lets out a long breath as she looks at the time on her phone. "We have two hours to prepare, so we better get to it."

We head back out into the main room. Tristan and Katka are standing off to the side, whispering. I frown, still not trusting either of them. Tonight would be the perfect opportunity for them to set us up to be taken by the Nazco guards while they slip away secretly with Estrella. I wouldn't put it past them. Tristan's eyes cut to mine as I cross the room to the kitchen table, and I spy the same distrust in his eyes.

I guess we both have something in common then.

"BJ will be overseeing tonight's rescue operation as commander," I announce, clearing plates and pizza boxes off the table. "From now on, he's in charge and we follow his orders if we want to all survive the night."

BJ hurries to my side and starts unloading his waterproof travel bag, taking out paper, notes, and a computer. Mara, Jamie, and Estrella circle the table, watching with interest.

"Why is he in charge?" Tristan questions. "Katka is our top operations expert back in my kingdom."

"Because he knows the facility and the Nazco better than either of you do," I say, biting back a snarky comment.

"If you want my help," Tristan says and comes to the other side of the table, placing his hands on the top, eyes boring into mine. "Katka will be co-commander of this mission."

My jaw clenches and I assess the group. Estrella's eyes flicker between the two of us, but she keeps her lips sealed. She can amplify our powers but has no powers of her own to fight other than the martial arts Ami taught her. Mara and Jamie are helpless. Which means that if this is going to work, I need Tristan.

And he knows it.

Blistering stars, this guy is really getting on my nerves.

"Fine," I finally acquiesce. "The two of you can be co-commanders. Just try to not get us killed, will you?"

"I want them to stay alive just as much as you do," Katka says, eyeing me warily as she joins us at the table. "Tell me what you have planned, BJ, and then I'll add my thoughts. We don't have time for childish squabbles."

"Excellent." BJ rubs his hands together excitedly, looking around the group. "For this to work, you all must each play your part. Now listen carefully."

35
IT REEKS OF SUSPICION
LEXI

Florida

How did I get in my room at Nadia's? I'm so confused. My legs wobble like I haven't walked in a million years. My side aches like someone punched me. I pull up my shirt to see a bruise blooming across my skin. Memories of being dragged and hauled through the Midnight Kingdom shudder through me.

I push my shirt down and shove those thoughts away. Instead, I move around, touching my desk, running my fingers over my school books, staring at my clothes piled haphazardly on my chair.

I'm like a ghost, standing in a room that's mine, and yet, knowing full well I shouldn't be here. I should be in that cold, stinking prison clinging to Conrad as he fights for each breath he takes.

The room is exactly how I left it when I went to school the morning those strange immortals kidnapped us. A Mountain Dew can sits on my desk by my books. My jacket is slung over the edge of my chair. The once-soaked socks I tossed aside after stepping a the mud puddle lay on top of my play script.

"This is so weird," I mutter.

Was everything that happened before just an obnoxious dream? And now I'm awake, back to reality? My hand rubs my side, a reminder that no, it all really did happen to me. A crawling fear swims through my stomach. I need to get out of here. Away from this place. I shove on my shoes and reach for the door handle.

I half expect it to be locked, but it turns easily. The hallway is empty so I pad down the stairs, my muscles tight, ready to run. Sparks of fire sputter from my fingertips. That only happens when I'm really nervous or worried. Quickly, I fist my hands to keep my fire in check. As tempting as it is, this is not the time to burn down the building.

When I reach the main floor, music pounds from the piano in the living room and then there's silence. The downstairs hallway is also empty. I eye the exit at the end of the hall. Can I just leave without anyone stopping me? My feet hurry down the hall. The doorknob bites cold against my skin as I open the front door.

Warm sea breeze washes over my face and the chimes that dangle from the porch's ceiling ting and clang. I'm about to step out into the twilight when I see them.

The Wraiths, shifting around the driveway like demons ready to strike at my soul.

A shiver curdles down my back.

BANG!

I jump in place and quickly shut the door, pressing my back to it as if that would keep the monsters outside.

BANG!

Relief washes over me. The sound isn't from the Wraiths. It's from Min. She does this thing where she'll just sit at the piano for a long time and then smash her hands on it. I can't get upset at her about it, though. I'm sure it's just her way of venting her frustrations at her messed-up brain.

We all have our problems.

"Lexi!" Cook calls to me and bustles down the hallway, wearing her apron. "Don't tell me you're leaving. It's time for dinner."

BANG!

My body startles at the sound, so sudden and unexpected. Cook's attention whips to Min at the piano and she hurries to her. "Min, practice hours are over. Time for dinner."

Cook helps Min stand up. The colored crystals hanging from the chandeliers in the living room catch the fading light, refracting like a prism and making the room and even Cook and Min seem otherworldly. I blink, shaking my head. I'm starting to lose it as much as the other girls here.

Cook herds Min and me to the dining room. Nadia is already settled at the head of the table, but the empty chairs sour my stomach. Especially Estrella's. I sit in my chair, unable to stare at her vacant one. Was it a dream that I told the Empress where Estrella was? Or had that been real? Gosh, I hope she's okay and staying far away from this place.

"How are you feeling, Lexi?" Nadia asks, pulling my

attention to her at the other end of the table. Nadia picks up a bowl of mashed potatoes and plops a spoonful on her plate before passing it to Flora. "We were so worried about you."

My eyes narrow on her. The wicked witch knows something, but how much? I decide to use the tactic less is more. "Really? Why?"

"You've been so sick," Nadia says, shaking her head with worry. "You've been in bed with a fever for a whole day now."

Man, this lady really knows how to act. She picked the wrong profession.

"A whole day," Izzy repeats as she starts loading her plate with corn. "A whole day."

Izzy keeps repeating the phrase and that's when I realize Mara isn't at the table because she always knows how to get Izzy to stop.

"Where's Mara?" I ask, looking around. "And Jamie?"

Nadia sighs. "We have no idea. They didn't come home from school today. It's very concerning. I do hope they didn't get lost or hurt."

"Lost, lost, lost," Zayla says happily while Izzy passes me a now empty bowl.

Guess I won't be eating corn tonight. But that's not important. The fact that both Mara and Jamie aren't here is ringing every warning bell in my head. They're the only ones in this room who have been going to school, which means one of two things.

They escaped.

Or they were kidnapped.

My stomach sinks and I nearly drop the empty bowl.

"You haven't heard from them, have you?" Nadia asks, eyeing me carefully.

I glower at her. "Apparently I've been sick with a fever. How could I know?"

"Of course." Nadia smiles sweetly at me. "You poor thing."

Something is off. Not that it hasn't always been off here, but something about the place stinks of suspicion. Just a few months ago, this table was practically full. But now that Tiffany, Estrella, Mara, and Jamie are gone, it feels almost empty with only eight of us remaining. In the past, new girls have replaced those who left, but that obviously hasn't been happening.

"I could go to school and look for them," Sally pipes up, flashing us with a smile. "I've always wanted to go to school. Plus, I've always wanted to be a detective just like the guy on TV."

"You're not going to school," Nadia says firmly.

"Not going to school," Izzy sings. "Not going to school."

Instantly, Sally starts wailing. I groan. *Fabulous.* Once Sally starts her crying fits, it doesn't stop until the orderlies come and give her an injection.

"The reason," Nadia says loud enough to be heard over the wailing, "is because we're all going on a trip!"

Sally shuts her mouth. Zayla switches her empty plate for Sally's full one when Sally isn't looking. She winks at me when she sees I've noticed.

"A trip?" I ask, my curiosity piqued. "What kind of trip?"

"We're going to the mountains," Nadia says, smiling at us like we're her beloved children. I'm so tempted to set the tablecloth on fire. "We have had some difficult times lately.

This will give us a chance to get out and have a little adventure. Now that you're feeling better, Lexi, I think you can travel, too."

"Yay," I deadpan. Because if the room stank before, it reeks now. "But aren't we going to first look for Mara and Jamie?"

"We're going to leave that to the experts." Nadia cuts her chicken with the precision of a surgeon. "The police have assured me they won't rest until my two girls are found. But I know how the stress of it all has been tough on each of you, which is why I thought this would be the perfect time for a little getaway. Won't that be nice?"

"Can I be a detective on the trip?" Sally asks. "We're going to the mountains? Oh! I could be a mountain singer. Or a mountain climber. Or a mountain rescuer."

"I have a brochure here to show you some pictures of... where did that go?" Nadia looks around for it and then her eyes land on Zayla, narrowing. "Zayla, pass the brochure around so the other girls can see it."

"I don't want to go," I challenge Nadia, lifting my chin. "You all can take your trip, but I'm staying here in case they find Mara and Jamie."

"You'll be coming with us," Nadia says firmly.

"Plus I've got the play performance this weekend," I add, scrambling for an excuse. My gut warns me that once I go on this supposed trip, I'll never see Jamie and Mara again. "I can't miss that. I've been working on it for months."

"Don't you worry about that," Nadia says.

"Don't worry, don't worry, don't worry," Izzy chants.

"We should be back from our trip in time for your play," Nadia continues.

I don't have a comeback for that. Why would Nadia want to suddenly take a trip in the middle of the week? It doesn't make sense. I add a chicken leg and some green beans to my plate. Flora has now woven together her green beans into a halo. She sets it on her head with a proud sigh.

"Voilà!" she says and holds her hands in the air in a pose.

"Yes, that's very nice, Flora," Nadia says, but her face is strained like she's barely holding it together. "Plus, here's the best news of all. We're leaving tonight right after dinner."

Flora gasps, making the beans fall off her head. Sally cheers. Min bangs her spoon. Izzy adds more food to her plate. Zayla disappears under the table.

But I'm still as stone. There's nothing coincidental about this trip. It can only mean one thing—they're finally going to get rid of us for good this time.

36

THE STEALTH STRIKE

ESTRELLA

Florida

The darkness wraps around us as we hunker in the thick, shadowy bushes, waiting for the transport to pass by us. Adrenaline pumps through my veins, spurred on by anticipation and fear. I review BJ's plan in my head along with his instructions.

Don't get too close, he reminded me. *Stay alert and see if you can identify any of their immortal powers.*

But it was Dion's warning that sent a spike of fear into my chest. *Whatever happens, don't get captured.*

The gates of Nadia's Home creak and inch open. The two Wraiths perched on the posts beat their wings and lift into the air, denizens of darkness.

"Those creatures terrify me," I whisper to Dion, crouched at my side. "Where did the Nazco get those?"

"The Empress probably bred them in a lab," Tristan mutters from my other side. The heat drifting off him makes it feel like it's summertime rather than a chilled January night.

"No one knows," Dion says. "They appeared with the Empress when she took the throne."

I frown. "Things don't just magically appear. They come from somewhere."

"Shhh," Katka warns from behind us. "Focus."

Across the street, Jamie scurries into the street and drops the road spikes before ducking back into the shadows like a thief in the night.

"Go," Katka orders Mara.

Mara grumbles under her breath, "Can't believe I'm actually doing this." But she steps out onto the pavement just on the other side of the spikes.

BJ had been worried the guards wouldn't open the doors to the transport with just the tires going flat or he thought they might have two vehicles, so Mara became the bait to ensure they got out of the vehicle. Sure enough, not just one van, but two emerge through the gates.

The headlights of the first van illuminate Mara standing in the middle of the road.

My heart pounds, begging for this plan to work.

Mara waves her arms, and the transports slow. While all the attention is on her, Jamie darts back into the road behind the vans and lays a second road spike, cutting off their escape.

Right on cue, the first vehicle's tires run over the spikes.

The front tires pop, blowing out. The van swerves as the

driver loses control. Mara darts in the bushes, and I pull her in beside me to safety.

"Good job," I tell her.

She shivers with fear.

Screeching fills the air and the van careens across the pavement. It topples sideways, landing with a thump on the ground. The second van slams on its brakes. It spins around and takes off in the other direction, only to hit the second trap Jamie laid.

Its tires also pop, except this van barrels down the street as if desperate to escape. The rims of the tires squeal in resistance against the pavement. Sparks fly into the air. With a screech, the second van jerks to a halt.

Instantly, Jamie tucks herself against the side of the second van, waiting for the door to open, knives in hand. Her eyes glitter gleefully in the muted light from the head-lights as she waits. That girl was born for this, I decide.

The first van's door slides open and a man steps out. He's wearing a similar black elemental-resistant jacket like the one Dion and I got from Ami, and he's holding a glowing stick in one hand and a flashlight in the other.

"Mara?" the man calls. "Is that you? Are you okay?"

"The voice is familiar," I whisper. "Wait. That's Val, our gardener."

"Looks pretty fierce to be a gardener," Tristan notes. "Can you tell what his power is?"

I concentrate on Val as he flicks on the flashlight and pans it into the bushes where we're hiding. His boots crunch on the gravel as he creeps closer to us.

"Anything?" Tristan asks, pulling his sword from its sheath.

It's hard to focus on Val's powers with Dion's and Tristan's so close, practically screaming at me. I close my eyes, reaching out my senses. The scent of earth fills my nostrils, and I feel the ground quiver. My eyes blink open.

"I think it's something to do with the ground or dirt," I whisper.

"An Earthbender," Dion says. "I can deal with that."

"On the count of three," Tristan whispers. "One, two—"

They leap from the bushes and attack Val. Tristan's sword flames and Dion's palms illuminate with sparkling light. Except Val is expecting them. He slams his fists down, and the pavement breaks apart like cookie crumbles. With a flick of Val's hands, the chunks lift off the ground and he flings them at Dion and Tristan. Asphalt pieces fly at them like an exploding grenade.

Dion shoots out a bolt of lightning seconds before a large piece of asphalt slams against his chest, sending him tumbling backward. The lightning hits its mark, landing on Val's face. He screams in pain and falls to the ground. His body lies still as stone.

"One down," Tristan says, advancing warily toward the van's door. "Who's next?"

The door to the second van slides open, but Jamie is ready. Her knives find their mark and her victim falls silently to the ground. There's something familiar about her moves. A flash of pain slams into my head as I watch her work. I press my hands to my head, grimacing.

"You're up," Katka's voice cuts through the pain.

I yank my gaze from Jamie and seize the crowbar at my side. Mara snatches up hers and the two of us race out toward the first van. We smash the crowbars against the windshield. The glass splinters. I continue swinging, working to break the glass. The need to rescue my friends drives every blow. Fearlessly, Tristan hops up onto the hood of the van, waiting.

He looks like a sun god. His whole body blazes with fire and his sword is lifted, ready to strike. He's terrifying and beautiful. I gulp at the sight of him.

Finally, the windshield shatters, creating an opening for us.

"You have a choice," Tristan calls into the van. "Get out now or wait until I set your vehicle on fire."

Both Mara and I step away from the van. I pray they won't call our bluff. Meanwhile, Dion runs to the second van, shooting bolts of electricity at the guards trying to exit it.

"Watch out for the Wraiths!" Katka screams at us.

Sure enough, the two Wraiths circle above like giant bats ready to devour us. Except they haven't attacked yet—which is odd.

The van door slides open, yanking my attention back to the ground. Girls pour out of it, screaming and crying. My focus scatters and I run to them.

"Izzy! Flora!" I call out their names. "This way!"

Izzy cries out when she sees me. "You!" she says. "Weird eyes!"

You've got to be kidding me. She isn't going to start a fight with me now, will she?

"Come on." I grab the girls' arms as fire engulfs the front of the van. "Hurry!"

Terror sends them running with me. I direct them down the road. Right on cue, a black van barrels up. BJ hops out of the driver's side and throws open the side door.

"Get inside," I order the girls.

Flora doesn't hesitate, but Izzy stops abruptly. "Are you kidnapping us?" she asks.

"I don't have time to deal with her," I tell BJ. "I need to get the other girls."

"I've got this," BJ says. "Go!"

I race back to the inferno, pulling out my sword. Tristan is battling one of the guards with a green spear, their weapons clashing against each other with sparks and flames. Thankfully, Mara is helping Zayla and two other girls to BJ's van. I reach the second van to find Dion standing in front of Nadia. She's holding a girl with a black hood over her face.

"Release the girl," Dion orders, "or I will electrocute you."

"If you miss," Nadia taunts as she holds a knife to the girl's neck while backing them both up, "you'll hit the girl. If you hit me, I'll cut her."

"It's a trap," I say, counting the last girls that Jamie is escorting to BJ's van. "All the girls have been accounted for."

"Are you sure?" Nadia grins that victorious smile that I came to hate while living at her home. Then she whips off the black hood, revealing a girl with red hair. Green eyes look over at me.

"Estrella?" she asks.

"Lexi!" I half-scream. "You're here! I thought you were kidnapped!"

Another guard appears from behind the van. He roars with anger and pushes out a palm. Wind slams into both

Dion and me. We fly through the air. My body hits the ground and I land on my right arm. The bone snaps and the sword falls out of my hand. Pain screams through my body and stars whiz through my vision.

Dion's body crashes into the first van. He slumps to the ground, clearly stunned.

Desperately, I sheath my sword, now too heavy for me to fight with, and pull out my dagger instead using my left hand. As I climb to my feet, dizziness swirls through me. The world spins like a merry-go-round. The only thing that keeps me grounded is Lexi's screams. I grit my teeth and move toward the sound.

Except pain sears my shoulders. Talons sink into my skin. The stench of rotting meat fills my nostrils. I'm lifted off the ground, rising into the air.

I look up and horror consumes me. I'm caught in the grasp of a Wraith.

37
OOPS! WERE YOU POISONED?
ESTRELLA

Florida

Desperation claws at my chest. I try to wiggle free, swinging my body forward and backward to throw off the balance of the Wraith. It only results in searing pain on my shoulders. I cry out. Liquid drips down my arms.

Blood caused by the Wraith's grip.

I try to lift up my dagger, but the pain holds me in check. The ground falls farther away. Where is it taking me? Time is slipping away. A wave of the creature's power ebbs off it. I hadn't noticed it when I fought the creatures before, but now that I've been training with Ami, I recognize its visik.

It's similar in some ways to other immortals, and yet...it feels inherently different, too.

Instead of having substance, there's an empty void. It's

calling me deeper into a pool of darkness. Forgotten caverns and lost hollows. An ache of secrets echoing through me like someone is crying from an abyss.

Deeper and further my mind falls, my cries echoing against an endless darkness.

"Estrella!" Dion screams, pulling me away from whatever enchantment this creature must have had over me. I blink and shake my head.

Below, Dion is sprinting, trying to catch up with us. A bolt of lightning shoots into the sky. My heart zings with hope. Smart. He knows I can use his lightning. I just need to pull out my sword. I exchange the dagger for the sword, twisting and causing the Wraith to screech in anger, but it doesn't try to hurt me. The Empress must want me alive, I realize. I can use that to my advantage. Wings snap at the air and the creature cries into the night.

He shoots off another bolt of electricity, aiming for my sword. It hits! I shove my powers into the blade, amplifying the strike, and plunge the sword into the belly of the bird-like creature. An ear-splitting screech emits from its beak. Its whole body shudders. A tingling ripples across its leathery wings until it sinks into its body.

The Wraith dips and swerves, but it doesn't let go of me or stop flying.

"Hit me again!" I scream down at Dion.

He cups his hands, staring at them as if gathering up his strength. Then he hurls back his arm and throws a rippling bolt, shining star-bright. The creature twists to avoid the impact, but I stretch out the sword. My shoulders burn. My arm wavers. Tears stream down my face.

The flash hits the blade, so sharp and fierce I nearly drop

the sword. But I hold tight, screaming against the pain. I suck in the power of the element and kick up my leg and hook it around its arm.

And I plunge the sword into its belly. Finally, the creature's grip loosens.

A plume of fire encompasses the Wraith and me.

Tristan.

Flames snake up my body, reaching the Wraith. Its cloak catches on fire. A curdling scream fills the night, and it releases me.

My body plummets.

I crash into a tree and then hit some branches, landing in a bush. My leg is twisted and my whole body feels like it's on fire. A buzzing fills my ears. Tristan hovers over me. He's saying something, but it sounds muffled. I merely blink up at him, unable to speak.

"You did great," I finally hear him whisper into my ear as he scoops me in his arms. He takes off running, but he stops suddenly as he's faced with some other guy.

Crap. Could he be out of power? He and Dion used so much of it tonight. We put everything we had into saving the girls, and we knew if one thing went wrong, we were in trouble. I just hadn't expected it to be me.

"Use my poowa," I say, my tongue thick and sludge-like. I try to find a place where my skin can touch his, but everything is burning. My body refuses to work.

"Move out of my way if you want to live," Tristan says, his voice sounding a little louder now.

The guy chuckles. "Hand her over and then I'll let you live, you Sabian dog."

"I'm starting to get annoyed with your terms of endearment," Tristan says. "If you don't get out of my way, we'll just have to move you ourselves."

The guy raises his hands but before he can do whatever he had planned, a burst of sizzling energy hits him. White light zips over his body as he's electrocuted. BJ's van comes racing down the street, pulling up right in front of us. The side door flings open and Katka jumps out.

"Get in!" She waves for us to come. "Is she okay?"

"I don't know," Tristan says as he leaps into the van while Dion hurtles into the front passenger seat.

"Drive!" Dion yells.

The tires squeal as BJ takes off. I vaguely notice the girls huddled together. Lexi crawls over to me.

"Will she be okay?" she asks Katka.

"Get back," Katka orders. "I need to attend to her wounds."

Lexi kisses me on the forehead. "You were amazing. Thank you for coming for us."

"We did it," I whisper to Katka as she inspects my body. "Saved 'em."

Katka looks anything but happy. She hovers over me, her brow knitted. "Estrella, are you in pain?"

"No."

"That's not good." She rips at my jacket.

"You wook worried," I say.

"That's because I am." She huffs as she studies my shoulders like I've annoyed her.

"What is it?" Tristan asks. "Is she going to be okay?"

"No, she's not going to be okay!" Katka yells. "She's got a broken arm and leg. Her shoulders are shredded by the

Wraith's claws and she's been poisoned. She needs a Healer. Now."

"Give her some antiqual," Tristan orders and rummages around in a case beside him.

"That won't last," she says. "We have to take her back to *Stará*. Immediately."

"There's no way you're bringing her back to Sabian territory," Dion snaps.

"You'll just have her die then because of your pride?" Tristan shoots back.

"We'll take her to Ami's land," Dion says. "She has a Healer there."

"Give me anqua." My words are slurred. "I'm fine."

"You're definitely not *fine*," Katka says. "Your shoulders have been cut with a Wraith's talons. They're poisonous, and by the looks of your shoulders, the poison is working fast."

Tristan pops open the cork and pours the liquid down my throat. It cools my burning throat and my head clears a little. Still, my body is shaking like it's in shock, and I'm forced to lay back down on the van's floor as we bump along.

"I thought Ami said we couldn't go to her land," BJ says.

"She'll change her mind," Dion replies. "She has to."

"You better be right," Tristan says darkly. "At the first sign of trouble, we're taking her back to my home. No questions asked."

"Fine," Dion says.

I don't miss the fear in his voice, but I'm in too much pain to argue.

38
TRAVELING TROUBLES
DION

Florida

I jump out of the van, assessing the pond and scanning the shoreline for any signs of Nazco. The night is quiet, stars thrown across the sky as if it hasn't a care in the world. The breeze is cooler, sighing through the pines and palms. Everything looks clear, so I give BJ a thumbs up.

BJ and Katka start unloading the group of girls and leading them to the Traveling Pool.

BJ's voice rings through the quiet. "The most important thing you must remember is to never let go of your companion."

"What if we do?" Mara asks.

"You'll get lost and we won't be able to find you," Katka says curtly, hurrying them to the shoreline. "So don't let go."

The thought of taking these girls unnerves me. One slip

of the hand, and we could easily lose them forever. Tristan carries Estrella out of the van. Blood cakes her clothing and parts of blonde strands have fallen out of her braid, telling signs she just survived a brutal battle. I swallow my worries like a bitter drink and quickly punch in Ami's number.

"Dion," Ami answers in her velvety voice, "such an unexpected surprise."

Meaning she was waiting for my call. She knew we'd have problems and I'd need her help. Irritation grates at my nerves.

"Estrella is hurt," I get right to the point, "we need a Healer."

"I have a Healer here, but it will cost you. An addendum to our blood contract perhaps?"

"That isn't going to happen."

"Bringing a horde of clueless Nazco into my land along with an ex-Conduit hunted by the Empress is a terrible option for me. I have nothing to gain from it, so my answer is no. Unless you want to offer yourself in exchange. I'll take you any day."

I roll my eyes. "Send your Healer to where we're going."

"Again, nothing in it for me. Also, must I remind you that if you don't have your sweet Estrella take me to the Temple of Fates, you fail your side of the contract? Which means all of your power transfers to me."

Blistering stars, she's right. I pace along the van, running a hand over my face. I'd been so caught up in saving Estrella and getting these girls free, I hadn't thought through the consequences of how this could play out. Blood contracts only lead to disaster.

Father had been right and that makes me even angrier.

"If Estrella survives the night," I say, not hiding my irritation, "I'll be in touch about the Temple of Fates."

"Excellent. Until then."

I hang up and march to our ragtag group huddled on the shoreline. My anger sends sparks along my palms, but right now I don't care. The weight of the responsibility of this group hangs heavy on me. We've literally ripped these girls from their home and now they have nothing except the clothes on their backs.

"I hate vacations," one of the girls is saying. "This sucks."

"Vacation, vacation, vacation," one of them sing-songs.

"We weren't going on a vacation," Lexi adds. "That was another lie that Nadia fed us."

"I want to go home," another wails.

"That wasn't a home, Sally." Mara crosses her arms. "That was a prison."

"Well, I liked it!" Sally snaps.

"No one is stopping you from leaving," Mara says, waving her hand back to the road. "Feel free to go."

Sally glances at the road, rubbing her arms.

"I don't recommend leaving," I tell her. "The best option for us all is to keep moving forward. BJ, you have the coordinates for Madagascar?"

"Madagascar," one of the girls whispers. "Isn't that like on another continent?"

"It is. Which is why the Water Channels are our best option," BJ tries to explain and then to me, "I'll let my contact know we're on our way."

"Excellent," I say.

"Madagascar?" Katka lifts her eyebrows. "That's Caladrian territory. Are you sure that's a good idea?"

"What about Estrella?" Lexi asks. "She isn't in any shape to travel."

"I'll take her through the Water Channels," I say. "She'll be fine."

"I was going to take her," Tristan says, a bit protectively if you ask me.

"Oh, Fates save us," Katka grumbles, rolling her eyes. "Just let Dion take her."

"Actually," I say to Tristan, "you said you had a Healer. Could you bring the Healer to Madagascar? If you hurry, you can get there not long after we arrive."

"If he goes home," Katka says, "his father might not let him leave. He's still ticked off about Tristan leaving without warning."

Tristan glances at Katka and then down at Estrella in his arms as if trying to decide what to do.

Estrella's head lulls against Tristan's arm like she's fallen asleep.

"Is there something we can do?" Lexi asks, wringing her hands. Fire sparkles from the tips of her wild hair.

"I'm afraid not." Tristan's jaw tightens. "He's right. I'll go home. Get a Healer. It's our best option."

Then he whispers something in Estrella's ear and kisses her forehead before setting her on the grass. I'd be lying if I said jealousy wasn't curling its way through my heart. I try to quelch the feelings because what we're doing is bigger than my emotions, but it only tightens firmer.

"Katka, you okay staying with this group?" Tristan asks, brow crinkling with worry.

"You mean stay with a bunch of dangerous Nazco who are being hunted?" she asks sarcastically. "Sure. No problem."

One of the girls drops to the ground and starts crying again. Another girl takes off along the pond, plucking blades of grass off the ground, making a bouquet.

"Good luck." He nods to the girls. "I think you're going to need it more than me. Send me the coordinates, okay?"

"Be careful," Katka says, her voice surprisingly warm. She touches him on the arm, her fingers lingering.

"Hurry," I remind Tristan.

He sloshes into the pond and then dives beneath the surface, vanishing. All that's left are bubbles, glittering in the starlight.

"Where did he go?" Lexi asks, her eyes flickering between all of us.

"To the Water Channels," Katka explains.

Some of the girls start murmuring, voicing their worries. I don't blame them. The channels are terrifying even for a seasoned traveler. The girl with the grass bouquet sets it on top of Estrella.

I clap my hands. "Alright. Everyone into the water. We're going to team up in groups of four. You need to make sure you travel with either BJ, Katka, or myself. Like BJ said, whatever happens, don't let go of your partner."

"I'm scared," one of the girls says as she wades into the water.

"I'll protect you," Jamie offers and takes her hand. "You can do this."

Jamie's bravery works because the girls follow her into

the water. I scoop up Estrella and then wade into the pond. BJ is waiting for me.

"You okay?" He puts a hand on my shoulder.

"If someone told me I'd be taking a group of cast-out Nazco and Sabians through the Water Channels into Caladrian territory six months ago, I'd have laughed at them."

"I just hope we can pull the rest of this operation off," BJ says. "We still have a long journey ahead of us. We've been lucky so far."

I frown at that. "Maybe. I was surprised they only had two Wraiths and their guards were easy to defeat. We got away too easily."

"I was thinking the same thing," Katka says, splashing over to us while adjusting her backpack. "You know what I think? That they didn't care about the girls. They used them as a decoy to grab Estrella. They knew she'd be there."

"You may be right," I say. "The sooner we leave this place, the happier I'll be. It's too peaceful. Too easy."

"Yeah." Katka bites her lip and glances around nervously. "I agree."

Whatever liquid Tristan gave her seems to be working. I hope the poison doesn't do any long-term damage. Everyone gathers into their groups in preparation for our trip. I cast one last glance at the shoreline, expecting Nazco assassins to show up, but all is quiet.

And that worries me the most.

39
NEW BEGINNINGS BRING NEW PROBLEMS
ESTRELLA

Mahajanga, Madagascar

My screams wake me. The memories of the Wraith's claws sinking into my skin, being flown into the air, lightning and fire surrounding me, and rescuing my friends all shudder through my body in a repeated nightmare. My eyes fly open and I sit up, a cry on my lips.

Two women I don't recognize hover over me. One has pale skin with white-blonde hair tucked into a bun while the other has darker skin with black plaited hair, wearing a brightly colored wrap. I don't recognize either. Frantically, I scan the room for my sword, but the dark-haired woman shushes me.

"Calm down, my love," she says, patting my shoulder. "You must rest. You are safe here."

Her power wafts through the air, smooth as honey and sweet as lavender. My head falls back against my pillow.

"You're Healers," I state, relaxing.

She nods, smiling. "Took both of us to heal you of your wounds and the poisoning. I didn't think I had enough strength to do it, but the Prince arrived with Elda. Just in time, at that."

"Thank you for coming, Elda," I say.

"You're welcome, but I did it for the Prince," Elda says.

Of course she did. They all adore their prince. Me, not so much. "Even still," I tell her. "I'm grateful. And what's your name?" I ask the other Healer.

"Anja," she says. "How do you feel? The poison nearly reached your heart."

I vaguely remember Dion carrying me out of the water and through a deluge of a rainstorm.

"Dion," I say. "Where is he? Are the other girls okay?"

"You lost a lot of blood," Elda says. "You should rest."

"I feel great." It's a total lie, but I'm desperate to see my friends and make sure everyone is okay. I sit back up and swing my legs over the edge of the cot. Dizziness causes my body to sway a little, but I grit my teeth and stand. "Where is everyone?"

"They are here in my village, likely still sleeping or eating breakfast," Anja explains.

"I appreciate you letting us come here. We had nowhere else to go."

"Enemies of the Empress of the Nazco are friends to us," she says.

"We won't forget your kindness," I say.

"You should know that there are only a few of us who are immortals. Most of the town is oblivious to us."

"That's good to know. We'll keep the secret of who you are safe."

I strap my sword onto my back and head to the door, but I realize my feet are bare and I'm wearing different clothes, a soft cream-colored linen tunic and pants. Thankfully, Anja fetches me a pair of sandals and Elda helps me strap the sword beneath my tunic. I explain to them that since I left Ami's kingdom, I'm terrified to go anywhere without it.

When I step outside into the bright morning light, the salty tang of the sea washes over me. Anja's home is made of red brick with a thatched roof. It sits in the center of a narrow street lined with similar styled homes. Tall trees with gnarled roots hover over the buildings like sleeping serpents protecting the village. Three children are jump-roping up ahead, but when they spot me they pause to stare and then burst into giggles, running away.

It makes me wonder how much they know about who I am.

A few merchants are setting up their wooden stalls, creating pyramid displays of bumpy red fruit and long sticks that I think are vanilla beans. They eye me nervously as I pass by, and I wonder if they aren't pleased with us invading their small village. But then two women balancing baskets of mangos on their heads smile at me.

"Estrella!" Lexi calls out from up ahead. She rushes up and throws her arms around me. "You're walking around. This is great!"

I squeeze her in a tight hug before pulling back,

assessing her. "And you're here. We thought the Nazco imprisoned you."

"They did, but they let me go." Her green eyes flash. "Their prison was dreadful. Cold and dark. And the Empress was terrifying."

"You saw the Empress?" I gasp.

"She was all white and silver. Cruel as winter." Lexi shudders.

"Why did the Empress let you go?"

"Don't know. Maybe because I didn't have any information on where you were."

A chill snakes across my skin. "The Empress was asking about me?"

Lexi nods. "Now I'm glad you didn't tell me where you were when I last talked to you. But they still have Conrad. We need to find a way to rescue him. I'm so worried."

"We will." I squeeze her hand, studying her face. She's lost some weight, her cheeks are hollow, and her bright red hair is duller than I remember. "You care about him, don't you?"

"Yeah. A lot. The last time I saw him, they'd brought him back from being tortured. It was..." She presses her lips together and her eyes water. "We just need to help him, okay?"

"Absolutely." I give her a hug. Except I don't tell her that the thought of infiltrating the Midnight Kingdom is daunting. I barely made it out alive just rescuing the girls. My stomach growls, pulling me back to the moment. "I don't know about you, but I'm starving. Do they have food here?"

"Of course!" She laughs and hooks her arm through mine. "I'm headed back to the house now for breakfast."

She leads me down the dusty street while we catch up on what we've both been up to. She points out the house BJ arranged for them to live in and how generous the villagers have been in providing food and clothing for them. According to BJ, this is a small village in the countryside, outside of Mahajanga. All the villagers except the Healer and her family are mortals, which should help keep the girls hidden since this is not an authorized immortal town. This place feels like time forgot it—a perfect hideout from the rest of the world.

"He's been so kind setting us up," she says, "but it all feels so weird, you know? Like he gave us everything to start out, but I don't feel like I belong here. I feel guilty because you all literally put your lives in danger to rescue us."

I take in our surroundings. The dirt road, the thick jungle surrounding the village, the thatched huts. "I get it. It's the perfect place to be forgotten, but it's not home."

"I'm glad you understand." She hugs me. "But enough about me and my woes. Tell me how you got to be so kick-butt. I saw you fighting off those horrible creatures! And since when do you carry a sword with you?"

She points to my sword strapped to my back, and I laugh. So I tell her about my training with Ami and then she tells me how Conrad has been trying to show her how to use her powers.

"I haven't gotten more than a few flickers of fire," she says, "but it's still kind of exciting. Except for Conrad and the idea of living the rest of my life in the middle of nowhere. How am I going to get my shopping fix?"

She's trying to make light of the situation, but her worries are real.

"I'm sure it's just temporary," I say. "Once you all get on your feet and your minds heal, we'll find a better place."

"With lots of shopping."

"With lots of shopping," I parrot, laughing.

We head inside a larger thatched building, the home BJ set up, and are met with the scent of steamed rice and cooked vegetables. I don't see Tristan or Dion but some of the girls are here, sitting on woven mats and eating breakfast. Flora is humming as she nibbles on a red fruit, a wreath of flowers on her head. When she spots me, she waves happily as if she hasn't a care in the world.

Mara and Jamie are huddled together, whispering, while Min hits her spoon against her tin cup as if trying to make up a new tune. Gaia is making a design on the table with her food. I almost miss Zayla. She's crouched in shadows in the corner of the room, shoveling food into her mouth, her large eyes taking everything in. My heart warms seeing her again even if she looks terrified. I make a mental note to tell her not to steal from the villagers. I don't doubt that she will try.

"It's so good to see everyone is here safely away from Nadia," I tell Lexi as we each grab a plate and load it full of rice, veggies, and mango.

"I agree," Lexi says, "but I'm worried about them. Some of the girls aren't able to handle the real world. Sally and Izzy won't leave their beds and Min might be here in body, but I don't know about her mind. And then there's Zayla. She still hasn't said a word since we left Nadia's and she refuses to sleep with the rest of us. Honestly, I don't know where she goes off to half the time."

"Probably stealing the villagers' forks." My eyes drift to Zayla. "I'll talk to her."

"She always did like you best," Lexi says, looking relieved.

Lexi sits down with Mara and Jamie while I crouch in front of Zayla. "Hey, it's good to see you again," I say. "Do you want to come sit with us and eat?"

She starts rocking back and forth. I've made her nervous.

"I'd love for you to join us," I add. "We're going to make some plans and I really want you to be involved."

"Plans, plans, plans," Zayla whispers.

"Remember when we snuck into Nadia's house?" She eyes me warily but nods, so I continue. "They're plans like that, and I really need your help because you're so good at stealth. I'm going to sit over there with the others but feel free to join us if you like."

I leave her and join the girls, sitting crisscross on a mat. They ask me how I'm feeling and what I've been up to. I give them a brief overview of where I've been. I try to answer their questions, but it seems to lead to more confusion. I get it—it's a lot to unpack.

"I'm glad to get away from Nadia's," Mara says, "but how long are we going to stay here? You're not expecting us to live here permanently, are you?"

"I don't know," I admit. "Ever since I ran away from Nadia's, I've just been trying to survive and stay alive."

Then I tell the girls how I've been training with the hopes of getting my memories and powers back. Zayla slips in closer to listen, and even Min stops banging her cup for a little while.

"So far nothing I've done has worked." I bite my lip and look down at my hands. "I even went into the World of Between, hoping that would spark my memories."

"What's the World of Between?" Lexi asks.

"The place where our power source comes from," I explain, realizing how weird and foreign this must sound.

"This whole powers and immortality thing is super weird," Mara adds. "Do you really believe we're immortals who have lost our powers? That's what Tristan told me."

Min starts hitting her cup again. *Bang, bang, bang!*

"Min!" Mara snaps. "Enough. Jamie, take that cup away from her. She's driving me mad."

Jamie reaches for the cup, but Mara holds it out of her reach. Thankfully, Zayla scrambles up behind Min and snatches it from her hand, scurrying to the other side of the mat before Min even realizes what has happened. Min spins around, searching until she spots another tin cup and grabs that one. She starts up her banging again while Flora hums to the beat.

"See?" Jamie waves at the girls. "This is what we're dealing with. They can't even get through breakfast without making a scene."

"Each of us was once immortal and had power," I tell them. Instantly, Min and Flora go silent again. Zayla creeps closer. "But the Empress took that away from us and sent us to live as mortals at Nadia's Home."

"That's what Tristan told us." Mara crosses her arms. "Sounds like something from one of Sally's TV shows."

"What if I were to tell you I might know how to get your powers and maybe even your memories back?" I press. "Would you help me?"

"Count me in," Jamie announces, pointing her fork at me. "I always feel like my body wants to do things but it doesn't work properly."

"Yes, yes, yes," Zayla whispers, but her eyes are shining bright.

"You already know I'm in all the way," Lexi says. "If I can get my powers back, I might be able to help Conrad."

"Fine. I'm in, too." Mara huffs, rolling her eyes. "Not that I have much of a choice."

"You all have a choice," I say, looking at each of them. "But I think if we can work together, we have a better chance of success."

"So what's the plan?" Jamie asks.

"There's this temple." I switch to a whisper. "I believe it holds an elixir that can give us our powers back."

"Seriously?" Mara's eyebrows rise skeptically.

"What are we waiting for?" Lexi asks. "We should go today."

"There's just one problem." I grimace. "It's lost."

"Ohhhh!" Zayla gasps, clasping her hands together. "Lost, lost, lost."

"That's one big problem, if you ask me." Mara shakes her head and focuses back on her plate of food.

"Do you have any clues to where it could be?" Lexi asks.

"We have a general idea, but we need more time to find it. Dion was in the middle of researching it when we found out about you all being transferred. It was a great opportunity to rescue you. But now that we're here, I think it's the perfect time to move forward with our search. If you want to help, raise your hand."

One by one each of them raises a hand. Even Flora and Min. Which means deep down, they understand what's happening and their bodies are crying out to be saved.

"Excellent," I say, grinning. "While the others work on

trying to find the location of this temple, I want us to start training."

"Yes!" Jamie punches her fist into her palm.

"Training for what?" Mara asks.

"I'm going to teach you as much as I can about how to access whatever powers you have left," I tell them. "I'm going to have to leave soon, but I want to make sure you're prepared for any enemy you may encounter so you're able to defend yourselves. The Empress may have made us outcasts, but she didn't realize she forced us to become far stronger. She turned us into something she one day will come to fear."

40

SHE MADE US INTO SOMETHING SHE WILL FEAR

ESTRELLA

Mahajanga, Madagascar

When I leave the house, I'm intent on finding Tristan and Dion to discuss my idea to train the girls, but it doesn't take long. I spot them across the street having what looks like a heated discussion, based on their furrowed brows and stiff stances. Seeing them together reminds me once again of my conflicting feelings for the two of them.

Tristan has stood by my side and always told me the truth each step of the way. He's been my rock when I felt myself falling apart. The thought of our fiery kisses sends a rush of heat through me. There's no doubt that I've been falling for him, and for a time, I thought he was the only one I could love.

But then Dion came back into my life at the masquerade ball and my emotions and feelings for him only confused me. I touch my lips, remembering that electrifying kiss we shared in Japan. It felt forbidden and wrong, and yet also so right. It's like the part of me that had been forgotten rose up, reminding me how much I cared for him. Our relationship has been rocky, to say the least. I thought he had proven he was committed to me, but after overhearing that conversation with his father, I'm wondering if I'm just a pawn in his father's plan to overthrow the Empress.

I growl in frustration at myself. Why did I let Dion kiss me? And why does my relationship with Tristan have so many obstacles standing in our way? It's like the immortal world refuses to let us be together.

I rub my temples and remind myself that my feelings can't keep me from my one task to find the Temple of Fates and recover my memories. Until then, I need to close the door to my heart and focus on what's ahead. Clenching my fists, I cross the street to join them.

"I don't like it," Tristan is saying. "I know you trust your guy, but there are too many variables."

"What you like or don't like is irrelevant," Dion snaps back.

"Hey," I greet them.

Instantly, both of them move to me, but then stop abruptly, glancing at each other. Yep. This is all very weird.

"Estrella," Dion says, his eyes searching me. "It's good to see you walking around. I was worried."

"You're looking great," Tristan says. "I talked to Elda and she said that you're healing."

"I am," I say, but I can't help but feel guilty. "Thank you

for helping me. If it weren't for you both, I'd either be carried off by those Wraiths or dead. You both have worked so hard to save me. I hope I can recover my memories and make it all worthwhile for you."

The two eye each other warily, but nod. There's an uneasy alliance between the three of us and somehow I need to keep us all from falling apart.

"You were having a pretty heated discussion," I continue. "Is something wrong?"

"I just don't think this place is secure enough for these girls," Tristan says.

"BJ says it's the safest place for them," Dion adds. "And I trust him. I've already checked and we weren't followed. There are only a small group of Caladrians in this area so it's the perfect place for your friends to escape the rest of the world."

"I talked to the girls and they appreciate being rescued," I say, "but they can't live here forever. This isn't home for them."

"It's going to have to be unless you can come up with a better option," Dion says.

"I don't have one." I cross my arms and gaze across the street at the girls' new home. "We need to get to the Temple of Fates sooner than later."

"You found out where it's located?" Tristan's eyes widen in surprise.

Dion eyes him warily. "You sure you should tell him?"

"He deserves to know as much as you do," I shoot back. "But yes, when I went into the World of Between, I found out that it's located at the Acacus Peaks."

"This is incredible news," Tristan says, and his body leans forward as if he yearns to give me a hug. "Great work."

"I did a quick search while you were resting," Dion adds. "I'm thinking you might be talking about the Acacus Mountains, a mountain range in the desert in western Libya. Since it's a part of the Sahara we'll have to search miles of sand and desert."

"That sounds difficult," I say, feeling deflated. "Why does everything seem to be so hard?"

"But the Dragon Seer was right," Tristan adds. "That is something."

"As much as she hated me, she told me the truth," I agree. "But the issue right now is I can't leave these girls here unprotected while we go looking for the temple. I told them I'd train them to use whatever powers they have left so they can defend themselves in case something were to happen."

"Not a bad idea," Dion agrees. "But I don't want to wait long. A day or two at most. Every hour we delay gives the Empress and her assassins an advantage in finding us."

I swallow, remembering the assassins Tristan and I faced in Florida. "Good point."

"How about BJ and Katka work on finding us the best route to the temple," Tristan says, "meanwhile, the three of us can do an intense training course with the girls?"

"Sounds like a plan," I say, eyeing the two of them. I can't shake the awkwardness of the three of us working together. "Jamie said there's an open field on the other side of the village. Meet me there in an hour."

"Are you feeling strong enough to do the training?" Dion asks.

"I don't have a choice. Like you said, we're running out of time."

Tristan finds the empty field not far from the village for us to practice. Mara and Lexi help gather the girls out to the field. Jamie even managed to drag Sally and Izzy out of bed, but both look a bit freaked out. I count the girls as they sit on the ground. Eight, which means we're all here. Tristan and Dion are standing off to the side, arms crossed, speaking to each other in low tones. Their worried expressions don't calm my fears. I join them.

"You think this is a safe space?" I ask.

"Considering the extent of their powers, this field should work," Tristan says, rubbing the stubble on his chin as his sharp blue eyes assess the area. "But we'll need to be careful. I'd rather not alert the villagers that we have special powers."

"Do we know what powers these girls have?" Dion asks me. "If we knew more, it would help."

"Lexi has fire power." I point to her sitting in the center with her arm around Min, whose brown eyes are eyeing the guys fearfully.

"I'll work with her," Tristan says.

"If I can touch the others, I might be able to figure out what their powers are," I say, "but I'm pretty new to all of this, too."

I move to stand in front of my friends, assessing them. I take a deep breath, hoping my words will help ease their worries.

"It feels like yesterday that I arrived at Nadia's and joined you for the first time for afternoon tea," I begin. "My biggest worry was trying to remember who I was and hoping I could remember each of your names. We were complete strangers, but since then we have survived an attack and traveled across the world to start a new life. To add to that, I've learned that each of us has special abilities that normal people don't."

"How do you know we have abilities?" Jamie asks.

"And how do we know we can trust these guys?" Mara nods to Tristan and Dion with a scowl.

Lexi rises and comes to stand with me. "I learned I can make fire. It was actually Tristan's friend who taught me. It's not much, but before, I was only able to make sparks."

She holds out her palm and a tiny flame flickers across its surface. The girls gasp. Min starts humming while Izzy holds her head, rocking back and forth as if the fire is upsetting. I don't blame her. She hasn't had any of the special tea Nadia used to give us.

"If your head hurts as I'm talking to you," I quickly explain, "that's your mind's way of trying to access the memories taken from you. Those memories not only were about your past but they are also tied to your powers. The tea helped suppress your memories so it will take time for your body to adjust."

"What if it's too painful?" Sally asks. "Do you have something that can help?"

"I don't." I shoot her a sympathetic look. "I'm sorry. But I want to train you how to access and use them just like Lexi can."

"What's your power?" Mara asks me.

"I'm a Channeler." I swallow, deciding now might not be a good time to tell them I can take their powers from them. "One of the things I can do is find out what powers other people have. If you're okay with it, I'd like to touch your hand and see if I can find out what powers, if any, that you have. They will stem from one of the four elements: fire, wind, air, or water."

"You can start with me," Jamie offers, leaping to her feet and coming to me. She shoots Mara a wicked grin, saying, "I'm not scared."

This earns her a dark look from Mara.

I take her hand and try to focus on the power within it. A quick movement flutters across my skin. I frown, wishing I was better at this.

"I think your powers come from the air," I tell her. "Are you fast?"

She shrugs, running a hand through her short blonde hair. "I suppose. I never really thought about it."

"We used to know each other when you attended the Midnight Academy," Dion interrupts.

"What?" Jamie asks, jerking back in shock.

"That's right," I say, remembering what he told me on the train. "Do you know what her powers are?"

"You were close friends with Estrella and Lexi," Dion continues. "You were especially good with throwing knives, or any weapon really. You used to carry around a slew of knives tucked into your clothing."

Jamie leans in as if she's holding onto his words. "I don't remember that, but it sounds like something I would do. Thanks."

"Fine," Mara says once Jamie sits back down. "I'll go next but I think I already know."

"Really?" I touch her hand and instantly a shadowy darkness seeps out of her palm. It's visible to all of us, and the girls cry out in surprise.

"Your shadow power is strong," I say. "You've known about this for a while, haven't you?"

She nods and then tucks her hands into her armpits. "It's weird, I know."

"Absolutely not!" I say and then look at Tristan and Dion. "If she could develop this, it could hide us, couldn't it?"

"Definitely," Tristan says. "In fact, there are some shadow wielders who are able to cloak themselves into being invisible."

"Well." She brightens at this and her chest lifts. "That's pretty cool, isn't it?"

"It really is," I agree.

I continue testing the others. Flora has the power to create vines and flowers. Zayla is true to her nickname of Sneaky with the power to seek things out. Min's power is obviously tied to music in some way. I have a hard time pinning Izzy's power down, but it reminds me of the ocean waves crashing. Gaia is something with the ground, but I can't pinpoint the exact power. Sally is the only one I can't feel any power coming from.

"Are you saying that I'm not special?" Sally asks. Tears start pouring down her face.

"You are incredibly special," I say, but my heart aches because I know exactly how she feels. "My powers aren't strong either so I might be missing something."

"But you found everyone else's," she points out.

"I know this is hard and not just for you, but for all of us." I pull her close and wrap my arms around her. Even with her encased in my arms, I feel nothing. This means the treatment plan at Nadia's worked, and it makes me furious.

I look out at all the girls, their eyes trained on me, desperate for truth, for purpose. "We're each trying to find our place in this world. If you're like me, that need to belong is screaming from deep within and every day you wonder if this life is too hard because you feel so alone and disconnected. But I'm here to tell you that no matter what, we belong together. We might be weak on our own, but together we can be stronger than we were ever meant to be."

Flora comes and hugs us. Lexi joins in, and before I know it, all the girls are wrapping their arms around us so we've become one giant group hug. Their powers sing around me, through me, and then back out again like a song.

It's the beginning of something. I'm not sure what, but I know our friendship is bigger and more powerful than I could've ever imagined.

41
TRAINING THE UNTRAINABLE
ESTRELLA

Mahajanga, Madagascar

For the next two days, we follow the same routine—eat breakfast and then head out to the field to train. Nights are dinner, washing up, and then falling asleep exhausted. It feels good to help others for once, and it's so fun to see my friends become more in tune with their powers. Most still can't do much with them, which has caused a few of the girls some frustration.

Lexi hasn't gotten more than that flickering flame, but Tristan has done well with showing her how to use that small flicker to her best advantage. Meanwhile, Dion has been working with Mara, explaining how to cover her whole arm with shadows.

Giving these girls a reason for their weird behavior and

purpose has energized and united us. But I'm worried that if another immortal found them here unprotected, they'd be killed without much of a fight.

This morning, I head out to the field after breakfast, mentally planning out some of the fighting moves I want to teach the girls. Behind me I hear Tristan call out my name, and inwardly, I cringe. But I stop and smile, waiting for him to easily jog to catch up with me. He's wearing khaki pants and a black shirt. It's very, very hard not to notice his muscular build or remember how passionate our kisses were.

The best part about all the training and the girls is they've been a distraction for me from having to talk to either Dion or Tristan. I don't even know how to act around either one. Do I tell Tristan I kissed Dion? Even though we broke up, I know he'd be hurt. If he were to kiss Katka, I would be crushed.

My heart is so confused. I care deeply for both guys and that's the part that scares me.

"I wanted to talk to you alone." Tristan glances over his shoulder to see if anyone is nearby and then takes my hand, dragging me behind a thicket of bushes. "You've been avoiding me."

I swallow, hating how well he knows me. "It's been hard."

"I feel the same way." He steps closer and the heat of his power drifts around me. "I know we agreed that we can't work, but who cares about what my people think? I certainly don't. My parents believe in you. Even the Dragon Seer gave you a prophecy, which means you're one of us."

"Except I'm not." A pang hits my chest. "You saw that

mob trying to kill me. They would never want me or have their prince be with me."

"If they knew you, they would love you just like..." His words fall away, and my heart clenches. "I've been thinking a lot about us...and the possibility of there not being an us. And that was when I realized I couldn't imagine my world without you. I've fallen for you, Estrella. I walked away from you in Japan and it nearly killed me. It made me realize I can't ever let you go."

He takes my hand and rubs his thumb across my palm. My breath catches as my defenses start to fall apart, but I can't let my emotions lead me. Not when there is so much at stake. I don't need to just protect myself anymore, I need to protect my friends.

"And I've fallen for you too," I say, whispering the words as the wind might take them away like a thief. "You were there for me when no one else was. You believed in me when no one else did and I can never express to you how grateful I am for that. But right now, I need space to figure out who I am. Will you give that to me?"

His knuckles run along my cheek, a beam of sun caressing my skin. "Of course."

We move apart and step back onto the path just as Katka walks up. Her green eyes flicker between the two of us and then darken.

"I came to tell you that I have put together an expedition plan to find the temple," she says stiffly. "After practice, if you two can keep your hands off each other, come see me and I'll show you."

"Thank you," I say, but she's already spun around and is marching away.

I sigh. "She loves you."

"I know," Tristan says, thick with guilt. "And Dion loves you."

"Yeah." I nod and we continue down the path in silence, both of us feeling the pull of the rest of the world ripping us apart. "Why can't life be simple?"

"What's the fun in that?" Tristan asks, that wicked grin returning, and I laugh because with Tristan the world is always bright and real.

As soon as we arrive at the field, we are back in the thick of training. Time flies by as I teach the girls the forms that Sensei Haruki taught me. After warm-ups, I choose to work with Zayla. If she's truly a Seeker, I can't let go of the possibility that if her powers could be developed, she might be useful for finding the Temple of Fates. I start her out with a game of hide and seek. I'm surprised she can find some of the closer objects that I hid.

I'm hiding a fork from breakfast in the bushes when I spot Sally sitting on a blanket talking with Katka. It's the first time Katka hasn't just dropped off the lunch basket and left. Curious, I tell Zayla we'll try again tomorrow and join them.

"You look tired," Katka tells me as I settle onto the blanket beside them.

"You know, I think I am," I say. My head aches and my muscles are sore.

I stare out at the girls practicing. Dion is working with Min and Izzy, who are mostly just staring at him in awe, while Tristan practices with Mara, Jamie, and Lexi. Flora seems to have lost interest and has resorted to picking flowers while Gaia is making piles in the dirt, which now I'm thinking is actually a good thing.

"You've been through a lot," Katka offers. "It makes sense."

I eye her warily. She's being awfully nice, which is super weird. "So what have you two been up to?"

"She was telling me about her job," Sally says. "She doesn't have powers either."

"I was explaining how not all of us immortals have the high powers," Katka says. "But that doesn't mean we aren't useful."

"That's true," I say. "No matter if you have powers or not, you're still one of us, Sally."

She nods, eyeing me uncomfortably. "But maybe my powers will still show up, right?"

"Maybe. I wish I was better at my own abilities so I could help you," I say.

"Why don't you go find out where BJ is?" Katka tells Sally. "He's supposed to be here with the drinks."

Once Sally leaves, Katka turns her focus on me. "I know that you think you love Tristan."

Yikes. Way to jump in and tell me what you think. But that's more like the Katka that I've come to know. I lick my lips. "I don't know if he told you, but we aren't together anymore. We don't really make sense. Plus, I don't think your people would exactly welcome me into your kingdom."

"I admit that I was very upset when I saw you both...you know. But I was wrong to judge you. Tristan is a wonderful man. You wouldn't be the first to fall for him." She chuckles. "Honestly, I think half of the kingdom is in love with him."

That makes me laugh, too. "I get why. He's very kind and loyal and…" *I think I'm in love with him.*

My eyes drift to where Jamie is arguing with Tristan about something. She's throwing her hands in the air and pointing at him. As if he can sense us talking about him, he glances our way. Surprise lights his face, seeing the two of us sitting together, and his brow furrows in worry, but he nods.

"I've been selfish," Katka suddenly admits. "I wanted him for myself but when I told him I loved him more than just as a friend, he couldn't reciprocate it. I was devastated."

"I'm sorry." I want to reach out and touch her hand, but as a Channeler, I know that would only make things worse.

"I've tried to put those feelings aside because as much as I hate it, the Sabians' powers are depleting. In a few months, we'll need the Numinous Flame renewed, but there's no one to take Ivana's place."

My heart aches for the Sabians, but also for all of us as I think about what Ami and Zola said about the Numinous Flames depleting. "I was able to touch the Sabian fire without it hurting me."

She gasps and her large green eyes widen. "The Queen was right."

I nod, staring down at my palms, remembering. "I actually didn't realize it at first because being in the World of Between is so confusing. It was Ami, the Eien Conduit, who pointed it out."

"This is why I can't let my emotions stand in the way of us getting our powers renewed. Despite how much people hate you, I can't deny that we need you."

"I wish I could be the Conduit you want me to be, but I

couldn't enter the World of Between on my own. I needed help. And I definitely wasn't strong enough to carry the Sabian fire out of the land."

She nods, eyeing me closely. "But if this Temple of Fates is real, then we can fix that."

"If we can find it."

"I think I figured out where the Temple of Fates is in the Acacus Peaks."

"Seriously?"

"It's not on any maps. I'm guessing it's hidden within one of the mountains. And based on some ancient texts, I think I know which one."

Hope surges inside of me. "That's the best news." Except if we know where to go, nothing is keeping us here in Madagascar. I rub my forehead. "It's going to be hard to leave these girls. I don't know if they can survive on their own."

"I'm worried we've already waited too long."

A scream interrupts our conversation. I leap to my feet to find Zayla clawing at Lexi. I rush over to them just as Tristan lifts Zayla into the air and clamps his hands around her, pinning her body into place.

"What's going on?" I ask, running to them.

"Her nails cut my skin!" Lexi exclaims, lifting her shirt to show long scrapes down her side. Blood drips from the wounds.

My eyes widen. "Zayla? Why did you do this?"

Zayla starts muttering under her breath, staring at the ground.

"I think we should take a break," Dion says, coming over to inspect the situation.

"Good plan," Tristan says. "Katka brought lunch and I see BJ has finally arrived with the drinks."

"Do you want to go see the Healer?" I ask Lexi, but she waves me away.

"I need to toughen up," she says. "I always heal fast anyway."

The girls head over to the blanket where Katka spoons rice and stew into bowls and passes them out. Meanwhile, Dion, Tristan, and I hang back.

"Katka thinks she found the mountain we are looking for," I say. "She thinks we should leave soon, but I can't imagine leaving the girls here."

I nod to where Flora is now placing a crown of flowers on Katka's head.

"I agree with Katka," Dion says. "We should leave at dawn. This waiting around makes me nervous."

"You think the Nazco can find us here?" Tristan asks.

"I think we should never underestimate the Empress," Dion says, his gaze scanning the perimeter of the field. "If you ask me, she let us go too easily."

"I hope you're wrong." I swallow as a heavy pit forms in my stomach. "But in case you're right, let's leave at dawn. I'll let Mara and Lexi know and put them in charge."

"I'll call Ami to meet us here," Dion says. "We'll go together."

We join the others at the makeshift picnic lunch, but my stomach twists into a knot from a foreboding of dread.

42
BETRAYAL FROM AN UNLIKELY SOURCE
ESTRELLA

Mahajanga, Madagascar

The screams wake me. I leap off my mat and reach for my dagger, but it's gone. Confused, I blink against the semi-darkness.

"Help!" Lexi cries out.

"I'm coming!" I choke out, fear clawing at my throat.

Fire sparks in the air. That has to be Lexi. She screams for help again. I scramble across the room, stumbling on the corner of Mara's mat. Mara swears while I smash into someone trying to get away. I reach to grab the intruder, but they slip out of my grasp. Thankfully, Jamie appears behind me and tackles the person.

"I've got the culprit!" she says.

The door flies open and Tristan appears, sword in hand. "What's happening?"

A few seconds later, Dion and BJ also arrive, flicking on the lights. I gasp when I see who Jamie is holding.

"Zayla?" I gasp.

She bursts into tears. "Secrets. Secrets."

Lexi's cries yank my attention back to her. Quickly, I race to her bed. She's holding her side, hands soaked in blood.

"She's bleeding. A lot," I say. "Get the Healer!"

"On it!" BJ says.

Tristan points the tip of his sword at Zayla's neck. "Don't move," he warns, "or this will be your last breath."

Zayla starts crying, but I'm too busy worrying about how Lexi's flames now hungrily consume her blankets.

"Help me put out the fire," I say and start beating at the blankets. A searing pain shoots across my head and a flicker of a memory shudders through me. I must have done this before.

Dion and Mara join me and within moments we've put out the fire. Smoke fills the room, causing us all to start coughing. Dion opens the window and I check Lexi's side.

"Are you okay?" I ask her, inspecting the wound and then pressing a bunched-up piece of clothing against it to stop the bleeding.

"She cut me. Zayla literally cut me!" Lexi lays back down, pain stretching at her face.

The other girls now crowd the doorway, eyeing the situation warily.

"You should all go back to sleep," I tell them. "We have everything under control."

Katka appears and scans the room. "Looks like she needs

some of your flame-resistant bedding, Tristan. Come with me, girls."

As soon as Katka herds them out of the room, all our attention shifts to Zayla.

"Why did you do this?" Dion demands of her. His gaze lowers to her hand holding a weapon. He snatches it from her.

"That's my dagger," I say, running and taking it. "How could you hurt Lexi?"

"Secrets," Zayla says again, tears filling her eyes. "Getting secrets."

"Not the secret thing again," Mara mutters.

"What should we do with her?" Jamie asks, still holding her firmly.

"What's in her other hand?" Dion asks, pointing to her clenched fist coated in blood.

Tristan yanks out the object she was holding. "Where did you get this?" he asks.

"Lexi," Zayla whispers, her face pale as death. "The secret inside her."

"What is it?" I inspect the tiny golden glass ball in Dion's palm.

"Blazes," Tristan whispers. "Is that what I think it is?"

Dion stares at it and then presses a finger to his lips, warning us to be quiet. He drops it on the floor and smashes his boot on top of it. It shatters. We all stare at it in shock and then Tristan swears under his breath.

"This is bad," Tristan says.

"Very bad," Dion agrees.

"What's bad?" I look between the two of them. "What was that?"

Dion turns to Zayla. "You cut that out of Lexi?" he asks.

She nods, tears pooling down her face. "I got out the secret."

"Why does she keep saying secrets?!" Mara demands. "What is happening?"

"That was a listening device," Dion explains, holding up the tiny black square that was inside the smashed orb. "The Nazco must have planted it inside of her. You were trying to get it out, right, Zayla?"

She nods frantically.

"Next time, talk to us," I say. "You could've hurt Lexi."

"But it's good she found it," Dion adds. "Because based on what I know about these devices, they can transmit everything we are saying."

"Every conversation," Tristan says. "Blazes, they have a tracking system in them, too."

My heart hammers against my chest as the realization slams into me. "Which means they know where we are and everything we've been saying."

"Exactly," Dion says, grimly.

"We need to leave," I say. "Now."

An explosion booms against the front door, shaking the small house we only just started calling home.

"Sounds like we're too late," Tristan says.

43
WHEN ALL YOUR PLANS ARE UNRAVELED
ESTRELLA

Mahajanga, Madagascar

Tristan and Dion rush out of the room and down the hall. I turn to Jamie, who is still holding Zayla.

"Let her go," I say. "You're the best fighter here. We need you."

I pass her my dagger, and she releases Zayla, who sags to the floor, still crying.

"Get dressed quickly," I order and race over to my side of the room. Frantically, I pull on the protective pants and jacket Ami gave me. "We have to leave this place."

I grab my sword, unsheathing it. Anger floods my system. We finally found a safe place to stay and it was all ruined. Lexi moans, trying to get dressed with Jamie's help. Her blood seems like it's everywhere. It's terrifying.

"How did that device get inside of her?" Mara asks, shimmying into her jeans. "Was it there the whole time?"

"This was a trap," I say, gritting my teeth in understanding. "They must have planted it inside of her while she was kidnapped. That's why they let her out of prison. They wanted us to escape so they could see where we would go and what we were up to."

"That's why they let us go so easily," Jamie says as she shoves her feet into her shoes and then puts on Lexi's.

Katka appears in the doorway, her face set with purpose. "Come with me. We have a way out."

"Lexi's still bleeding," Jamie says, helping her to her feet. "She can't move fast. Why did you have to cut her open like that, Zayla?"

Zayla shakes her head and huddles onto the floor. I grab Zayla's arm and lift her to her feet. As angry as I am at her, I get why she thought she was doing the right thing. Besides, I'm not leaving any of my friends behind.

"Come on," I say, dragging her across the room. "You're coming with us. But from now on, do not use a knife on any of us, got it?"

"Hurry!" Katka says, glancing down the hall as another explosion booms through the house.

Fear slams into me as I step out of the room and peer down the hallway. The front door is open. Fire and lighting clash against the darkness. Dion and Tristan are out there fighting for us. If anything were to happen to them, I don't know what I'd do.

"I can't leave them to fight alone," I tell Katka.

"You have to," she says. "They are fighting so you can

stay alive. We can't afford to lose you. All of us are depending on you."

Indecision pulls at me, but Katka pushes me toward the back of the house with the others. Right now, I need to make sure my friends stay safe. When we step into the backroom, Elda and Anja are there along with BJ. He yanks a rug off the floor and pulls on a board. But it's not a board, it's an opening to a trap door on the floor.

"Hurry," he tells us. "Climb down. Follow the tunnel. It will take you to the edge of the forest."

No one moves, so Elda goes first. Izzy climbs tentatively down the ladder.

"Faster!" BJ says. There's real terror in his voice, which spurs her to scamper on down. Min follows, but Sally doesn't move from the corner of the room where she's huddled in her covers crying. Flora stares down into the opening, wringing her hands.

"Estrella goes next," Katka says, pushing me toward the trap door.

"I go last," I say, my eyes drifting to the window where lightning lights up the sky. "I need to make sure everyone is safe."

Her eyes flash in anger but then she says, "They need you to lead them to the pond. Wait for us by its edge. Can you do that?"

She's right. I hate it, but I can't argue with that. "Okay."

I scamper into the darkness, hoping I'm making the right decision.

44
UNTIL DEATH DO US PART
DION

Mahajanga, Madagascar

The pale moon illuminates the carnage around us, making me sick to my stomach. Tristan and I managed to kill three of the assassins, but we weren't quick enough. Two of the buildings are destroyed, fires feast hungrily on the thatched roofs, villagers lie dead in the dusty street, and the wails and screaming of those still alive ring in my ears. Their deaths are on me. I'm the one that brought Estrella and her friends here. Before we arrived, they had been living simple and peaceful lives.

The guilt threatens to cripple me.

None of this would've happened if I hadn't helped Estrella get her powers back. And now I might not only lose her, but all of us will die. My best friend, BJ, has been trusting me with his life and for what?

My feet are spread apart. My palms are at my side. I glare across the village center at Chandra and her group of assassins. There are at least thirty of the Empress's most powerful warriors. Tristan stands on my right, sword hot as the underworld.

The odds of our survival are not good. I can only hope Katka and BJ got Estrella and the girls away in time.

"You have killed enough innocent people," I tell Chandra. I roll my shoulders, preparing for my next attack. My powers are waning, but I shove those thoughts aside. "Leave before you join them."

"You know better than that, my love," Chandra says with a laugh. A breeze of her own creation whips her long dark hair around and the flames of the burning buildings cast twisted shadows over her face. "You could never kill me, especially after all we've been through together."

"What is she talking about?" Tristan mutters beside me.

"She's my ex," I say. "Big mistake."

"The Empress sent me a message," Chandra continues, and her eyes sparkle in the firelight. "Her offer still stands. Bring Estrella back to her and she will wipe all of Estrella's memories of Tristan. You will be free to love her as you should've in the first place."

My heart dives. That agreement with the Empress was between only the two of us. It had started out as a way to get the Empress to trust me, but I'd be lying if I said I hadn't considered it.

"What is this?" Tristan turns on me. "You made a deal with the Empress?! You filthy piece of scum."

"I pretended to make that deal," I snap, but from the burning anger in Tristan's eyes, I know he doesn't believe me. This is exactly the sort of thing the Empress is so good at. Making people not trust each other. It's one of the ways she gained her throne and kept it for hundreds of years.

"Are you sure?" Estrella's voice asks from behind me.

I spin around to find Estrella standing behind us, holding her sword, her face as white as the ashes caught in the air. Tears glisten in her eyes.

My whole body chills cold and dark as the Arctic winds howling across their icy plains. She's the last person I wanted to find out about this.

Because lies have their way of burrowing in deep and latching on like ticks, sucking the life out of their victim.

"Please," I beg. "You have to believe me. I needed the Empress to trust me so I could work freely to help you."

"Honestly, I don't know what to believe anymore," she says, and I hate how empty and heartless her tone is.

There's a ripple of laughter from the assassins, and their bodies shift as if preparing themselves for attack. My body tenses.

"Estrella, I'm so glad you joined us," Chandra says, her mouth twisting into a smile. "You can come with us peacefully or we can kill everyone here, including your friends by the pond. I know you left them there, thinking they were safe. But they're not."

"I'm not going to let them take you," I tell Estrella. "I will do everything to protect you."

"Really?" Tristan's tone is deathly. "Because it sounds a lot like you were planning on it."

"If I wanted them to take you," I say, "I would've done it a long time ago."

"Or maybe you were just waiting until you got everything you needed from her," Tristan says with a growl.

Estrella eyes me and her glare spears at my chest. Her gaze flickers to Tristan. My heart aches realizing this has only strengthened their bond.

"I refuse to be captured," Estrella tells Chandra. "I won't let myself or my friends become pawns of the Empress ever again. So I choose to fight to the death." Her gaze shifts to Tristan and me. "Will you stand with me?"

She's asking both of us, but mostly me.

"Always," Tristan says.

"To death," I agree. Then I turn back to Chandra. "You've made your choice and we've made ours."

"We shall see, won't we?" Tristan mutters suspiciously. "Actions always speak louder than words, and lies always are exposed when tested against truth."

I swallow, but give him a resolute nod. "Put me to the test."

"That I will do gladly," Estrella says, chin lifted at me as she moves to stand between us.

"Don't let her touch them!" Chandra screams. She lifts up her arms and throws out a wind force.

I hold up my hands just as Estrella presses her palms on Tristan and myself. Instantly, the surge of my power rushes out of me, sucked away in a tidal wave. Terror strikes my chest. Estrella is going to turn against me.

Chandra's wind smashes into the three of us, knocking us backward. Dust and debris from the earlier devastation whirl around us. A beam of wood hits my stomach and I'm thrown to the ground. But Estrella has crouched on a knee, arm held over her face as if she was expecting Chandra's impact.

The moment the wind finishes surging over us, Estrella leaps to her feet and takes off in a sprint toward Chandra, sword pointed before her. A cry erupts from her lips. A burst of fire and electricity explodes from the sword's tip. It's a mix of blinding white and inferno red.

She's a storm of danger.

Death on the run.

An indestructible warrior.

"Blazes, she's extraordinary," Tristan says, rising up from the ground.

Her bolts of electricity hit their mark down the line as her sword arcs through the air. Cries pierced the night. Bodies drop, shaking from shock, while others run off screaming as flames lick their skin.

Fear floods Chandra's face. Desperately, she pulls out a long chain. Estrella plunges her sword into Chandra's side just as the spiked ball at the end of the flail whizzes through the air. It strikes Estrella's chest. She tumbles backward.

In seconds, the swarm of assassins descend on Estrella.

Without my powers or weapons, I'm helpless. I heft up the beam that hit me, now my sword. Ash swirls around me. Terror sings on the wind.

I stride into the madness, ready to face my end.

Mahajanga, Madagascar

"No!" I yell, watching Estrella fall beneath the bodies of the assassins.

My gut twists. Fury erupts from within me.

If she dies, none of these maggots will live. Their bodies will burn and fuel her soul's journey to the heavens.

I leap into the crowd with a roar. From somewhere deep within, fire rushes into my blade. It's as if it knows this is where my destiny lies. My prophecy from the Dragon Seer screams at me, a memory I've always wanted to forget. The truth I kept buried because of fear and shame knowing I would lose the one thing that meant the most to me—my power.

Your flames will shield the one destined to save your people—the very soul to whom your heart is eternally bound—but to fulfill this prophecy, you must give it all, leaving yourself empty and cold.

Tonight, I'm embracing my prophecy.

It's mine to claim, and I will fulfill it.

My sword swoops and arcs. Limbs fall. Heads topple. Blood coats the ground.

My path to Estrella is lined with the fallen. My focus is only on where I saw her fall. Finally, I spot the face I've come to love. The face I'm going to die for.

I will my arms to move faster. Quicker than death's grasp.

An assassin is clamping resistant bracelets on her wrists. Another snatches up her sword. I've almost reached her.

They're dragging her away.

A burst of lightning from Dion illuminates the sky and vanishes. Has something happened to Dion?

My pulse drums against my ears. A man comes at me with a growl. My sword hits his neck, but it bounces off him. His skin is stone. He plows into me and our heads butt.

Stars swirl in my vision. I stumble, my knees buckling.

A knife plunges into my back and darkness swirls around me, clouding my vision.

NO! I can't fall.

I've been training for this moment all my life. They took Ivana from me. Her blood still screams for vengeance. I will not let them take Estrella, too. Not when I still have breath inside of me.

I roar, calling on the last of my visik. The final dredges of my immortality. Unlike when I faced Roach, this time Estrella isn't here to channel my powers and save me. This time, I'm alone.

Fire erupts from my sword. My blade consumes the darkness. It slices through the knife of the attacker before me. I duck around the stone wielder and two more assassins step in my path. Water floods me, dousing out my fire, but my blade finds its mark.

Heads roll.

Estrella screams. They're dragging her down the street. I follow, sprinting.

Chandra stands before me, blocking my path to Estrella. One hand holds her side, blood dripping from it. My long hair hangs over my face, wet with blood. My power has vanished, replaced by an empty hollowness. My clothing is torn, but I refuse to die.

Not until I'm finished.

"You," I growl.

A whimper squeaks from her mouth and she backs away. "Kill him," she orders the two Nazco at her side.

A humming noise thrums above. I look up. People are flying toward us. Then I spot Ami floating in the air, her arms touching two immortals who must have the power of flight. Her hair floats around her like ribbons of night.

Flaming arrows and bolts of electricity rain from the sky.

Ami drops to the ground in a glow of emerald light and pulls out the katana strapped to her back. The second her heels hit the ground, her sword clashes with a Nazco. She deflects an oncoming strike and spins to retaliate with another attacker at her back. Each move is effortless, precise, perfect. Her warriors follow her lead and descend on the Nazco.

Hope surges through me. Using the distraction, I duck

and roll, avoiding my attackers until I've broken free of the blockade.

I run down the deserted street, kicking up dust. I reach Estrella's two kidnappers. My arms won't quite move properly. I roar, calling up the last ounce of my strength. When they see me, their eyes widen. They don't bother fighting back. Instead, they scream and run off.

"Tristan!" Estrella says, wobbling on her feet. "You're alive."

She falls into my arms, sobbing. I wrap her close to my heart. My body shakes as a chill shudders over my skin.

"You're cold," she whispers and looks into my face. Her eyes widen. "Your hair. It's gray and so are your eyes. Why don't I feel your powers?"

"You're safe," I whisper into her hair, pulling her against me. "You're here. That's all that matters."

She clings to me. Despite the chill creeping through me, all is right with my world. But then she's ripped from my arms, straight into the air. A scream curdles from her lips. Two Eien fliers have grabbed her, lifting off into the night. I chase after them, but something smashes hard against the back of my head. Darkness swoops over me.

46
I WILL HAVE MY REVENGE
ESTRELLA

Mahajanga, Madagascar

The bodies of the fallen Nazco burn. Their deaths should fill me with some sort of victory, but I find no joy in their demise. We never found Chandra's body. She must have escaped, which means the Empress will get a full report on how we're working with the Eien. Plus, if they were listening to our conversations, they already know about the Temple of Fates.

Not good.

The worst part is Tristan has vanished. The last time I saw him was when Ami's people came to save me by grabbing my body and flying me away to safety. As they whisked me away, Nazco were swarming him. Katka and I scoured through the wreckage but had no luck in finding his body.

The memory of his gray hair and ice-cold body sends

another stream of tears down my face. He sacrificed his powers to save me. The thought torments me. No one should be sacrificing themselves so I can live.

If I hadn't yanked all of his powers from him, maybe he wouldn't have used up the last of his visik. I asked BJ if something like that is even possible, and he said he's heard stories of immortals who burned out when they knew they would die. My only hope is that the Nazco captured him. If he's still alive, I'm determined to find this Temple of Fates and the supposed elixir and then rescue him. Except, what if this ancient place is merely a myth and doesn't really exist?

My eyes drift to Dion, standing on a rock, staring at the sun creeping up on the horizon. I haven't spoken to him since the battle. The fact that the Nazco didn't kill him or capture him makes me suspicious. Chandra said he was working with the Empress. Is there truth to her words? Maybe she's allowing him to stay so that once we find the temple, he'll give her the information. Or give me up?

A part of my heart dies just thinking about the possibility of betrayal.

I shake my head of my terrifying thoughts and focus on the fact that BJ, Katka, and the girls are all safe. According to Lexi, she, Mara, and Jamie were able to use their limited powers to hold off the assassins until Ami's warriors arrived at the pond and saved them.

"We should leave," Ami says, coming to stand at my side. "I know you're upset about Tristan, but the Empress might send more warriors when she discovers she has failed to capture you."

"I just need a moment." No, I need time to be reverted so I can fix all the ways I failed.

"The Empress is crafty. I heard how she found you."

I clench my fists at her words. The Empress had come so close to killing everyone I cared about and wiping my memories again.

"Thank you," I say. "I owe you not just my life, but all of our lives. I will never forget it."

"I only came for selfish reasons," she says stiffly. "You know the location of the temple and we need to find out how to renew the Numinous Flames once again."

"You could've used a Truth Seeker to get the information from Dion and me but you chose not to, so don't act like you didn't sacrifice to be here."

"You are an unexpected surprise, Estrella. I see why the Empress fears you."

I stare at her silhouette, sharp and cutting against the purple dawn. "You're tough as nails and a warrior, but to me, you're also so much more."

She casts me a confused look.

"I don't want to be wary allies anymore." I take her hand. She startles and her gaze darts to our clasped palms, but she doesn't pull away. "I want to be Conduit sisters just like we were when we were in the World of Between. I want us to stand against the darkness that is threatening the world of immortals. But I can't do this alone. We must stand together because together we are stronger. Will you join me?"

"Yes. You have my allegiance." Her lips tip into a dangerous smile. "And friendship."

I nod, and a whisper of hope flickers inside my chest. "Then let's go. We have a temple to find."

If you enjoyed this story, I'd appreciate your time and effort if you'd leave a review and share with other readers what you loved about the book. Are you Team Tristan or Team Dion? Let me know!

Would you like a little more? Head over to my website and get a special bonus scene with Lexi and Conner. https://christinafarley.com/the-immortal-bound-series/

I've got you covered! You can read the next book in the series, THE IMMORTAL CROWN, and join Estrella on her journey to finding her powers and true love.

Continue the adventure in

THE
IMMORTAL
CROWN

The Immortal Bound
Series Book 4

YOUR NEXT ADVENTURE

The Immortal Crown (Book 4): Continue Estrella's journey!

The Dreamscape Series: A thrilling near-future adventure where your dreams are no longer safe.

The Gilded Series: A contemporary fantasy set in Korea.

The Princess and the Page: Get enchanted in this magical, fairytale mash-up set in France.

The Thief of Time: A magical school for librarians.

Fairy Tale Road: Choose your fairy tale ending in this adult romance.

About the Author

CHRISTINA FARLEY writes romantic fantasy and thrilling adventures inspired by her travels. When not wandering the world or creating imaginary ones, she spends time with her family in Florida where they are busy preparing for the next World Cup, baking cheesecakes, and raising a pet dragon in disguise as a very furry cat.

Visit her online:
ChristinaFarley.com
Instagram: @ChristinaLFarley
Facebook: @ChristinaFarleyAuthor
YouTube: @ChristinaFarley
TikTok: @ChristinaFarleyAuthor

Join Christina's Newsletter, the Travelogue: Exclusive access to videos, book updates, giveaways:
https://shorturl.at/anNzs

STAY IN TOUCH

I hope you'll stay in touch by joining my newsletter group, The Travelogue, or Keeper of the Realms so we can continue to take more adventures together. If you sign up, you'll receive a free book as my way of saying you're awesome.

Christina's Newsletter, The Travelogue: Reader news, writing tips, giveaways, and book updates: https://shorturl.at/ZQn5G

Christina's Keepers of the Realms: Join Christina's VIP Reader Club called the Keepers of the Realm. This community is designed for passionate readers like you to not only dive deeper into my stories but also help spread the magic of my books. Gain exclusive content, have a say in my worlds, and join the monthly giveaway! https://shorturl.at/nwAho

ACKNOWLEDGMENTS

Psalm 46:1-3

I can't believe I'm here writing these acknowledgements after finishing another book. My heart is especially full because if you are here reading these words, it means you are still here on this wild adventure with me! I'm so grateful.

I wanted to highlight and give a special shout out to some readers who have been sharing my stories with others. They are Kelli Justine, Brittany Rinehart, Emily Bueckert, Ravyen Allen, and Erin Brubach. You helped make this series a success and every post and message touched my heart.

A special thanks goes out to my Keeper of the Realm Group: Laura P, Mila C, Beth G, Andrea M, Ava M, Kendra P, Laziz T, Ana B, Amanda F, Jennifer A, Aziza E, Marisela Z, Eva M, Jenny H, Christina V, Amber J, Shana D, Kelli J, Bert B, Dianna B, Tez M, Bri L, Candi M, Julianne J, Amy P, Kris D, Sheree W, Jamie G, Jan W, Stephanie B, Ells, Heath W, Willa Z, Jerry N, Kate H, Joyce K, Tiffany L, Vivi B, Alison R, Callie T, Sarah W, Sunny B, Finely T, Margaret T, Billy F, Jocelyn M, Laziza T, Merry M, Megan B, Susan L, Emily I, Yvonne V, JB, Theresa L, Adalyn B, Jamie, Christy S, Jennifer J, Susan L, Megan L, Jasmine B, Lolly G, Theresa L, Bonnie M, Maria V,

Monica, Kristian B, Michael E, Ashley S, Megan B, and Misty P. You all are the best!

Paul at Trif Book Design did it again! Thank you for creating another beautiful cover. Veronika Wunder, I'm so glad you created another map. This one was so worth the extra time!

Thank you to my copyeditor, Sarah Ward, for making this manuscript shine.

To Julianne, I'm so glad you encouraged me to make this idea into a series.

To Caleb and Luke for being my champions. Finally, to my husband, Doug, who has been there from the beginning.